THE LOCKET

BOOK ONE OF
THE TALES FROM AVENRAND
SERIES

THE LOCKET

BY

K.S. BRIXEY

TALES FROM AVENRAND

BOOK ONE

In memory of Caden Michael White
2003-2009

Your contagious smile is forever etched on our hearts

ACKNOWLEDGMENTS

I truly believe no book gets written in a vacuum. If you know me and you think you didn't contribute to the story, you may need to read it again!

First off, thanks to my mom for being so excited about getting to read my book. To my sister, Carol, who loves everything I write and thinks some of you will, too. And to my brother, Jim, who has over the years always been supportive of my creative tangents because he has had a few of his own.

I want to thank all the Springfield Writers Guild members that have given me so much encouragement along the way. They were the first group to call me a writer and convince me to call myself one. They were kind when they critiqued my first pages and gave me the confidence to keep on getting words on pages.

Thanks to the Sci-fi/fantasy (now Speculative Fiction) genre group that meets twice a month with all kinds of things they make up that have helped my writing and the crazy idea that I could pull this off. Also, a special thanks to WritingMoments.com. This group got my butt in the chair and in front of my book every week.

I owe a special amount of debt to my first group of beta-readers. They took almost 200 pages of messed up manuscript and told me I had a great story idea from a draft that was nowhere near ready for anyone to read. Their feedback was honest and encouraging. I am so grateful to them for plugging through those first pages and sharing their ideas.

I feel like this book didn't become a real book until my editor, Shelby Hild, put her touches on it. This was the first time I had gone through an editing process, and she was kind and encouraging while at the same time she let me know what a mess it was. I spent months with her in my head as I made that first run through those massive edits. Thank you, thank you, thank you for all you taught me about story and writing and words and research and all the things during this process.

And no story would be a story without having a group of story lovers you can jump off the page with. Thank you to my imagination sharing brainiacs; Connor, Amanda, Christina, Amy, and Haley; for never tiring of letting me bounce ideas off them.

A special thanks to A.L.Guilfoyle for her creative talents producing our first book trailer. All I can say is, "Wow!"

To my friends, family, and strangers who have become friends along the way, all of you who inquired about the book and gave me opportunities to practice pitching it. I am grateful. I hope it lives up to your expectations.

And to you the reader, who I hope read this far to be recognized. No story feels like it is complete until someone reads it on the other end. I hope it helped you escape for a few hours into a world of your imagination, leaving the cares of your world behind. Thank you for joining me on this adventure.

I can't wait to share more great escapes with all of you.

The questions will progress through the story in chronological order. To avoid spoilers, make sure you have read through the chapter listed before reading the question.

1. Why do you think everyone is worried when Lacy begins telling stories of seeing Willy?
2. Have you ever experienced seeing a loved one after they have died? Can you relate with Parker when he said it was normal?
3. What is the significance of Lacy's obsessions with the time of Willy's death?
4. Do you think Raelynn should have stayed longer to help Lacy or is it better if she and the girls muddled through on their own for a while?
5. Can you identify with Lacy's relationship with Willy? How does the banter between Raelynn and Lacy help you visualize the state of Lacy and Willy's marriage? (Chapter 5)
6. The Locket is introduced in the first and fifth chapter, other than the title of the book. What is the significance of the Locket at the time of its introduction(s)? (Chapter 5)
7. What would it be like to wake up in the past and still be able to remember the future you just left? (Chapter 6)

8. Have you ever had a vivid dream that seemed real? Or thought you've seen a loved one that has died? Maybe you thought you heard their voice? Do you think this is just our minds playing tricks on us? (Chapter 8)

9. What if you could go back and alter an event in the past, what would it be? How would you change it? How would your life be different now if you did? (Chapter 9)

10. Our lives are narrated by the stories we tell, how we remember things may not be the same as others who go through the same events with us. What events have Lacy and Raelynn shared? How do they see them differently? (Chapter 10)

11. It took a lot of encouragement to get Lacy to go to a counselor the first time. It has only been three months, do you think Raelynn is pushing her too hard? Why or why not? (Chapter 11)

12. Let's talk about Raelynn. What kind of friend do you think she is? Is she doing too much for Lacy or should she back off and give her some space? Does Lacy rely on her friend too much?

13. What made Lacy blame Raelynn for having her daughters taken from her? Were you rooting for Lacy to finally start standing up for herself?

14. Why do you think Lacy initially chose Dr Garamondy to be her doctor? (Chapter 16)

15. When Lacy goes back to Avenrand the second time, what are the rules of magic that Hope explains to her? (Chapter 19)

16. What do you think about Raelynn and Lacy's relationship? Lacy let's Rae cry on her shoulder but she doesn't return the "I love you" … do you think she is still holding a grudge over not being invited to dinner or did she accept Raelynn's excuse? (Chapter 20)

17. What are the treasures you remember from your childhood? Did you have any secret nooks and crannies you liked to hide in? Did your family have any mantras or sayings that helped guide your behavior? (Chapter 21)

18. Which side of the argument between Raelynn and Lacy's family in Salina did you tend to agree with? Were you surprised that Lacy's parents didn't seem concerned or was Raelynn just being controlling as she was known to be? (Chapter 25)

19. If you meet your future self in an awkward encounter, what would you ask her? What would you tell your younger self?

20. Talk about a time in your life when you had to convince yourself you were brave and courageous. How did that turn out?

21. When do you think Lacy finally realizes her future is worth fighting for, if she let's go of the past? (Chapter 37)

22. Talk about the struggle between the dark shadow (the traveler) and the light. (Chapter 43)

23. Have you ever been expected to know what to do, like when Caden told Lacy she would have a "mother's instinct', but felt lost instead? (Chapter 46)

24. Do you think Lacy has a 'mother's instinct'? Give examples to prove your answer.

25. Who found the girls and brought them back to the bridge? (Chapter 50) How did they explain their rescue?

26. So when Raelynn meets Dr Garamondy on the farm, what was Lacy being suspected of? (Chapter 52) Why do you think the author didn't specifically tell you?

27. It's obvious why Lacy was ready to throw away the key to Dr Garamondy Sr's work, but why do you think Dr Garamondy, Jr agreed to do it? (Chapter 53)

28. Were you surprised when The Locket reappeared? What are the clues throughout the story that would explain how the locket could show up at the end? (Chapter 54)

The red glare from the alarm clock's digits radiated across the bedroom, capturing Lacy's attention. The zero on the far right rolled to a one. 4:01 illuminated the corner of the dark bedroom. The sun wouldn't be up for hours but trying to go back to sleep was impossible. Where was he? She stared at the clock without blinking. As if fixated in time, she watched each digit crawl to the next.

4:02... 4:03... 4:04.

At 4:15 she blinked, picked up the handset, and dialed Willy's cell phone one more time. Surely, he would answer this time.

"You've reached Willy Donathon. Leave a message at the beep and I'll call you back."

"You keep saying that," Lacy growled under her breath, "but I have been calling you since midnight."

Lacy slammed the handset into its bedside cradle.

"Where the hell are you?" she stared at his empty side of the bed, a knot tightened in her gut. "We were supposed to continue this party when we got home." She threw his pillow at the bedroom door with all the force her anger could muster. When her attempt to use magic didn't make him appear, she sighed and shook her head. "Some things never change, do they?"

Dinner the previous evening had been amazing. The idea that he had planned the whole evening himself raised her hopes that things really would be different. She could imagine him now reaching his hand across the private table for two, the candle light flickering across his arm, smiling down at her. At Willy's request—and more than likely due to the large tip he gave them— the small, three-piece band played the first song the two of them had ever danced to. "Can I have this dance," he had whispered, "for the rest of my life?"

Lacy played along taking his hand as she stood up and he led her to the small dance platform in front of the band. She couldn't remember a time when he had ever been so romantic.

For a few hours at least, she believed Willy wanted to change and that he could become a full contributing partner in this marriage.

"Let's finish this evening right," he proposed. "We'll tuck the kids in bed, open a bottle of wine, and put on some quiet music. Who knows where we'll end up?"

"Sounds wonderful," she replied with a smile, amazed her face still knew how. "You know you surprise me sometimes."

"I've been an ass," he confessed. "You have always been there for me. I want to show you how much I care about you and how much I appreciate you. You grew up way before me, Lacy. It's time I grow up and get on board. I mean it this time."

"Flip you for who goes and gets the kids." Lacy laughed as they headed out into the parking lot.

She was still high on his promises to make up for the years he had been absent from their marriage. His promise to be a better husband and father to the kids had echoed in her head.

This time she had believed him.

They both knew Lacy would have to be the one to pick up the kids. After all, she had the car and he had a motorcycle but playing the game had been fun. Willy walked Lacy across the parking lot, his hand around her waist holding her close to him. Their long embrace solidified her faith in him this time. He had lifted the face shield on his helmet for one last kiss before he whispered, "I'll be waiting for you. Be careful with our precious cargo."

"Of course. We'll be right behind you."

He had straddled his bike and road off.

Although he was supposed to be there waiting for them, Willy wasn't home when she returned. She had tucked the kids into bed, slipped into something sexy, poured a couple glasses of wine, and waited. Sipping the wine, she had reveled in the lingering sensations left behind by his touch, the long embrace, and the slow dances.

The warm feelings had cooled when both her glass of wine and his were empty.

"I believed you," she whispered in defeat. Picking up the handset again, she dialed the only other person she could call no matter what time of night it was.

"Lacy? Slow down," Raelynn said. "Honey, I can't understand a word you are saying. It's four o'clock in the morning. What did he do now?"

"It's a quarter to five," Lacy corrected. "And I am really worried. At first, I was hurt and mad. Now I can't help but wonder if I should be worried this time?"

"You worry every time he pulls this shit," Raelynn reminded her. "Why do you let him get to you like this? If you want, I'll come over and wait with you as long as I can kick his ass when he comes staggering through the door."

"What if something happened to him?"

"Nothing happened to him," Raelynn assured her. "You know Willy by now. He's out partying and lost track of time. Same old Willy."

"Right," Lacy agreed. "Same old Willy."

After a long silence, Lacy muttered under her breath.

"What did you say?" Raelynn asked.

"He was so great last night, Rae. I thought for sure he was going to change. How could he not come home after we made plans?"

"You act surprised even though staying out all night partying has been his mode of operation since you've known him. How many times have we had this conversation?"

"Tonight was different," Lacy assured her. "He planned this entire, perfect evening. He even danced with me! He brought me flowers and a gift. You should have seen it Raelynn, he made me close my eyes and he put this beautiful locket around my neck. It has the most captivating gem on it."

"Hmmm? Sounds like a make-up date. What did he do? Did he buy another motorcycle without discussing it with you?"

"Not that I am aware of."

Lacy was pulled into Raelynn's interrogation. Raelynn had always controlled Lacy's emotional life since Parker, Raelynn's husband, and Willy were first deployed together almost ten years ago. Raelynn was there to hold Lacy's hand through miscarriages and deployments, through near breakups and fallen comrades. Raelynn was there for her more than Willy ever was, even after he was discharged from the military.

"Did he fool around with another woman?"

"No! Of course not." Lacy reacted as if that had never happened—or at least as if it could never happen again.

"Maybe he quit his job and then drained your bank account."

"Stop it, Rae," Lacy demanded. "You know he wouldn't do that. Willy has always been a great provider for his kids."

"I wonder how many kids he actually has," Raelynn wondered aloud, as if she was joking but Lacy knew she was serious.

Lacy's heart raced as she heard the chimes of the doorbell. She imagined Willy standing on the front porch with a guilty look on his face, and the thought made her feel angry and betrayed.

"It's the doorbell. I have to go," she told Rae, her voice trembling with emotion.

"Why would Willy ring the doorbell? Unless he is too wasted to find his key. Make sure you look through the peephole."

Lacy hung up the receiver, trying to ignore Raelynn's dissension. In a way it felt good to have a reason to cut her interrogation short. Thinking about Willy staggering up onto the front porch after forsaking their after-dinner plans infuriated her. She jerked the new locket off her neck and threw it across the bedroom. The doorbell rang out again.

Lacy's blood pulsed like a raging river as she descended the stairs. She could feel her heart thumping against her chest as she wobbled toward the front door. Would she hug him or hit him? As she walked down the hallway and across the living room, she rehearsed a few lines to yell at him.

"So much for a special night, you kind of blew that one. Good job with that growing up thing. The kids will be grown up before you. You know, Willy, I thought you wanted this to be the night I finally forgive you, a night to change the course of our marriage—oh, wait a minute!—that was just cheap talk."

Lacy reached for the door, then hesitated. Resting her hand on the doorknob, she heard Raelynn's voice in her head, "Check the peephole first, no surprises."

Pressing one eye up to the peephole, she focused on what she expected to be Willy's head. That wasn't the motorcycle helmet she thought she would see. Instead, she saw the top of a black felt hat, similar to the one she had seen before when law enforcement had been called to their home in the past. Even angrier, she opened the door expecting to hear that Willy had been arrested for another DUI. She was going to make sure she knew the exact time he got pulled over. Was it right after they left the restaurant or had he gone somewhere else first?

Fixated on the time, the thoughts of the financial burden another DUI would cost them: lost wages, fines, loss of driving privileges; whisked by. All of that would be a hindrance to them getting ahead financially, but they had made it through before. The time stamp on this ticket was what was important. It would make or break their marriage altogether.

"I know, I know," Lacy repeated as she opened the door. "I know why you're here."

"Ma'am," the officer tried to interrupt, but Lacy kept insisting she already knew why he was there. "I'm Deputy West from the Escambia County Sheriff's Department."

"I know you're the sheriff. I know why you're here and I don't care. I can't care anymore," she went on. "He can rot in hell for all I care. But tell me one thing, what time was it? What time did you pick him up? At this point the only thing that matters is the time."

"Hey, baby, someone is beeping in." Raelynn stared at the phone sitting on the table next to her chair. "I missed what you said."

"Do you need to go?" Parker asked.

"No." Raelynn shook her head even though Parker couldn't see her. She was desperate to hear his voice during these long and way too often deployments. "I will talk to you as long as you can stay on the line. Lacy can wait."

She shifted back into her cozy, upholstered wingback chair. Even though it seemed a little out of place in the narrow hallway, it was the one place she wanted to be when her husband wasn't home with her. As long as Parker was the one on the other end of the phone, she could sit here all day.

"Lacy again? Kind of early, isn't it?"

Probably found himself a girl, Raelynn thought.

"Funny, Willy says Lacy has been sleeping in till noon."

Raelynn didn't want to argue with Parker about Willy. She wiped the sleep out of her eyes and sighed. She knew as his deployment dragged on; the calls would come less often. This could be the last call she would have with him for months.

"Willy didn't come home again." Raelynn ignored more beeps.

"I thought I had him straightened out. He told me he had a big plan to make it right with her. I am going to have to kick his ass when I get home."

"Stand in line. You'll have to wait your turn for that." She continued ignoring the beeping.

Parker went on to explain the new terms of his deployment. "Good thing Willy didn't reenlist. This deployment is going to be the worst yet. I sure miss him on the ship though."

"I know you do, baby." She held back what she wanted to say about Willy. Although he had always been a great friend to Parker, Raelynn had never approved of the way he treated Lacy.

"I miss you, too," Parker chuckled. "Two more months and we can make up for lost time."

"I look forward to making up for lost time with you." Her laughter was cut short by the thumping of little feet above her. She gasped as Ella darted down the stairs. "Slow down." Ella ignored her and hit the bottom of the stairs running toward the phone.

"Daddy!" Ella screamed, sliding across the terrazzo-lined hallway in her socks and stopping just short of slamming into the wall. The grin across her face complemented the dimple on her right cheek.

"I told you not to do that," Raelynn reprimanded. "You are going to break your neck."

"Is that Ella?" Parker asked.

"Yep, our little early bird. I'll put you on speaker."

"Hi, Daddy." Ella started talking before she got up to the phone, grinning as she pressed her lips up to the speaker. Raelynn put her hands on her shoulders and pulled her back a few inches.

"Hi, sweetheart. How is my little angel?"

"I'm not little anymore, Daddy. And I'm getting bigger. Are you coming to my party?"

"A party?" Parker acted surprised. "What kind of party?"

"I can't believe you forgot it's going to be my birthday in three days."

"Your birthday!" Parker gasped. "You mean another birthday? Are you going to be two already?"

"No, Daddy," Ella laughed. "You are teasing, right? You do know how old I am going to be, don't you?"

"Are you going to be sixteen already?" Parker asked.

"No!" Ella giggled twisting her thin hair around her finger.

"Are you going to be forty-two? Am I too high or too low?"

"Way too high."

"Too high, hm…" Parker took a second to respond. "Then you must be turning eleven!"

"You remembered!" Ella laughed. "Daddy, I am setting a place for you at my party. I want you to be here."

"I want to be there but I have to work."

"On a ship?" Ella asked.

"Yes, angel," Parker said. "On a really big ship."

The call waiting beep interrupted and without thinking Ella clicked the call button before Raelynn could intervene.

"Hello, Mason's residence."

"Miss Mason, this is Deputy West," the officer said. "May I speak with Raelynn?"

"That's my mom. We're talking to my daddy."

Raelynn picked up the handset and switched the phone off speaker. "Parker?"

"Mrs. Mason?" Deputy West asked.

Raelynn clicked the call button again. "Parker?"

"It's still me."

"Oh, that is wonderful. Thank you for dropping our call. Now, my daughter won't get to talk to her father for several months. He's in the navy and getting ready to set out on a ship. Not to mention it's her birthday."

"I do apologize, Ma'am. This is Deputy West. I'm calling on behalf of your friend, Lacy."

"Lacy?" Thoughts raced through Raelynn's mind. Did Willy come home drunk and hurt her? Did she hurt him? "What happened? Is she okay?"

"Mrs. Mason," Deputy West lowered his voice to a soft tone. "Lacy is okay. However, she could use some company. Her husband was in an accident. Could you come by her house and spend some time with her?"

"Of course, I can come by," Raelynn said, beginning to go through a mental checklist. "Does she need a ride to the hospital? I have to drop my daughter off at school and then I can be there."

They had been there for each other for over ten years, so Raelynn was used to taking care of Lacy. Military wives stick together through it all and are bound for life. Often to Lacy's ridicule, Raelynn considered herself an older sister even though she was a few months younger than Lacy. Parker had seniority over Willy and so Raelynn took the senior role over Lacy.

Parker had reenlisted a few months before Willy got out. Willy had announced his decision to not re-up without hesitation. If he had reenlisted, it would have been because of Parker. They had been battle-buddies for eight years. They'd trained together, deployed together, and buried comrades together. They knew each other long before their wives knew each other. A relationship that tormented Raelynn even to the point of her questioning who Parker was more loyal to: her or Willy.

Disappointed she wouldn't be able to reach Parker after losing his call, she threw Ella's clothes on the bed in a huff. As they pulled into the drop-off lane at the before school day care, Ella blurted out, "Are you mad, mommy?"

"Of course, not, sweetie," Raelynn sat up and forced a smile across her face. "Have fun at school today." As Ella skipped up to the door, Raelynn shouted, "I love you!"

The real questions she wanted to ask spun around in her head all the way to Lacy's house but when she got there, she froze. Standing in Lacy's living room, the officer seemed out of place. She couldn't remember any of the questions she'd rehearsed in the car, "What did you say?"

She made the deputy repeat himself several times.

When the words, Willy is dead, eventually hit, the look of grief on Parker's face was all she could think of. This will devastate him. He was deployed. He didn't need any distractions. Military wives must protect their sailor from bad news because they are already in harm's way. They do what they can to keep them focused on the mission.

How would she be able to tell him his battle buddy for life was dead? How could she not tell him?

Then she remembered Lacy's fear that something had happened. Despite trying to convince her otherwise, she was right. What must she be feeling?

Her cell phone vibrated in her pocket and without looking, she flipped it open and froze.

"Raelynn," Parker's voice sounded concerned. "I've been trying the home phone, but you haven't answered."

"Sorry," Raelynn took a few steps into the hallway. "Lacy isn't doing too good. She's just sitting there staring out the window."

"What's wrong?" After an awkward silence, Parker asked, "What is going on?"

"Oh, Parker, I'm sorry. I don't want to tell you this because you are not supposed to get bad news from home."

"We can get bad news, hun. If something bad has happened, we have to know. We can't come home and find our world turned upside down."

"Are you sure? This is bad. It is going to hit you pretty hard."

"Well, you are going to have to tell me now or I'll be wondering what it is. You can tell me, Raelynn; we have ways to deal with bad news over here. If it's too bad, I'll ask for leave." Silence lingered until Parker broke. "For crying out loud,

Raelynn, did someone die? Cuz you are acting like someone died."

Raelynn took a deep breath. "It's Willy. He didn't come home last night."

"That's nothing new. He never comes home on time."

"I know," Raelynn's elbow followed her head, holding her phone to her ear as she shook her head. "But it's different this time. Remember when we got disconnected this morning? It was the sheriff trying to get me to come over and take care of Lacy. They said Willy was in an accident. He's …" The words stuck in the back of her throat.

The silence between them lingered.

Raelynn waited a few minutes. "Parker? Are you alright?"

"Damn it, Willy," Parker's voice trembled. "Tell me he isn't dead."

"I can't."

"Damn it, Willy."

"I knew I shouldn't have told you. I should have waited till you got home."

"No, no… You had to tell me. All the times I thought that clown was going to kill himself in combat—it was that damn motorcycle, wasn't it? I told him not to buy it."

There was nothing more to say and they promised each other to stay strong for Lacy.

When Raelynn put her phone down on the coffee table, Lacy was still staring out the window. The same place she had been when Raelynn arrived. Staring, as if waiting for Willy to come home. Raelynn picked up the business card the sheriff had set on the table before he left. Deputy West. She approached the window and eased her arm around Lacy's shoulders. "How are you holding up?"

"We don't know anything for sure." Lacy continued to stare out the window. "You know that sheriff didn't have any proof it was Willy. All he knew is that it was a man on a bike."

"They must have something," Raelynn explained. "He did track you down."

Lacy began shaking her head. "No, this can't be right."

CHAPTER 3

2001

"You and the girls can move in with us," Katlyn Johnson patted Lacy's leg as if that would fix everything. She smiled and turned her head towards the front of the sanctuary.

"Mom, please," Lacy put her head into the palms of her hands and leaned forward in the pew ignoring her mother's hand resting on her leg. "Please just stop."

She didn't want to be told what to do, not now, not until she could convince herself Willy was gone. Not until the pressure of appearing sad was over. What was wrong with her that she couldn't even muster a tear at Willy's funeral. All she wanted right now was to get this awkward social convention over with.

Katlyn had always tried to manage Lacy and her older sister, Jolene, but Lacy's love for Willy had been out of control from the moment of their first kiss. Katlyn was very vocal about how she regretted allowing Jolene to have that New Year's Eve party.

Jolene had invited a group of boys, including Willy, to ring in the New Year 1990. Lacy told everyone it was love at first sight. Katlyn made it clear that Willy Donathan was not the man she had in mind to capture the heart of her youngest daughter.

"You are going to need to do something." Katlyn moved her hand to Lacy's back, rubbing with gentle strokes. "You can't stay here all alone with those girls."

"This is our home," Lacy squirmed out of her mother's grip. "We aren't alone."

"Willy is dead." Katlyn turned her hips to face Lacy. "You are alone. You and the girls can come back to Kansas and get on with your lives."

Lacy got up, squeezed between her mother and the back of the pews in front of her.

"Excuse me. Can we just get through this fune—this thing… and then I'll let you know what we are going to do. Right now, let's just get this thing over with."

Katlyn stood up and started to follow her. "Lacina, dear, I just think—" Her mother was the only one that still called her Lacina, and it always felt like she was in trouble.

"I need to go check on Olivia and Alice." Lacy raised a straight arm back toward her mother as she turned away and walked down the aisle of the church. Sensing the upcoming lecture, she intercepted, "Let me find my girls."

Katlyn eased back down onto the bench.

Somewhat lost in the church, Lacy looked around for her sister who had been watching the girls. She hadn't been in a church since her first communion back at Piper Lutheran Church. The nursery in the basement where all the young communicants had to serve to earn their service hours had always given Lacy the creeps. It was down a dark, musty hallway and the thought of the girls being taken down there was making Lacy anxious. She stared down the stairwell trying to muster up the courage to descend.

"Lacy?" Joe Johnson turned to his daughter with a concerned look on his face. "You look like you need a hug." Joe took her into his arms and gave her a gentle squeeze.

"Thanks, Daddy. I don't know where Will… I mean Jolene took the girls."

"I'm sure they are fine." Joe swept Lacy's hair behind her ears. She ran her fingers through her ruffled hair and pulled it back out. Tossing her head, her hair fell down over her shoulders.

"I need to find them. We're supposed to wait in the fellowship hall while the guests arrive."

"Jolene will get them in there. How many guests are you expecting?"

"I don't know, Dad. It's not like we sent out invitations."

Lacy couldn't focus. One minute she was looking around for the girls and the next trying to figure out how many people might show up. Did Jolene take the girls outside to play? What friends did Willy have except Parker? As much as she hated funerals, it made her sad to think that in the end even his best friend couldn't be here to send him off.

Raelynn walked up and nodded a hello to Mr. Johnson. "Some of the ladies from the church are preparing dinner for your family after the graveside services. I was sent to find out how many people they could expect."

"This isn't right," Lacy said without thinking.

"What isn't right?" Raelynn asked.

Mr. Johnson motioned them to head into the fellowship hall. The room was off the church's kitchen and filled with tables and chairs lined up ready for the dinner being prepared.

"It's not right that Parker can't be here." Lacy almost felt tears emerge but none came. "Willy needs his best friend right now."

"I know." Raelynn reached out to hold Lacy's arm and patted her back. "I'm so sorry he can't be here."

They held each other. Raelynn shed tears. Lacy felt numb. They were now the center of attention of the relatives gathering in the fellowship hall. Of all the things, Lacy felt more emotion over Parker not being here than any of the other chaos happening around her.

"Do you know where the girls are?" Lacy looked around at all the family looking at them. "They need to be here."

"They are with your sister. She is taking them to the bathroom. They'll be here in a few minutes." Raelynn looked around the room. "Big turnout, don't you think?"

Lacy peeked out the door at the other guests gathering in the lobby. "Where did all these people come from?"

"My guess is from the base," Raelynn looked out and then pulled the door shut.

Lost in her thoughts, Lacy tried to remember the last time Willy had mentioned hanging out with any of his military buddies.

"Most of them seem to be from the church," Parker surprised them. "Willy's been talking about the church a lot these last few weeks."

Lacy and Raelynn jumped with delight and ran to hug Parker. Wrapping arms around both of them, he gave them a big squeeze.

"Oh my god, Parker." Real tears rolled down Lacy's cheeks for the first time since learning that Willy had died. "You made it."

Olivia, Alice, and Ella ran through the swinging door to the fellowship hall and raced each other to Parker. They clung to him as if he was their last hope. With a little reassurance from Parker, went right back into play mode.

"How did you make it?" Raelynn peeled the girls from their grip on him.

"There were some guys getting ready to come back," Parker explained. "One of them gave up his seat for me. We'd both served with Willy back in Operation Desert Storm, and he knew how much Willy meant to me."

"This means so much to him." Lacy took a tissue offered to her from a woman she didn't recognize. "This means so much."

Lacy leaned forward and gave Parker another hug. She tried to hide in his arms as the room began to feel as if it was closing in on her.

"Lacy," Parker whispered. "I think it's time to let your guests show their respects."

Lacy looked up and saw a line forming behind them. She began going through the motions of greeting and hugging one person after another. All of Willy's relatives gathered in the fellowship hall to wait with her family. There were dozens of cousins, aunts and uncles, and a few Lacy didn't even know existed; so many that her own family seemed to get lost in the crowd.

Halfway through the greeting line, Lacy called out to Raelynn, "Could you find Willy? He needs to be here."

The room fell silent.

Raelynn squeezed through the crowded room to get to Lacy and rescue her from the never-ending line of attendees extending their condolences.

"You doing okay?" Raelynn put her arm around Lacy's shoulder. "Why don't you come sit down?"

"I need to find my girls," Lacy said.

"We're still here." Jolene stepped up beside her and pointed to the Olivia and Alice playing with Ella in the back of the fellowship hall. Their matching black dresses, colors that Lacy tried to discourage but Katlyn insisted on buying them, billowed as they twirled.

"How are you holding up?" Jolene asked.

"A little dizzy. I want to get this over with."

"Understandable." Jolene gave Lacy a quick hug. "Girls, why don't you give your mom a hug and then it's time to go celebrate your daddy's life."

"Can we stay with you?" Olivia asked.

The crowd in the fellowship hall thinned as Willy's family found their way to the sanctuary for the service. An usher stood at the door to the hallway that led to the sanctuary. "They are ready for you."

Lacy took the girls hands, one on each side of her, and trudged toward the sanctuary. Entering through the side front door, she guided the girls into their seats on the front row. She felt the eyes of the congregation on her, staring, looking for signs of the proper grief she couldn't seem to muster.

It didn't seem like much of a celebration to Lacy. There was a lot of singing about God and stories from Willy's new church friends Lacy had never even met. All this time Willy had some secret life he'd never shared with her that wasn't drinking or fooling around. It was very confusing.

Then his military service buddies got up to talk. They told stories Lacy could relate to. They shared some wonderful times of partying and staying out late, making their wives worry. Several of them even asked Lacy to forgive them for all the times she'd needed to bail them out of jail.

Lacy smiled. It was somehow comforting reveling in any memory of Willy that seemed real, that somehow let her feel his presence.

After the service, she stood next to his casket. Reaching out to touch his hand, his cold, hard skin made her snap her arm back. She jumped again when her father put his hand on her shoulder. His hand was strong and warm.

Flower arrangements surrounded the casket. Bright, wonderful spring displays stood on either side of where Willy lay. The blooming Peace Lilies with their white blossoms crowded the small area in front of the altar. Lacy stared at Willy, waiting for him to sit up, hoping they would both wake from this nightmare.

Her dad grasped her hand with both of his palms.

"Whenever you're ready," he whispered.

"I'm not ready for any of this," Lacy cried. "Dad… I don't know what to do. I can't leave him. I can't just leave him here alone."

"It's okay, baby," he said. "You don't have to go yet. We'll stand next to him and let the rest of the family come up and say their goodbyes."

"Lacina," Katlyn said, standing on the left of the casket. "Come stand over here, honey. Next to me. People are waiting."

"Okay," Lacy said, letting her mother control the situation. Always, except when it came to Willy. Katlyn would be the first to let the world know that she didn't approve of him. Lacy had followed him to Pensacola against her mother's best judgment. There'd been no sympathy the many times Lacy called late at night crying because Willy hadn't come home. She had tried to talk to Joe, but Katlyn was the gatekeeper of the family phone. Lacy only got to talk to her dad when it was allowed. Soon she stopped calling home at all.

Lacy did as she was told and stood off to the side of the casket. She greeted each and every person that went by until she was exhausted. After the line dwindled, her immediate family waited with her. Lacy stepped up close to Willy. She wanted to hold him, to kiss him, to wake him up, but she remembered that cold touch and froze in front of him. She set her hand on the edge of the casket. Then leaned over hoping to feel his breath on her face.

"Goodbye, baby," she whispered.

"When is Daddy going to wake up?" Alice asked. Standing on her tiptoes, she tried to peek over the edge.

Lacy reached over and picked her up.

"He's sleeping forever, now." Lacy forced the words out through her sobs.

"Ma'am," in a soothing voice the usher interrupted. "Whenever you're ready."

"For what?" Lacy looked at her dad for answers.

"When you give the word," he said, "we can proceed to the graveside."

"I'm not ready," Lacy cried out. "I'm not ready!"

Alice began to cry. Jolene came and took Alice out of Lacy's arms and consoled her.

Joe took his daughter in his arms and held her.

"Take your time," he consoled. "Take all the time you need."

At the graveside, Lacy sank into the seat in the front row, staring at the casket as it hovered over a deep hole in the ground. Olivia sat to her right side between her and Jolene. Alice sat on her left with Katlyn next to her. Joe stood behind Lacy and placed his hand on her shoulder. Lacy was too exhausted to cry anymore. She just sat in a trance and stared at the casket as Willy's family gathered up close behind them under the graveside tent.

"Mommy," Olivia said. "Who is that man in the uniform?"

"The police officer?" Lacy asked.

"No," Olivia said. "The sailor."

"Oh, Parker," Lacy said, not remembering Parker hadn't worn his uniform. "He got to come home to be with us."

"Not Uncle Parker," Olivia said. "It looks like Daddy under the box." Olivia pointed beneath the casket but Lacy didn't see anything.

"Yes, Daddy is in the casket, honey," Lacy said. "He is sleeping."

"I think he's flying," Olivia insisted.

The pastor called for everyone's attention for a short graveside service that ended in more hugging and consoling.

CHAPTER 4

2001

Lacy sat as still as possible at the island counter in the middle of her kitchen. She didn't want to be hugged or consoled anymore. She did her best to ignore the arguing between her mother and Raelynn. Both women thought they knew what was best for Lacy and her children. Katlyn insisted that Lacy and the girls come back home with them. Raelynn insisted that Lacy was home.

"Mom's right," Jolene said. "Raelynn, I know you love Lacy, but she needs her family right now. We can take care of Alice and Olivia. Besides you have Parker and Ella to take care of."

"We have been taking care of each other for years," Raelynn persisted. "Mr. Johnson, you understand. Even though Willy was discharged, we were still here for him. We took care of each other when our husbands deployed, and we will do it now."

Lacy sunk her head as far down as she could without sticking her nose in her mug of warm tea. As much as she had found Chamomile tea soothing in the past, nothing was calming her today.

"I have to agree with Jolene." Katlyn put on the sweet motherly voice she conjured up from some dark place within her. "I'm not going to make my daughter go through this alone."

"Did anyone think to ask Lacy?" Mr. Johnson placed his palms flat on the counter across from Lacy.

Joe's hands diverted Lacy's attention away from her mug. She had always found comfort in those strong hands, never afraid of hard work. Her eyes quickly shifted back to her mug of tea when her mother interrupted.

"Oh now, Joe, Lacina isn't thinking straight right now." Katlyn stepped around the island and gently put her hand on Joe's arm. "You heard that nonsense about seeing Willy at the graveside. She's not currently capable of taking care of her children by herself."

"You're right, Mr. Johnson," Raelynn said. "Let's ask Lacy what she wants to do."

"Raelynn," Katlyn snarled. "This really doesn't concern you anymore. Thank you for your help today but maybe it would be best if you run on home."

"Mom!" Jolene yelled. "Please."

"Well," Katlyn explained. "This is a time for us to figure out how to move forward."

"One thing you don't understand, Mrs. Johnson"—Raelynn stood up and pushed her chair back from the bar—"Lacy and I have been together a long time. We are a military family and you can't get any closer than that. Tell me where were you when Lacy spent those months and years worried about Willy while he was deployed? Where were you when he kept her up all night worrying about his partying ass? Where were you when he didn't come home that night? My place is right here. The real question is where is yours?"

Lacy slid her half empty mug across the counter. Sighing deeply, she scooted her chair back.

Not making eye contact with any one of her self-appointed advocates she muttered, "I think I'll go lay down."

Quietly, she shuffled out of the kitchen.

Shaking her head at Katlyn, Raelynn stomped out of the kitchen and followed Lacy up the stairs to her room.

CHAPTER 5

2001

"I know we aren't getting along but they leave in the morning, you know?" Raelynn tried to convince Lacy to come down for dinner with her family.

"Yes, I know." Lacy said. "But I don't have any energy at all."

"Your mom is putting food on the table, and I've already laid out your clothes. Of course, no one cares if you go down in your robe."

"My dad would." Lacy forced a grin on her face. "He won't say anything, but he would mind."

"Well, getting dressed might convince your mom you're handling things here by yourself." Raelynn tossed a pair of socks on top of the pile of clean clothes.

"I don't know if I can," Lacy said. "I don't think I can take care of Olivia and Alice all by myself without Willy."

"What are you talking about, Lacy. Of course, you can. You have taken care of them by yourself plenty of times when he was deployed. Think of this as an extra-long deployment."

"During deployment I can talk to him on the phone and look forward to him coming home."

"You never looked forward to him coming home. You always said y'all got along better over the internet."

"Why is this happening to me?" Lacy plopped a pillow on her lap. "We were finally getting things put together in our marriage."

"You sound a little crazy. Last week Willy was a waste of your precious youth and now you sound like he was your prince charming." Raelynn grabbed the pillow from Lacy's hands and tossed it to the other side of the bed. Then she picked up Lacy's shirt and pitched it to her. "Get dressed. We're having dinner with your parents."

"I'll never forget our first kiss. It was—"

"I know. I know." Raelynn interrupted, rolling her eyes. "It was like a magic carpet ride. Not to mention it was your first New Year's Eve kiss and you were drunk."

"It was a first kiss that lasts a lifetime." Lacy's smile was short lived. "It was supposed to last a lifetime anyway. How could he do this to me?" She slipped on her shirt and hung her head down toward the ground.

"I am sure as unthoughtful as he was…" Raelynn thought being frank would help Lacy realize it wasn't the end of the world. After all, Willy was not a prince charming and though she wasn't privy to their sex life, the rest of the way he treated Lacy was not worth grieving over as far as she could tell. "As unthoughtful as he could be, Lacy, I am sure he didn't die and leave you on purpose."

"You think he committed suicide?" Lacy lifted her head and scowled at Raelynn.

"No," Raelynn protested. "Of course not. I just said I didn't think he did that on purpose. And that's what I meant. I'm trying to explain that your first kiss… it was a long time ago."

"No, it wasn't that long ago," Lacy said. "It was our last one too. You should have been there Raelynn."

"Apparently not!"

"He was so charming. A true prince. We danced and we laughed. We hadn't had that much fun and romance in such a long time. It's like he had some kind of epiphany. It was magical…" Lacy said, drifting off.

"I am so glad you have that wonderful memory with him." Raelynn only half meant it and the rest she had to force out of her mouth. She never did understand what Lacy saw in Willy.

"He gave me a gift," Lacy said, hopping out of bed. "I almost forgot all about it."

Lacy pulled open the dresser drawers and sifted through the clothes searching for the necklace. She slid open the cubbies on the headboard. She searched through the pockets on her dress jackets hanging in the closet.

"What is it?" Raelynn asked. "Maybe I can help."

"It's a locket." Tears began streaming down her cheeks. "I have to find it. It's the last thing he ever gave me. It is a very precious gift from his heart."

"We'll find it. I promise." Raelynn doubted anything from Willy was from his heart, but she knew she needed to be supportive if she was to convince Lacy's family that Lacy should stay here. Raelynn put her arm on Lacy's shoulder. "We will find it."

"Time to eat," someone shouted from downstairs, startling them both.

"We'll search all night if we have to," Raelynn promised. "But we should eat now."

Lacy moved a few more piles of clothes, hoping to find the locket as Raelynn tried to get her out the door.

"Dinner is ready." Jolene's slender build stood rigid in the doorway, her long hair settling on her shoulders. "Everyone is waiting on you."

This week had been all about Lacy, the grieving widow, and it was becoming evident that it was wearing on Jolene. Raelynn knew Jolene was not used to having to share much of the spotlight with her sister.

"Thanks, Jolene," Raelynn said, putting her arm around Lacy and leading her out the doorway. "We're starving."

Lacy laid her head on Raelynn's shoulder and walked down the stairs to the dining room as if she was going to her last meal.

"Olivia, I found your library book in my backseat." Raelynn passed by Parker and followed the girls in through the front door. "I put it in your backpack. Don't forget to give it to your school tomorrow."

"Thanks, Aunt Rae." Olivia giggled and gave her a hug. "What's for dinner?"

"I got this." Lacy, still in her bathrobe, stood at the top of the stairs. "You go on home. Spend some time with Ella."

"At least let me help with dinner," Raelynn offered.

Parker blocked her as she tried to make her way into the kitchen. "I think if Lacy says she's got this, we should respect that."

Lacy creeped down the stairs holding the rail with both hands. The eyes of her guests gazed up at her.

"I'm sure she can use the help." Raelynn furrowed her eyebrows in her husband's direction. "You know you can spare me."

"No," Lacy insisted. "I've got this. You've been such a big help. I need to do this."

Lacy took Raelynn's arm, gave her a quick hug, and ushered her toward the front door.

Parker tried to put his arm around Raelynn as they walked down the front walk but she shrugged him off. Their voices got louder as they walked toward their car.

"What is wrong with you?" Raelynn yelled. "You know she's not ready yet. What about those girls?"

"If you don't let her start doing things for herself, she will never get ready," he insisted.

As he opened the car door for Raelynn, she took a step back.

"Please, let me do it myself," she scolded. "Or I might get used to you doing everything for me."

"You're enabling her. You need to let her try. I thought that's why you didn't want her to go home with her overbearing mom."

"Are you saying I am overbearing?" Raelynn reached out for the door.

"I want you home with Ella and me." He took her shoulders in his hands and turned her to face him. "Let's enjoy the time I have left at home as a family."

"Doesn't seem fair, does it?" Raelynn teared up. "That we get to be a family and the Donathons can't. I feel so bad for those little girls."

"And yet…" Parker hesitated.

"What?"

"They seem to be the ones doing better than any of us."

Lacy searched the refrigerator and the freezer but there were no more pre-made meals to be warmed up. The breadbox was empty, and the pantry was down to two cans of tomato soup and a box of Corn Pops. Why did she let Raelynn leave? Maybe she wasn't ready after all. She scrounged around and found some milk to put on the cereal to give the girls.

"Come on girls," Lacy said. "It's time to eat."

"That's breakfast," Olivia snarked.

"Haven't you ever heard of breakfast for dinner?" Lacy asked. "Daddy used to make it all the time?"

"I remember," Olivia only acted as if she actually remembered.

"Breakfast for dinner!" Alice cheered.

Lacy watched her daughters eating their cereal. She was quite proud of herself for actually pulling it off. It was the first meal she had prepared since Willy died. Maybe they could be normal again after all.

Milk dripped off Alice's spoon and a corn pop slopped onto the counter. She quickly pinched it between her fingers and slid it into her mouth.

"Disgusting." Olivia murmured.

"Finish up you two. It's time to get ready for bed then you can play for a few minutes." Lacy put the jug of milk back in the fridge and wiped down the counters.

"I can't find my homework," Olivia cried handing Lacy her bowl.

Homework. The word echoed in Lacy's head. Homework. What was Parker talking about? Did Raelynn help the girls with that?

"Do you have homework? For God's sake, you're only in second grade."

"Sometimes," Olivia explained. "Like last week we brought pictures of our pets. So Aunt Rae took a picture of a squirrel in the backyard. My teacher laughed."

"Would you like a pet?" Lacy asked.

"I want a baby squirrel," Olivia said.

"I want a baby monkey," Alice squealed. "And a banana."

Lacy smiled. "You girls are all I need. You make Momma smile."

They responded with two big grins that made Lacy feel almost normal again.

Normal meant reading a good novel while the girls played.

She slipped past the girls acting out their future family life with dolls that were a foot tall. While Olivia was more interested in engaging the characters in deep conversations, Alice was consumed by fashion, changing her dolls' outfits one after another. Lacy was happy that it entertained them long enough to allow her to delve into a fictional world of her own. They didn't even notice she had ascended the stairs and disappeared to find her book.

There it was. Message in a Bottle, the last book she had been reading, still waiting for her to return. She picked it up and stared at the cover. She loved the romances of Nicholas Sparks but not so much his endings.

Great guys should never die, she thought. She stared at the cover almost afraid to pick it up. Funny, it was about grief but also about starting over; something that seemed impossible to the protagonist, as well as to Lacy. As she opened the book to find her last page read, something sparkled behind the lamp. It was the locket Willy had given her on their last date. She picked it up, smiling as she put it around her neck, fumbling her fingers until the clasp was secure.

Then she took the book and skipped back downstairs to her recliner. Out of habit, she switched on the reading lamp next to her chair even though she didn't need it. The setting sun beaming through the window offered her plenty of reading light.

Opening the book to the last dog-eared page she had read, Lacy paused to watch the girls play out another round of fantasy on the coffee table.

We'll be alright, won't we? Lacy thought. Turning to look out the window at the world, she grasped the locket that dangled from her neck and squinted to block the sun's reflection.

CHAPTER 7

1993

"Lacy," Willy reached over and tapped Lacy's arm. "Hey, we're almost there."

Startled by the sound of his voice, Lacy jolted in her seat. The sun blinded her half-hearted attempts to open her eyes. Her body longed to remain in deep sleep where reality remained in some distant land even if she had only dozed off in her recliner.

"Lacy," Willy called out again.

Wiping away her blurred vision with each blink, Willy's profile behind the steering wheel began to come into focus.

Staring at the ghost of her deceased husband, her mouth moved but all that came out was a little squeal. The fuzzy dice dangling from the rearview mirror redirected her attention.

"I know you're sleepy, but I want you to be wide awake so you can enjoy our dinner."

"Something is not right," Lacy managed to say.

"It's going to be perfect. Absolutely perfcct."

Lacy sat up and searched the back seat. It looked like the back seat of Willy's '76 Camaro. How can that be?

"It's the old Camaro," she whispered.

"Old?" Willy acted surprised. "You love this car."

"Where are the girls?" She unbuckled her seatbelt and twisted around toward the back seat.

"What girls?"

"Our children," Lacy demanded. There were no car seats, no half empty bottles, no toys, not even a crumb. "Where are Olivia and Alice?"

"Oh my God, Lacy." Willy's voice turned dark and perturbed. "You are not going to start in on trying to have kids again, are you? Not tonight, our last night together before I get shipped out. Please don't do that."

"I'm not doing anything. All I want is to know where the girls are. Does Raelynn have them?"

"Lacy!" Willy shouted. "Wake up!"

He snapped his fingers in front of her face and then looked back at the road.

"I'm awake." Lacy shook her head, turning back around and staring through the front windshield. "At least, I think I am."

"You were acting crazy." Willy gripped the steering wheel with both hands. "Talking about kids. You even named them. What kind of crazy dream was that? And who is Raelynn?"

Lacy could tell that Willy honestly had no idea what she was talking about. Was this a dream? Was she here with Willy? Would it hurt to enjoy it? She closed her eyes trying to go back to sleep so that she could wake up with her girls playing on the floor in front of her.

She could remember them. She remembered their high-pitched voices squealing as she had drifted off to sleep.

"Don't go back to sleep," Willy demanded. "We're here. Surprise!"

He was very proud of himself for planning an evening with her at her favorite restaurant on Pensacola beach. The place where he had proposed one year ago.

"Well?" he asked. "Great place to have a going away dinner, right?"

"I remember," Lacy said thinking about the night Willy brought her here, not one year ago but almost ten.

"Of course," Willy said. "It's where we got engaged."

"And where you—" Lacy stopped short of telling him this was where he took her for their almost anniversary before deploying with Parker. It was the night Parker had shown up with Raelynn and introduced them to her.

Of course, she was having a very vivid memory dream.

"I reserved our exact table on the beach." His grin was like that of a small child showing off for his mother.

Lacy smiled.

Fine, she decided. Why not just go with it? Why not relive one of the better nights we had together?

Lacy wondered if things were playing out the same as they had nine years ago or if her mind was playing tricks on her.

Maybe she was filling in the gaps in her memory, maybe she didn't remember how things had gone. One thing was for certain, when she had worried about him dying in the past, it was always getting killed in the war that she feared most.

"This is it," Willy said. "Remember?"

He pulled Lacy's chair out and helped her slide it back in when she sat down.

"Yes, I do."

Lacy smiled kicking off her shoes and burying her feet in the sand. This place was her favorite. The tables were set with fancy linens and porcelain dishes right on the beach—and oh, she loved eating so close to the water. Each table had a different colored table cloth with a matching fabric umbrella over the table to keep the sun off patrons.

The outdoor setting offered sand volleyball courts, where you could play while you listened to a Jamaican band play. Past the levy, waves crashed onto the shore. It created a romantic setting as the sun went down over the gulf and the stars began to brighten the southern sky. She drew in the salty sea breeze and watched a seagull swoop down to snatch a French fry off an uncleared table.

Whether it was the wine or the warm breeze off the gulf, Lacy was swept into the moment, falling in love with Willy all over again. As he smiled and lifted his wine glass, she lifted her own. The glasses clinked as they touched each other.

"You're grinning," Willy said. "What are you thinking?"

"I am thinking how amazing this is." She sipped her wine and watched every move that her husband made.

He took his gaze off Lacy to watch the band as if waiting for a signal from them. When the lead guitar player nodded to him, he stood up and stretched his hand out to Lacy.

"My lady, may I have this dance?"

Lacy's heart began racing like it was her first embrace at the Homecoming Dance. She stood up and placed her hand in his.

"Why, yes," she replied in her best Southern accent. "It would be my pleasure."

They laughed and she followed his lead to the dance floor as the band played the song Willy had requested.

The lead singer began belting out the words to the first song they danced to the night he'd proposed, Could I Have This Dance by Anne Murray.

Lacy fell into a blissful trance as they rocked to the music and held each other close. The memory she had of this perfect evening from her past transformed into something that seemed real, normal. Thoughts of funerals and overdue bills—even her worries of unsupervised children were fading from her mind.

"Could I have you for the rest of my life?' Willy whispered in her ear along with the band.

Lacy joined in and they sang the rest of the song lyrics together.

At the end of the song, Willy dipped her and her heart raced. As Lacy reached her hand to her chest to catch her breath, she felt the cool metal from the locket. Within seconds, Willy dropped her and she landed on the hardwood floor.

Lacy squinted her eyes, bringing the light from the lamp into focus as she laid on the living room floor. The blades of the ceiling fan spun as she heard the muffled sounds of Alice and Olivia.

"Mom?" they were saying. "Mommy, are you okay? Are you okay, Mommy?"

Still trying to comprehend what had happened, she mumbled, "I'm okay."

It was like being plucked out of time or like waking up from a meticulous dream.

"Did you fall down?" Alice asked.

"I'm okay," Lacy pulled herself back up into the recliner.

The last thing she remembered was touching the cool metal on the locket that hung against her chest. She started to touch it, but then pulled her hand back. Reaching around her neck with both arms she felt for the clasp, unhooking it she let it fall into her hands.

Lacy looked at the clock to see how long she had been sleeping. It was 5:50. Had she been asleep under a minute. How could that be? It seemed to be a much too long and detailed dream for such a short span of time. She couldn't even remember that first dance with such details, but somehow, she felt his touch, smelled his scent on his scruffy, out-of-regulation whiskers, and heard his voice.

What just happened, she wondered.

CHAPTER 8

2001

Raelynn smiled.

While she didn't like the circumstances that brought him home, it was nice to see Parker at the other end of the table. As much as she disapproved of Willy's behavior, she was distraught at his death.

When someone close dies, there is always a mix of emotions. At first, they are raised to sainthood for the funeral, no one wants to speak ill of the dead. Then the real impact of their life, from start to finish, is revealed; like finishing a novel.

She avoided the fleeting thoughts that Lacy was better off without Willy. She tried not to think of the good that might come if Lacy could meet someone who would treat her better than he did.

Raelynn's heart broke looking into the faces of the bereaved. Looking across the table, she stared into the face of her own grieving husband. As much as Raelynn tried to deny it, Willy was Parker's best friend.

"Why are you smiling?" Parker asked.

Ella looked up from her macaroni and cheese at her mother's face.

"I want to enjoy this moment," Raelynn said. "It feels right to be here with my family together around this table. I could spend every evening just this way."

"Six o'clock," Parker said. "Dinner every night at six o'clock. Don't be late."

"Exactly," Raelynn agreed.

Ella shook her head. "You two are weird."

"You know, Ella. When I was a young boy at home, we were expected to be home by six for dinner. There were some exceptions, but you had to ask to be excused. My mom would only give us permission to be late if it was very important."

"Why didn't she just change the time like we do?" Ella asked.

"Dinner was at six. That's the way it was," Parker explained. "If you missed it, Mom would fix you a plate, wrap it in plastic wrap and put it in the fridge for when you got home."

"Why didn't you drive through and pick something up?" Ella asked.

"We only ate out on very special occasions." Raelynn set her water glass down in front of her plate. "Like after my dance recital, we got to go out for pizza. I don't ever recall my mom driving through anywhere."

"Is that why we have to eat at the table, even when you drive through and bring it home?" Ella twirled her fork in her noodles.

"It's important." Parker leaned forward and turned his shoulders toward Ella. "This is our family time and there is nothing more important."

"Daddy," Ella said. "Please don't go tomorrow. You said it yourself, 'there is nothing more important than family'."

"Ella, don't make Daddy feel bad for doing his job. You know he has to go."

"It's okay," Parker sighed. "I struggle with the conflict as well. Family versus duty. I have to believe, Ella, that my duty supports my family."

Ella finished her food and took her plate and cup to the kitchen sink. She bounced back through the dining room with an announcement that her friends were waiting online for her.

"Two hours," Raelynn reminded her.

Ella protested on her way down the hall.

"You heard your mom," Parker hollered.

The smile between them faded as the reality that their time together was drawing to a close. In less than twelve hours, Parker would be on a plane heading back to the front lines.

"I wish you could stay, I…" She wiped a tear off her cheek.

Parker got up to comfort Raelynn. Kneeling down, he cupped her face in his hands.

"Baby, we'll get through this," he stroked her cheeks. "We always do."

"I know," Raelynn tightened her lips. "I know we will be fine. It's just … it's just too much. I'm scared you'll lose focus, and I'm worried about Lacy."

"I'll be fine. I know how to work through this." Parker slid his hands down her neck with a gentle massaging motion. "And Lacy will figure it out. It's gonna be a little bumpy, but she'll get through it."

He gave her a hug and returned to sit across the table from her.

They gazed into each other's eyes until Raelynn broke the silence.

"Parker, Lacy is in trouble."

"What do you mean? Didn't Willy have any life insurance?"

"It's not that, I'm worried she is not grieving well."

"I thought she had been getting up and taking care of the girls?" Parker set his silverware across his plate signaling he was done with his meal. "You said that was going well."

"Oh, it is. Lacy is focusing on the girls, getting up and taking them to school and getting them fed, that's a big step forward. What I am concerned about is that she told me she saw Willy. They even danced."

"You know," Parker sat down next to Raelynn placing both of his hands on top of hers, "that's pretty normal when you suffer a great loss."

"Are you serious? It seems odd."

"Yes, many people report seeing their loved one. It may be someone they pass on the street that has similar attributes, and their mind plays tricks on them. It's part of the grieving process."

"You're probably right." Raelynn got up and stacked Parker's plate on top of hers. "I hope you're right."

Parker followed her into the kitchen. Reaching his arms around her waist, he turned her around to face him. "I'm not going away forever. I'll help you through this."

Raelynn pulled him close to her. His face was smooth shaven, like holding a cool apple up against her cheek.

"I should be helping you through this," she replied. "You lost your best friend and now you have to go back to that hellhole. I wish there was something I could do."

"Be there at the other end of the line when I call. Knowing you are here waiting for me is all I need to get me through."

"I'll be here, whenever you call."

Raelynn assured him again as they stood on the tarmac at the Navy airfield the next morning.

"I'm a phone call away."

She squeezed him to her as she looked over his shoulder at all the people gathering. Hundreds of family members and friends assembled behind the yellow tape to send off their sailors. Holding on to one more lingering embrace, one more kiss, trying to reassure themselves that this goodbye won't be their last.

As sailors began forming up with their units, the crowds thinned. Raelynn caught a glimpse of a familiar face. "Lacy?" she whispered.

"She'll be fine," Parker said.

"No," Raelynn clarified. "She's here."

They turned to face her slim figure sprinting across the tarmac. Her curly, dishwater blonde hair bounced off her shoulders.

"Parker," Lacy shouted waving both her hands in the air. "I found you." Lacy tried to catch her breath. "I can't believe they wanted to search my car and wouldn't let me through the gates."

"Those car seats in the back look pretty suspicious." Parker laughed.

"I know right?" Lacy grinned.

Parker reached out to hug Lacy. "I'm glad you made it."

"I wanted to thank you for coming to Willy's funeral. It meant so much to me and the girls. I don't know how you pulled it off. Parker, please…"

"I'm going to be okay, Lacy, and you will too. We have to. We both have people counting on us." Parker wiped the tear running down Lacy's cheek. "I'm counting on you."

Lacy put her arms around him. "Be careful, Parker, we need you to come home."

Lacy stepped back and let Raelynn and Parker say their final goodbyes.

Parker ducked under the yellow tape and turned back with a wave and a kiss. Raelynn gripped Lacy's hand—almost by instinct now—with one hand and waved goodbye with the other. The two friends had stood on this tarmac many times together as their men left them behind. Many tearful goodbyes never knowing if their husbands would make it back from their missions.

As the crowd dissipated, the women stood firm together, waving until the plane left the airstrip. They watched as it lifted up, made a sharp turn, and disappeared into the sky.

"You're not ready?" Raelynn questioned, coming up the stairs and seeing Lacy through the master bathroom door.

"I need to find something," Lacy slammed the vanity drawer closed and stepped into the bedroom. I can't find my locket."

"What's that?" Raelynn pointed to the cameo pendant on the night stand. Except for the pendant, the nightstand on Willy's side of the bed looked the same as it had the night he died.

"Well, that's weird. How did it get over there?" Confused and flustered Lacy carefully removed it from the night stand and put it around her neck.

"Pretty," Raelynn smiled. Girls' night out was an evening they spent forgetting their men. But with Willy gone and Parker on deployment, it was going to be hard to not bring them up.

"I'm ready." Lacy picked up her purse and swung it over her shoulder. "Let's go kick some ass."

"Don't even think about drinking vodka tonight. I am not spending the night in jail with you."

They laughed, which shocked them both. Laughter had been in short supply the last few months.

"Hurry, let's get our drinks, the movie is about to start." Raelynn rushed up to the bar and ordered her drink.

Avoiding vodka, Lacy chose a dark malt beverage. "Ladies don't drink dark malt," Willy had once told her changing her order to a red wine. Tonight, I order whatever I want.

"Interesting choice," Raelynn smirked.

After the movie, Raelynn insisted they go to a popular steakhouse—without considering how often they'd been there with their husbands. After ordering more drinks and appetizers, they asked the waitress to return for their dinner orders when the appetizers came out. With no intention of going bar hopping and the babysitter booked until midnight, there was no sense in rushing dinner.

"I have to pee," Raelynn giggled.

"Do you want me to go with you?" Lacy asked.

Raelynn bumped the table trying to stand up before sliding out of the booth.

"No, I got this."

She fell back into the booth as they both laughed. Raelynn tilted her head trying to keep things in focus. The light swinging over their table reflected from Lacy's locket.

"That is such a stunning locket." She seemed mesmerized by the intricate gem glowing from its golden case.

Without thinking, Lacy reached up to her chest and felt for the locket. Covering it, she blinked imagining it as Raelynn must have seen it.

"It is pretty, isn't it?"

"What's pretty?" Lacy heard Willy's voice ask.

Lacy opened her eyes and saw Willy sitting across from her. Her hands fell to the table in shock. Willy looked around at the other tables.

"What is it, Lacy? What's so pretty?"

"Your face," Lacy reached up for the locket. She gripped the locket in her right hand and squeezed her eyes shut. "It's your face, Willy. That's what is so damn pretty."

"What the hell?" Raelynn said. "Are you seeing things again?"

Lacy shook her head. As she opened her eyes, the figure sitting across from her came into focus, "Raelynn?" She jerked the locket off her neck and dropped it into her purse. It's just that Willy and I used to sit in this very booth together."

"I'm sorry, I didn't realize. Should I have picked a different restaurant?" Raelynn scooted closer to the end of the seat and waited for Lacy's response.

"No, it's fine. Go pee. I'm alright." Lacy giggled.

"But you were talking to Willy."

"Go pee." Lacy waved her hand toward the restrooms.

"I better go pee," Raelynn slurred.

As soon as her friend disappeared around the corner, she took the locket out of her purse and set it on the table. After staring at it for a few moments, she put it back around her neck. Testing it, she reached up and grasped the locket in her hand and blinked her eyes.

This time she was in front of a small video screen in a USO office where she had often videochatted with Willy when his ship was at port. Willy was on the screen in front of her, blabbering on about their lack of recreation on the ship. A familiar face appeared in the screen behind Willy.

"Parker? Is that Parker with you?"

"Hey, man," Willy said, grabbing Parker and pulling him into the camera view with him. "How do you know my old lady?" Willy teased, but Lacy sensed jealousy in his voice. "You two know each other, do ya?"

"It's nice to meet you, Lucy." Parker laughed. It was obvious the two had been drinking.

"It's Lacy," she corrected. "I thought you weren't allowed to drink on the ship."

"Thas right, ma'am," Parker slurred. "No drinking on this ship."

"I still want to know how you two know each other." Willy made a loose fist and pounded it on the table. "You got something going on I don't know about?"

"Parker, your battle buddy," Lacy explained. "He's all you ever write about."

"It's nice to meet you, Lucy," Parker slurred again.

Willy reached over and pushed Parker out of the camera's view. "It's Lacy, you drunk son of a bitch. Lacy."

"I've got to go, babe," Willy said. "Time to get Parker's drunk ass on that ship before they shove off without us."

"Be safe," Lacy replied.

The screen went black, and she reached up for the locket. Blinking, the light above the table blinded her. She closed her eyes again and tried to get the bright spots to clear from her vision. The seat across from her was empty. She wasn't sure who would be joining her but was relieved when Raelynn teetered back from the bathroom.

This is happening, she decided. I have to figure this time jumping thing out.

When they returned to Lacy's house, Ella was asleep with Alice and Olivia. The two mothers paused at the bedroom door to admire their sleeping angels. Olivia and Ella were sprawled across her twin bed horizontally, four legs dangled off the side. Alice was rolled up in a ball, one eye peeking out from her comforter.

Laughing they stumbled down the hallway to Lacy's room. Kicking off their shoes, although Raelynn only managed to get one shoe off, they fell into Lacy's bed. Their clothes smelling of smoke and alcohol, they fell asleep.

The children woke them up early, laughing and bouncing on the bed making Raelynn's stomach even more nauseated than it already was.

"Ugh," Raelynn moaned, rolling over and covering her head with the pillow.

That made the girls laugh harder.

"Hey," Lacy said. "No jumping on the bed. You girls head down to the kitchen, Aunt Rae is going to make pancakes."

"With chocolate chips?" Alice asked.

"Yep," said Lacy.

"Yippie," Olivia screeched.

The girls headed out the door, giggling.

"You rat." Raelynn's groans were muffled by the pillow.

"It got them to quit jumping on the bed, didn't it?"

"I don't feel so good." Raelynn wrapped both arms around her stomach. "I think I may have drunk too much."

"It doesn't help. It doesn't make them come home any sooner."

"You weren't too sober either. No disrespect, but you were talking to Willy."

"It wasn't that." Lacy rolled up onto her side, propped up on her elbow, head in her hand. "I know this sounds weird, but I think I am going back in time. I figured it out last night. It's the locket. I think it has something to do with the way light hits it."

"Lacy," Raelynn rolled onto her side to face her. "That is crazy talk."

"I was sitting there with Willy last night. And when you were in the restroom, I was back at the USO talking to Willy on the webcam. I saw Parker."

"You saw Parker?" Raelynn sat all the way up and glared down at Lacy. "Now you are freaking me out, Lacy. Parker is still alive. There is no reason you can see him."

"I don't think I saw him because he is dead. I see him because I go to a specific time and place in the past. I mean I don't remember talking to Parker before I met him but that's because I didn't know who he was. I always ignored other guys on the video calls and focused on Willy. This time I saw Parker and said hello."

"Hun, it's normal to see the dearly departed while you are grieving. Parker explained to me that lots of guys see their departed comrades. It's a common occurrence. What you are talking about isn't. It's not real. It's not part of the normal process."

"I know," Lacy agreed. "It's not."

The girls yelled for Aunt Rae, and the conversation soon turned to getting ready for breakfast. Raelynn splashed water on her face, tried to shake the fog out of her head, and met the girls in the kitchen. "Come on Lacy, let's get these girls fed so they'll quit terrorizing us."

Lacy moaned. She peeled off her stinky shirt, dabbed a deodorant stick under her arms, and slipped on a fresh t-shirt. She joined Raelynn in the kitchen to share in the duties of making chocolate chip pancakes. Her stomach turned at the thought of even a small sample of the chocolate.

Feeling victorious over satisfying the girls, they left them at the breakfast bar and slipped off with their coffee mugs to the dining room table. As they breathed in the aroma of fresh roasted coffee, the earlier conversation from the bedroom resumed.

"Lace." Raelynn reached out and touched Lacy's arm. "I know you must miss Willy very much. Knowing Parker is coming home again is what gets me through the days. I can't imagine what you're going through. But the whole idea of time travel, that is…"

"Out there, I know. Let me do a few more tests, and then I'll know if it's real."

"There are stages of grief you know." Raelynn set her mug down on the coffee table. "Time travel is not one of them." They both laughed because it sounded ridiculous just hearing the words. "Don't you think it would be good for you to go talk to someone who knows about this sort of thing?"

"I don't care what any expert, who has never lost a loved one, has to say about the stages of grief. I am not crazy, Raelynn. I know how it sounds, but I was with Willy last night. And what if…" Lacy paused to take a deep breath. "What if I could go back and tell him not to take his bike that night?"

Silence fell between them.

They stared at each other, both trying to take in the awkwardness of this conversation.

"I can't tell you I believe you, Lace. I don't. And I don't want to hinder your healing. As your friend—your oldest and dearest friend—with enduring love for you all I can say is that you need to get a grip on reality. You have to get help."

Lacy stared across the room toward the window. She wanted to get up and walk out of the room, but she needed to convince Raelynn she was not crazy. This is really happening.

"No." Lacy leaned in further, still staring at the clock above the counter. She crossed her arms putting her elbows on the table between them. "The clock is always the same when I get back. No actual time passes."

"Lacy." Raelynn squirmed, letting out a deep sigh. "Do you know how crazy this sounds?"

"Can I get you anything else?" the waitress interrupted.

"No, thank you," Raelynn replied.

Reaching in front of them and taking their empty plates, she asked, "Did you enjoy your breakfast?"

"Yes, ma'am," they both answered at the same time as the waitress set the check down between them. She exchanged a quick smile with them and then moved on to the next table.

"You go back in time but no one here notices you're gone because the locket brings you back to the exact time you left," Raelynn whispered.

"Exactly," Lacy sat up and squared her shoulders with the table. "It works. Do you want to try it?"

"I am not going to play into this game of yours. It's not healthy."

"I never told you why Willy married me. I had blocked it out of my mind altogether myself."

"You'd been in love since high school. I've heard the story numerous times."

"But then Willy went off to war, I wrote him but he pretty much forgot about me. He never wrote back."

"They get busy. It's hard," Raelynn assured her.

"He did make some time for me on leave—but only if no other girls were available. Then I got pregnant. I was seventeen and a senior in high school. I kept writing him, but I left out the details of my growing belly."

"Did he write back?"

"No, but my father sent his officer a letter against my mother's wishes. My mother wanted me to get an abortion and forget about Willy. She thought he was a worthless thug. But his commanding officer gave him leave to come back and move me to Pensacola, so he showed up and did the right thing."

"That was nice."

"We went to Pensacola and got married at the justice of the peace. My mother wasn't very happy. The Navy helped me get my GED, and I started prenatal care but too late. I was in my third trimester when Willy had to go back out to sea. A few weeks later I lost the baby."

"I was in the labor room with you. Don't you remember?"

"No. The first time I recall meeting you was in nineteen ninety. It was our first anniversary and you and Parker came by our table."

"We were roommates until they moved you out of the maternity ward to the OB-GYN ward. I visited you there."

"I still don't understand what went wrong. Maybe I should go back to nineteen eighty-nine and find out what happened."

Raelynn reached out and attempted to snatch the locket from Lacy's hand, "Okay I'll try it."

Lacy pulled it back. She unclasped the chain as she stood up and slid into the booth next to Raelynn. "Turn around," she twirled her finger in a circle. Running the chain around Raelynn's neck, she hooked the clasp with care.

Lacy moved back to her seat across the table. Raelynn gave her hair a quick fluff and then looked down at the locket, tightening one side of her lips into her cheek.

"Grasp the locket and blink your eyes. When you open them, you'll be in a different time."

Nothing happened, so Raelynn attempted the process again. Nothing.

Shaking her head, she removed the necklace. "I don't know why I started believing you."

Lacy took the locket from her.

"It's worked before." Clasping the chain around her neck, she blinked. There was no change.

"Did you go back in time?" Raelynn blurted through a deep puff of air.

"It didn't work." Lacy stared down at the locket on her chest.

Lacy shifted back in her seat until the sunlight from a nearby window reflected off the locket. Grabbing it, she blinked.

She squinted allowing in small portions of the bright light. It definitely worked. Where on earth am I?

Standing under a canopy of trees, she looked out over the rolling pastures of the most pristine farmland she had ever seen. The pastures were edged with woods and the trees glistened almost like the light that reflected off the locket. There were several ponds with water so clear she could see multicolored gems sparkling on the bottom. Rabbits, deer, and squirrels bounced around the tree lines, running in and out of the woods.

The sound of galloping hooves startled her as a herd of horses ran out of the woods and across the open field. Their precision as a group, changing directions in unison, took her breath away. As they approached the edge of the tree line where Lacy stood, some of them kicked up their back heels high in the air. She stepped back, hiding behind a tree as they halted near her and began grazing in the field.

As if calling to her, a silver stone sparkled in front of her. She reached out for it. A black stallion lifted his head from the grass, inhaling deep breaths of the warm, spring air. Then he walked up to where she was hiding. She slipped the stone into her pocket.

"I know you are there," the stallion said.

"You can talk?" Lacy asked, hoping that would be the end of the conversation.

"Can you?" the stallion asked.

"Yes." Now I know these are all dreams.

"Come out where I can see you," the stallion requested. "Then you will see I am a real horse."

Lacy crept out from around the tree. Although she loved watching horses from a distance, she had always been afraid of them. Even in a petting zoo, she'd never allowed her daughters to go near them.

"Lina!" the stallion exclaimed.

"I'm Lacy," she corrected, her voice shaking. "What is your name?"

"I am sorry. You looked familiar. My name is Hope." The stallion nickered.

"No need to apologize. May I pet you?" Why did she ask? She was petrified of touching horses.

"Of course." Hope lowered his head so that Lacy could reach his muzzle.

Lacy took a step closer and laid her shaking hand across his nose.

"Have you never touched a horse?"

She snapped her hand back. Childhood trauma.

"It's okay," he added. "I won't bite."

"What is this place?"

"This is Avenrand. Are you lost?"

"Avenrand? My grandmother told stories of a place she called Avenrand. Bedtime stories. Make believe. Her name was Lina."

The other horses in the herd crowded in and her heart quickened. She tried to step back but another horse was behind her. Feeling lightheaded, she struggled for a breath.

Hope pinned his ears and motioned the horses back. He nuzzled up close to Lacy. "Don't mind them. They just get excited when a nice human comes around. Everyone likes attention, don't you?"

But the attention overwhelmed her. "No." Her voice quivered. She saw a light reflect off the locket, her shaking hand reached for it and she blinked.

"Are you okay?" Raelynn reached out and touched Lacy's still trembling hand.

"It worked. I think." Lacy hesitated for a moment and then admitted. No, it can't be real, she thought. "I wonder if I am making this all up."

"You were here the whole time," Raelynn said. "Did you see Willy again?"

"No, I didn't see Willy. I saw… I saw a… I think… Was I here the whole time?"

"Yes. Well, I think so. I was talking to the waitress for just a moment. I mean if you had disappeared, I would have noticed."

Lacy began to cry. "I think you're right," she said through sobbing breaths. "What is wrong with me?"

Raelynn stood and scooted onto the bench next to Lacy. She put her arm around Lacy's shoulders.

"Nothing is wrong with you, Lacy, you're grieving. It's a lot of work to let your mind and body and emotions adjust to such a great loss. I can't imagine what it would be like if I lost Parker."

That made Lacy cry even harder.

"I'm sorry, Lace. I didn't mean to upset you more."

"You're not, Raelynn. You're very sweet to be here with me. I think all I needed was a good cry. Maybe I've been bottling it up inside me. All this time travel talk… You've been such a good friend to let me go on and on with this craziness."

Lacy removed the locket and tossed it into the trash receptacle on their way out of the restaurant.

Raelynn reached in and grabbed it as Lacy pushed the heavy glass doors toward the parking lot.

"Lacy, you'll be upset when you think that you threw away the last gift that Willy ever gave you."

"I know, but it makes me crazy. I can't be thinking like that anymore."

They walked across the parking lot and stared at each other across the top of the silver sedan.

"You're doing great. You recognize the power it had over you and now you can move on."

"I talked to a horse."

"What?"

"I saw a talking horse in my head," Lacy confessed.

"You're afraid of horses," Raelynn recalled as she unlocked the car doors.

"I know. I talked to one, and I petted it. See how insane this is? Proof it's not real."

Lacy flung the passenger door open harder than she planned. It tapped the car next to her, and she paused to inspect for damage.

Raelynn waited to put the key in the ignition until Lacy slid onto the passenger seat and closed her door.

"It's fine. Only moved a bit of dirt. That guy needs to wash his car."

"You know what I think? I think it's proof that you are healing. Overcoming your fear of being alone must be represented by you petting that horse."

"But the herd scared me and I bolted."

"Well, that means you still have things you need to work through, but you can get someone to help you with that. I'll put the locket away in a safe place and you can get some help. Promise me right now that you'll get some counseling."

CHAPTER 11

2001

“This is ridiculous. What a waste of money! Did you see how much this guy charges? One hundred and fifteen dollars an hour.” Lacy stood and looked down at Raelynn. “Let’s go get some lunch.”

Raelynn grabbed Lacy’s arm and motioned her to sit back down. She rolled her eyes and flung herself back into the chair. A plant caught her attention. It sat alone on a shelf. Odd that the bookcase did not contain any books. Just this one plant. Was it alive or plastic?

“Lacy Donathon,” a voice projected from behind the counter.

Lacy froze in her seat.

“Come on.” Raelynn pulled on Lacy’s arm when she hesitated too long. “I’ll walk you to the window.”

Lacy didn't know how to respond when the counselor asked what brought her in. Should she tell him she could go back in time or maybe that she felt alone without her husband? One seemed more realistic than the other. She hadn't seen the lockct in a week. Secretly, she yearned for the surprise of opening her eyes in another time or place. The opportunity to see people from her past with today's perspective. She couldn't stop thinking about it. She hadn't had time to grieve Willy when she knew she could use the locket and see him whenever she wanted. Where had Rae hidden the locket?

What was this counselor going to do for me that comes close to seeing Willy again? Would he be able to explain the talking horses?

"A friend brought me here." Lacy shifted back into the plush cushions of the couch. The counselor sat across the coffee table in an upholstered wingback chair.

"Whose idea was it to come in: yours or your friend's?" The counselor's eyes peered over his clipboard.

"She suggested it. But now I am not sure."

"Can you tell me why you ended up here?"

Lacy squirmed and pushed herself against the back of the couch as far as she could. The reason she had agreed to come was because she considered that maybe her time traveling had gotten a little out of hand.

When did talking horses ever exist? Never. What about the fact that she could spend an entire evening with her deceased husband, and no time passed while she was gone.

She was very confused about that. Although she was certain that the locket was taking her to these different times from her life, what if she could figure out how to control it?

Could she go back and tell Willy not to ride his bike that night? It would be the decent thing to do.

She had figured out how to blink whenever she wanted. What she didn't have control of was when or where she ended up after she opened her eyes. If she got the locket back, she needed to figure that out so she could go back and save her husband. They could get on with their lives. All this grieving nonsense would be over, and she wouldn't be alone anymore.

"My husband died in a motorcycle accident in April."

"'Your husband has been gone for three months?"

"I think so. Yes. He died three months ago."

"I am sorry to hear that." The counselor sat up, leaned forward, and lowered the clipboard onto his lap. "Can you share more about that?"

"It was after we went out. Willy decided we would start having date nights again, so we got a babysitter and went out. It was a nice evening. He was super romantic. He had even been so thoughtful he bought me a gift and gave it to me at the restaurant. It was a locket. A very special locket."

Even without its magical powers, Lacy thought about how sentimental the locket was.

"We had to meet at the restaurant. I don't remember why. We should have driven together. I took our car and he rode his bike. We flipped a coin to see who would pick up the kids from the babysitter. No matter who won or lost, I would be the one that had to pick them up. We laughed about that. Then he was supposed to go straight home and get things ready for us to finish our evening after we put the kids to bed. But when I got home, he wasn't there."

Lacy began to sob and couldn't get any more words out.

The counselor leaned even closer toward her chair and handed her a tissue, but remained silent. He let Lacy sit in the chair and cry.

When she was done, she took a deep breath and looked at the counselor for direction. He smiled at her sympathetically but said nothing. She squirmed in her chair, wishing he would ask her another question or say something. Was she supposed to keep talking?

"I am not sure what else to say," she broke the awkward silence.

"Whatever comes to mind."

Annoyed by the continuing silence, Lacy tried to wait him out but finally gave in.

"Nothing, nothing comes to mind. He didn't come home. He's never coming home again."

After another long silence, the counselor informed her that their time was up. As she was leaving his office, he recommended a support group for her.

"It's helpful to know that you are not alone in your grief. Being with others going through similar things is a great way to feel supported and move to the next level." He scribbled some contact information on a card and handed it to her.

She still had the card in her hand when she got in Raelynn's car. "He says I need support to move to the next level. Is this a video game? What does the next level even mean?"

Raelynn giggled. Trying to focus on her driving, she minimized her reactions as Lacy continued to rant all the way home from the counselor's office.

"I am never going to him again. He stared at me most of the session and said nothing. And this group, it sounds depressing. I don't need to be around a bunch of sad people making me feel worse. I …" She wanted to say that she hadn't given up trying to save Willy, but stopped herself.

"You should go. You paid good money for his advice. At least go to the group and check it out. You need others to help you through this."

"I have you, don't I?"

"You know how you said the worse thing people did after Willy died was tell you everything was going to be alright? And how upset you were because they had no idea what they were talking about? How could they tell you everything would be alright?"

"Well, it's true."

"We know these people have lost someone. And if you go to this grief group then if they tell you everything will be alright you can believe them. You will be around people who know what you are going through and they may be able to help you. Perhaps they can teach you how to cope with this loss."

I can't accept Willy is gone for good. How will I raise our girls by myself? "And help me move up to the next level?" Lacy asked sarcastically. "I wonder how many lives I get."

CHAPTER 12

2001

"When did your marriage end?" asked the young woman at the social security office.

"What do you mean?" Lacy responded. "My marriage didn't end—my husband died."

"Then use the date of his death," she said without any inflection.

Lacy turned the paper around so she could read it.

It said Marriage ended April 16, 2001.

I am no longer married, Lacy thought. Does that make me single? This isn't right.

Her hand shook. She didn't want to sign the form and admit that her marriage ended, but she had to to get help supporting Alice and Olivia. So, she did.

For the rest of the afternoon, she could not stop thinking about the young woman questioning when her marriage had ended.

The more she thought about it, the more desperate she was to find Willy. Where was he? If she could see him in the past, it was still possible to save him. She had to talk to him. She had to find out where Raelynn had hidden the locket.

As she grappled between time traveling to find Willy and moving on to end this agonizing grief, she decided to do something she had never done before. She was going to take herself out on the town. Maybe, just maybe, it was time to quit thinking about him and to get on with her life.

Lacy called up the teenager down the street. Always ready to make some extra cash, Melony seemed to be available whenever Lacy called.

"No." Melony shook her head. "Not that one."

Lacy hung the shirt back up in the closet and pulled out the purple, silky western shirt and held it up across her chest. "This one has glitter."

"Don't you have anything a little lower cut?" Melony suggested. "You're single. You need to show some cleavage."

"What on earth do you know about showing cleavage?" Lacy shook her head. "I hope you aren't teaching my girls about cleavage."

"Not until third grade," Melony teased. "In second, boys still have cooties."

"Boys had cooties well into junior high in my day. Willy was the first boy I ever kissed. It was precisely at midnight at my sister's New Year's Eve party. I was sixteen."

Melony grinned and handed Lacy a low-cut, turquoise blouse made of silk and a pair of low-rise designer jeans with faux gemstones on the pockets.

"Let's see if I can squeeze into these," Lacy took the stack of clothes into the bathroom and closed the door.

"You need to get all that reminiscing out of your system, or you'll be crying into your first glass of wine."

"How do you know all of this, young lady?" Lacy shouted back. Then sucked in her breath trying to squeeze into the jeans.

"I watch cable," Melony laughed. "You'd be surprised what you can learn."

"You'll learn more than I do watching Rugrats." Lacy presented herself somewhat excited about the new look, but also a bit petrified.

"It's nice," Melony said, repositioning Lacy's blouse a little lower. "Now for your makeup…"

After hugs and kisses, Lacy headed out for her first ever night on the town by herself. She decided to avoid all the places that she and Willy used to go. She could not risk crying tears into her drink. Tonight was about getting herself back out there, a trial run at her new life. It had been six months since Willy died. I can do this, she thought.

She started off with a drink at a small sports bar in an adjacent neighborhood. It was a way to loosen up a little before she moved on to the next club where she might get asked to dance. At least she could act interested in the game to keep from feeling too awkward.

As she scooted her stool up to the bar, she realized she was noticing couples everywhere. They seemed so happy and focused on one another.

"What can I get you?" the bartender asked.

She ordered her drink without taking her focus off the other couples. It made her feel more alone. Tears welled up inside her and she fought to push them back down. Some night on the town this was turning out to be.

Somehow instead of going to the dance club like she'd planned, she ended up knocking on Raelynn's front door. Hopefully, Raelynn and Parker weren't planning anything too intimate for his first night back home.

"Say hello," she whispered to herself. "Have a drink or two, and then stop by the dance hall and find a cowboy to hang onto for the night. "

"Lacy?" Raelynn looked shocked to see her.

"I wanted to welcome Parker home. Are you two busy?" She winked.

"Well…" Raelynn seemed a little on edge as she stepped out the front door onto the porch.

"What's going on, Raelynn? Is everything alright?"

Lacy couldn't help but peek around and try to see where Parker was. Was he beating on her or something? She acted as if she didn't want Lacy to see something. She heard quick steps rush to the front door, and Parker stepped out onto the porch.

"Welcome home! I hope everything is alright." Lacy reached up and wrapped her arms around Parker.

"It's fine." Parker gave her a quick squeeze and took a couple steps back toward the door. He seemed like he was hiding something too. "It's great to be back. What are you up to tonight? You sure look hot, like you're ready to hit the town."

"I am. Raelynn said I needed to move on, and I think I'm ready."

"That's great." Parker paused. "I think."

He looked at his wife for assurance.

"Yes, that is great," Raelynn said. "You look great, too."

Still curious as to what the big secret was, Lacy angled her upper body to take a peek inside when she saw a shadow move across the dining room window.

"I was checking to see if you wanted to celebrate with a toast, but we can get together later. It seems like y'all are busy."

Thinking she heard voices inside, Lacy looked through the blinds and saw several silhouettes around the dining room table. She leaned over and peered through the door.

"Oh, wow." Lacy's voice shook and her pulse quickened. "It's Darren and Marcy. Why didn't you tell me you have company?"

Lacy stepped inside the front door and waved innocently at their long-time mutual friends.

"Lacy." Parker walked up behind her.

As Lacy gestured to Darren and Marcy, she realized there were two other couples seated around the table and her heart sunk in betrayal.

"Hi. everyone," she faked a smile. "Enjoy your meal."

"Hey. Lacy," several voices greeted her.

Lacy turned and brushed past Parker as she stepped back out on the porch. She picked up the pace as she passed Raelynn.

"Have a good party," she choked out and sprinted down the sidewalk.

"Wait!" Raelynn ran to catch up, placing a hand on her shoulder. "Please, let me explain."

Lacy brushed Raelynn's hand off with a firm swing of her arm. "You don't have to, Raelynn. I get it. It's a dinner for eight—not for seven or nine. Who's the lucky couple that replaced Willy and me?"

"It's not like that," Raelynn said.

Lacy opened up her car door and paused before getting in.

"It's exactly like that," Lacy said.

She scooted into her seat and slammed the door. Raelynn motioned for her to open the window. Lacy started the car and drove off, leaving Raelynn standing in the middle of the road.

Tears streamed down Lacy's cheeks. Her body trembled so much that she had to pull off to the side of the road. Laying her head against the steering wheel, she cried until she couldn't anymore.

CHAPTER 13

2001

It was hard to ignore Raelynn's attempts to contact her, but Lacy felt like doing so made her point stronger. They had hurt her deeply. In the past, she would have stuffed those feelings down and pretended everything was okay. Being a widow seemed to give her permission to stand up for herself.

Lacy decided it was time to meet her people. She needed to be around people who weren't trying so hard to make her move on from Willy's death and those that hadn't moved on without her.

The musty smell reminded her of searching for Olivia and Alice at Willy's funeral. Walking down the stairwell, she wondered why church basements always seemed so dark and damp. A hint of Florida's salty air blew in through an open window. She took a deep breath, exhaled, and then walked into the fellowship hall filled with chatter from cliques of regulars catching up.

Chairs were placed in a circle, and Lacy passed by the one with a clipboard setting on it and chose the farthest one from it. She guessed that would be the leader of the group. Soon, she realized that sitting at three o'clock or nine o'clock would have been less intimidating than straight in front of her at six o'clock.

Fortunately—except for a quick hello—she never felt pressured to talk and remained quiet for most of the meeting.

"I cry every day," a young woman confessed. "I lost everything when my husband died."

"It can be overwhelming." The leader consoled her.

Several heads nodded in agreement.

"It takes time," a member said, trying to be supportive.

"Everyone says it gets easier in time," the young widow responded. "It doesn't get easier. It's been five years, but I still cry every single day."

Relieved when the leader announced a fifteen-minute break, Lacy continued thinking about the young widow.

Lacy longed to feel whole again. There was no way she was going to still be crying for Willy in five years. There had to be something that would snap her out of this fog she'd been living in.

Her shaky legs carried her back to the refreshment table. She stayed back a few feet and watched to see how many cookies seemed appropriate to put on her plate. Forgetting to eat didn't stop her from being hungry. Having food set in front of her, she could have easily taken more than her fair share.

Which punch was spiked? She laughed to herself.

A gentleman came up beside her.

"Can I get you a plate of cookies or a drink?" he asked.

"Oh, thank you. I was going to let it clear out a little before I went up."

"Well, don't wait five years or all the cookies will be gone."

Lacy smiled. She wasn't the only one who thought that amount of time was excessive but she wouldn't have said it out loud. Lacy wasn't sure if she should laugh or run away from this guy.

"Chris," he introduced himself and held out his hand. "Chris Manning. And you're Lacina Donathon."

"Lacy. My mother is the only one who calls me Lacina." She shook his hand.

"Oh, I have to agree with your mother. Lacina is a lovely name."

"Thank you," Lacy smiled, pushing her dishwater blonde curls behind her ears. "Nice to meet you?"

Chris replied with a chuckle. "I wouldn't be sure about meeting me either."

"Oh, no," Lacy explained. "I meant… Well, under the circumstances…"

"I am just giving you some grief." Chris laughed. "Is this your first meeting?"

Lacy squeaked out a laugh feeling the blood rush to her cheeks.

After a brief pause, she choked out the words, "Yes. Yes, it is. My husband died. I was told this would help."

"What would help is being around a little more uplifting crowd."

"I tried that and found out I'd been exiled."

"The not-a-couple-any-more curse. I've experienced that. I'm still trying to figure out if that means they were friends with my wife and I was her sidekick or they can't figure out how to set a table for an odd number."

Lacy smiled. It was good to meet someone who understood.

"All we had were couple friends, I guess that's why I ended up here."

"It seems that way for a while. I can't tell you how long you are going to cry. What I can say is that eventually you will stop zeroing in on all the couples and start seeing there are single people out there."

The leader called them back to the circle.

After the meeting was over, Chris approached Lacy again.

"We should have split when we had the chance," he said as they were leaving.

Lacy was disappointed to not find Chris at the next grief support meeting. All week she had been thinking about him. What if they had split when they had had the chance? Together.

She'd been doing well taking care of the girls and finding ways to stay busy. Most important of all, she wanted to tell Chris that she had made it a whole week without crying. That maybe— just maybe—he would want to cut out of their meeting early like she had imagined.

Since their last encounter he—and that young woman still mourning the loss of her husband five years later—had been all she could think about. Somehow it was motivating her to move on.

When Lacy looked around and didn't see Chris, she felt more alone than ever before. Her couple friends had moved on without her and the most understanding person she had met to date was a no show.

All she could think of on the way home was getting back to Avenrand and finding out if Hope was real.

In her eagerness to find where Raelynn had hidden the locket, she tried not to rush Melony out the door. She watched her babysitter walk down the street. She waited until the teenager entered her own home three houses down and flashed the porch light on and off a few times to indicate she was safe inside.

As soon as the light stopped flickering and remained on, Lacy closed and locked the front door. She sprinted up the stairs to the bedroom. Determined to find the locket, she pulled everything out of her closet, opened every box, and uncovered every pile of knickknacks.

Lacy realized she hadn't taken the time to see if the girls were asleep. Since Alice couldn't fall asleep in the dark, she would need to turn off their light. She caught her breath and took a moment to slow down, releasing the air through her mouth.

The locket isn't going anywhere, she thought.

She tiptoed down the hall and cracked open the door to the girls' room. They didn't stir. She kissed each one of them on the forehead, snugged their covers around them, and retreated back to the doorway. Before she turned off the light, she paused and smiled at her children.

When sleeping, they looked so innocent.

Then she flipped the light switch and paused for a moment.

"Mommy," a quiet whisper floated through the dark.

"Yes, baby girl," Lacy kept her voice to a hush.

"Can you tell me a story? One of Grandma's stories about Caden's Rose." Alice begged.

Lacy smiled. She loved her grandmother's stories. "Maybe tomorrow night. Your sister is already asleep and you should be too."

Alice let her head fall into the pillow in defeat.

Lacy pulled the door closed and returned to her bedroom.

Piles of items from her closet were strewn throughout the bedroom. There was a narrow path through them to her bed and one path to the closet.

She maneuvered to the bed where the clothes that were once hanging up were stacked on each other, still attached to their hangers. She began going through the pockets of each shirt. "What a waste of time," she thought. If Raelynn had hid them in a pocket, wouldn't she expect her to find it when she wore that shirt?

She might not expect her to check Willy's clothes.

Lacy looked at the pile of his shirts lying on the other end of the bed. As she walked toward them, a flickering light caught her attention from the floor of the closet. In the far corner, a beacon called to her from the dark.

The gem's brilliance eclipsed the glitter of the locket's gold casing. Lacy had never taken notice of the gem before. It had always seemed so dull and dark. Today, the polished, quartz crystal was gleaming, pulsating with life—in its pink and sapphire hues.

The beating of her heart vibrated against the walls of her chest.

This was what she wanted. With the necklace, she could go back in time and convince Willy not to ride his motorcycle that night. They could go together to pick up the kids and everything would be alright. They would still have a place at the dinners for eight. Willy may have cheated and partied too much, but even that didn't hurt as bad as being shunned by your entire friend group.

When your husband is deployed, you don't get uninvited, Lacy thought. Why had they uninvited her now?

How many times had they put a place setting out at an empty chair when their husbands were deployed? How many times did they promise to never forget them for one minute while they were gone?

Clutching the locket in her palm, Lacy contemplated its power. With her nail, she tried to pry it open, but the latch was frozen shut. Inspecting the intricate details, there was no doubt in her mind that at one time the hinges had worked. Someday, she would find out what was inside, but not today.

The gem began flickering in rhythm with her heartbeats.

Hypnotized by its cadence, Lacy slipped the necklace on. Heavier than any of her other jewelry, the cold chain soothed her stiff neck.

With a deep sigh, she closed her eyes and reached for the locket. She thought she heard the girls sobbing when she opened her eyes and found herself standing on a deserted road. The asphalt road dead ended by water in both directions. A short terrace of green grass surrounded the road on all sides

Who would design a road in the middle of a lake, she thought, trying to gain her bearings. Where is that cry coming from?

A small tree adorned the bleak roadside. Its branches hid something laying in the grass. The source of the crying became evident as Lacy approached an infant bundled in a torn sheet. It wasn't until after she held the baby in her arms and soothed him that she wondered if this was a good idea.

What time was she in? How old was she? Could this have been one of her miscarried babies?

She looked around at this small island created by flood waters. They were trapped here. It had once been a highway marked for two-way traffic with a double yellow line painted in the middle. The road ended in water on both sides. Lots of water. The nearest land she could see was a faint tree line in the distance. Roof tops broke through the surface of the water, too wide to swim across.

The sun—hanging low in the sky— reflected off a highway sign casting a long shadow across the green grass that surrounded the road. Lacy snuggled the baby up in her arms and walked toward the road sign.

PA 42, she read. Was she in Pennsylvania?

Scared and alone with a baby in her arms, she waited. There was no way to get off the island. No matter how many times she walked up and down the road, their predicament was not going to change. She watched the sun sink even lower—it would be dark soon.

At first, Lacy contemplated using the locket to take her back to her real time, but what would happen to the baby? If she held him, she thought maybe he would flash to the future with her. If he didn't, would he die here abandoned and alone?

Was she brought here for a reason? As time passed, she worked herself into a panic. Without food or drinking water, both she and the baby would perish sooner rather than later. Her stomach tightened into a knot she couldn't untie.

A misty blue haze remained as the sun disappeared over the horizon. Her search for material to make a shelter out of was futile. She prayed that the flooding had ceased, hoping the waters would retreat by morning. She'd experienced flooding before when Hurricane Andrew slammed the coast of Florida. The water rose for days before retreating.

Wrapping the baby in her arms, she sheltered against the one remaining tree above water on their little highway island. When he cried, all she could do was rock him, hoping she could soothe him with a soft lullaby.

Nothing frightened her alone in the dark, except the possibility of the water rising higher. There was nowhere else for them to go. No higher ground.

Under her breath, she prayed the prayer Jolene had always recited to her before they'd gone to bed.

"Now I lay me down to sleep," she whispered. "I pray the Lord my soul to keep. If I should"—She couldn't bear to speak the rest of the real prayer out loud, so she made up something new—"If I should cry before morning, Lord, turn my tears into your glory. If I should live for other days, I pray the Lord will guide my ways. Amen."

She smiled at her creativity, then wondered why someone would talk about dying in a child's prayer.

That is so bizarre, she thought. Especially here in the middle of a lake or river overrunning its banks.

The baby cried, and Lacy joined him in his tears. There was nothing she could do to ease his hunger. At first the rocking motion had soothed him, but then it didn't. Eventually, he was too tired to continue, and he fell asleep in her arms.

Lacy sobbed until she dozed off.

It seemed as if three things happened at exactly the same time: a bright light, the baby's cry, and the hum of a motor.

Lacy jerked awake and realized she was sitting in about six inches of water. Her worst fear had come true. The water was still rising. Along with it, debris floated along the shoreline. What appeared to be a child's teddy bear floated by just out of her reach.

She scooted back up the grass onto the shoulder of the road and stood up, trying to hush the baby so she could listen. There it was again. Yes, it was indeed the sound of a motor.

The baby's screams continued to pierce her ears. He was inconsolable.

"Help us," Lacy called out as she saw the small boat off in the distance. Waving one arm and holding onto the baby with the other, she frantically motioned to the boat. "Over here. We are over here."

The boat turned away from them.

Lacy walked to the highest point on their little island and looked around. Although the thought of being rescued seemed bleak, the fact that there was one boat out there meant there might be more somewhere.

Lacy gathered as many pieces of cloth as she could find washing up nearby. Using a few sticks that had floated up on the island, as well as some branches she broke off the tree, she tied the cloths into man-made SOS beacons. She posted them along the edges of the island. She couldn't be on both sides at once and any sign that someone was here might be what gets someone to stop and look around for them.

As the sun lowered in the sky, she was losing hope. The baby wouldn't survive much longer. He hadn't cried in what seemed like hours.

He laid in her arms, very still. Lacy put her ear down on his chest to make sure he was still breathing.

A baby boy. She never knew the gender of the first baby she lost. Was it a boy? Why didn't she know? Her heart raced. She'd never given it much thought before but now it grieved her that she hadn't taken time to know.

Lacy laid down in the grass happy to feel the sun warm her skin. She set the baby next to her and used her body to offer him shade. Exhausted, she dozed off.

"Ma'am? Are you okay?"

At first, Lacy thought she was dreaming.

"Hello?" another voice called out. "How are you doing?"

Lacy sat up, shaking off the groggy sleep in her head.

"I'm okay," she mumbled. Then she cleared her throat. "I'm okay," she yelled toward the boat.

Looking down at the baby, she saw pale, blue lips. He was quiet and still. She picked him up and squeezed him, as she ran down to meet the boat.

A stout woman stood in the water near the stern and slid a rope through her hands pulling the small vessel up closer to the bank. Inside, another fair-skinned woman held an elderly woman in her arms. They sat on the bench in the middle of the boat. Lacy quickly accessed the situation and knew there was no room for all of them.

"The baby," Lacy said, holding the bundle out in front of her as far as she could stretch. "Please take the baby."

"Ma'am," the lady with the rope said, "We are heading toward the main land and stopped to get your information. Are there any other survivors with you?"

"It's just the baby and me."

"We can send someone back for you. We'll leave you a few bottles of water."

"Please take the baby." Lacy waded out passed her.

Even though her jeans were soaked up to her thighs and getting heavier, she kept walking until she reached the side of the boat.

"There is no reason to split you up from your baby. We have to take her"—she nodded to the elderly woman, her lips were blue and skin pale—"to the hospital. They will have helicopters there, and we will tell them you are here."

"No," Lacy said. "He won't make it if we have to wait at all. He hasn't eaten. He's barely clinging to life as it is. Please take him with you. I will be fine."

The woman in the boat reached out her hands.

"We'll take him," she whispered.

"Thank you," Lacy handed the bundle over to her. "He needs food and water as soon as possible."

"That reads route forty-two, so I think I know where we are," the stout woman said pointing to the sign as she climbed back into the boat. "The hospital isn't far now, and we won't have to stop for any lights."

Lacy smiled at her attempt to lighten the situation.

"I promise, we will send someone back for you." She picked up a paddle and began rowing the boat in a big arc turning it around and heading out.

Lacy watched them disappear into the distance.

How close could that hospital be? She hadn't heard a single helicopter since she'd arrived. Her shoes squished as she trudged up to the top of the hill and sat on the asphalt of Route 42. She reached out for a small stone glistening in the sunlight.

Too numb to be frightened anymore, Lacy turned toward the sun and let it warm her face. She rubbed the smooth, flat stone between her thumb and index finger. Tucking her chin into her chest, a single sunbeam reflected off her locket. Without thinking, she covered the locket's gem with her free hand and closed her eyes. Blink.

Falling over the corner of her bed, she fell headfirst onto the floor. She was back in her bedroom, but it was like she stepped right off the island and onto the edge of the bed.

This felt different than before.

"Someone is upstairs," Lacy heard an unfamiliar voice coming from the bottom of the stairs.

CHAPTER 15

2001

"Who is there? Girls, where are you?" Lacy yelled from the upstairs bedroom.

"It's the police, ma'am." An officer looked up from the bottom of the stairs. "Your girls are down here with us."

Lacy appeared at the railing looking down at them. She looked confused and a little out of place.

"The police? What are you doing here? Did someone else die?"

Raelynn squeezed in front of the three sharply dressed police officers. Stepping around Alice and Olivia as they played with their dolls, she felt like she was staring at a ghost.

"Lacy?" They had already spent hours searching every corner, every inch of this house. Lacy had been nowhere to be seen. So, then, how did she appear at the top of the stairs?

"Is anyone with you?" the officer asked.

"No," Lacy hesitated. "Just me."

Raelynn met her halfway up the stairs.

"Where have you been, Lacy?" she whispered as she reached her. "We've been so worried about you. Where were you? Why did you leave your daughters here all alone?"

"Were you kidnapped, Mommy?" Alice asked, looking up for a moment then picking up her doll and turning away.

"Of course, not. What on Earth is going on here?" Lacy followed Raelynn back down the stairs.

"That is what we are trying to find out, ma'am." The officer pointed to the couch. "Please have a seat."

He motioned to the other officers, sending them back upstairs. Lacy followed her instructions and sat down looking puzzled.

"How did you get back upstairs?" Raelynn whispered, sitting down next to Lacy. "Were you hiding from us?"

"Ma'am." The officer looked at Raelynn. "Would you mind taking the children into the other room while I ask Ms. Donathon a few questions?"

"Of course." Raelynn turned toward Olivia. "I guess it's time to make those chocolate chip cookies, isn't it?"

The girls jumped up, giggling, and dashed into the kitchen. "I guess they're ready. I've been promising them we'd bake cookies for four hours."

"Four hours?" Lacy whispered.

Raelynn patted Lacy's shoulder, stood up and headed to the kitchen. What would have happened if she hadn't come over to check on Lacy this morning?

After four hours of scouring the house—no Lacy, no babysitter—she suspected foul play. Lacy would never leave her girls alone in the house without supervision. But she had. When the police had contacted Melony, they learned that the girls may have been alone a lot longer than four hours and it wasn't the first time. She had found Lacy sitting in her car distraught and drunk on more than one occasion.

Distracted by her crazy thoughts, she paid no attention to Alice and Olivia making a mess with the flour and sugar.

Had the babysitter left early? Had Lacy forgotten Willy wasn't here to watch the girls? Where had she gone for so long? Should she had come over earlier? Why didn't she call Parker first instead of the police?

Raelynn stepped closer to the door trying to hear what Lacy was telling the officer.

"No, Olivia," Alice shouted. "Don't put the outside of the egg in."

Raelynn refocused on the baking project. "Oh dear," she said looking at the havoc the girls had created. Flour was on the counter, on their clothes, on the floor…everywhere.

Olivia dropped the egg, smashed shell and all, into the flour as Alice poured half the milk in the bowl and half on the counter.

"Whoa!" Raelynn held both palms in the air. "Let's clean up and restart this project from the top."

The doorbell rang, and Raelynn peered through the doorway to see a sharply dressed young woman let herself in. A clipboard was visible in her hands. As she walked past the kitchen, she said a warm greeting to the girls. Raelynn nodded and turned back to the mess on the counter. But soon, she was distracted again, ignoring the girls as she crept over and peered out the kitchen door/ She listened intently to the conversation in the living room.

"Officer Adams." The young woman reached out her hand to shake his.

"Ms. Conrad, thank you for coming. This is Lacy Donathon." Officer Adams waved his hand toward Lacy. "Lacy, this is Ms. Conrad from social services."

Lacy crossed her eyebrows and frowned at Officer Adams. "I told you I've been upstairs. We are fine."

"Why don't you two sit down and talk?"

"We are fine," Lacy said firmly. Then she shouted, "Raelynn!"

Raelynn hesitantly walked into the living room toward Lacy and the officer motioned her to stop. The two officers came down the stairs and huddled with Officer Adams. "It's all clear. No signs of entry."

The two officers stood at the edge of the living room monitoring the conversation Lacy would have with Ms. Conrad. Officer Adams escorted Raelynn back to the kitchen.

"Thank you for calling us, Mrs. Mason."

He gestured Raelynn to have a seat at the small breakfast table in the corner away from Olivia and Alice. They continued making a mess unsupervised—giggling and laughing.

"Ms. Conrad will be finding a place for the girls to stay," Officer Adams said, his voice hushed, "while she finishes a standard investigation to determine if a long-term situation would be beneficial."

"Stay? You're taking the girls?" Raelynn shook her head. Officer Adams nodded. "Can they stay with us? My husband and I could take them."

"That would be up to Ms. Conrad. There is something very strange about the way Lacy just showed up at the top of the stairs, don't you think?"

"I don't know what to say…" Raelynn hesitated.

The last thing she wanted to do was make things more difficult for Lacy but what the heck did happen?

"Is she going to need a lawyer? Be straight with me, Officer."

"We present our facts to the chief, both yours and Miss Phillips testimony, and he will talk with the judge to determine what further action if any needs to be carried out. Ms. Conrad will conduct a standard investigation that is done when minors are left unattended for an extended period of time. If Lacy's story pans out and she was unconscious, then it would be in her best interest to determine what is causing that. Do you know if she is a heavy drinker or takes any kind of drugs?"

"She rarely drinks more than a glass of wine here or there. She's a good mom. She would never do anything to put those girls in danger."

"Sometimes people's behavior changes after a loss."

About the time edible cookies were baked and being consumed by Alice and Olivia, Raelynn finished cleaning up the mess the girls had created. Ms. Conrad entered the kitchen.

"Mrs. Donathon has volunteered to let social services take the girls without contest until we finish our investigation."

CHAPTER 16

2001

Intent on her search for anything she could find to explain what happened last night, Lacy ignored the fact that Raelynn was peering over her shoulder and typed into the search engine, time travel.

"You should know that Parker and I offered to take the girls. But they were concerned that Parker was getting shipped off soon."

"That's nice of you." Lacy remained focus on the screen.

"Aren't you worried? That sounds like they plan to keep them in the system for a while."

"I'm sure they will be fine," Lacy said, not looking up from the monitor.

"Lacy, you know I would do anything for you, but you need to tell me what's going on."

"I already have. Don't you remember? I've got to find out if this sort of thing is happening to anyone else."

"Even if it is, you won't find it on LookSmart or Google Search. People aren't going to spend money to build a web site to talk about something that'll make them look insane."

"You'd be surprised what is on the internet, Rae. There are these sites where you can post for free. They are called blogs. They're like personal diaries."

"So any nut can post whatever they want?"

Lacy stopped typing and turned to look at Raelynn. "You think I'm crazy, don't you?"

"Where did you go for over four hours?"

"Do you really want to know, Raelynn? Can you handle the truth? And frankly, can I trust you to keep the truth to yourself? What did you tell Ms. Conrad? It was convincing enough that they took Olivia and Alice from me."

"You think it was my idea to have them take the girls away? Ms. Conrad didn't just talk to me. She talked with Melony and her father too. They all have noticed you've been acting a little strange lately."

"Well, you did call the police."

"I was here for hours and you were nowhere to be found! I thought you'd been abducted or something."

"Rest assured; I was not." Lacy looked back down at her computer and started typing into the search bar again.

"What are you searching for, Lacy?"

"Like I said, I am trying to find out if there's anyone out there that has ever heard of anything like this."

"Like what?"

"Any of it. All of it. Time travel. Gem magic. Lockets. Talking horses."

Raelynn leaned in to see what Lacy was looking at. On the screen was a webpage with the words, Time Traveling Gems. A picture of a sparkling purple gemstone flashed in the center.

"What are you doing? Seriously, Lacy? Did you find the locket? Is this what this is all about? I thought you were going to leave it alone."

Raelynn didn't wait for an answer. She leaped up the stairs two at a time to Lacy's room and began searching through Willy's shirt pockets, looking for where she had hidden the locket.

"You won't find it," Lacy said, standing in the doorway watching her friend yanking shirts off their hangers. "If you would have waited a moment, I would have told you. Yes, I found it."

"Why, Lacy?" Raelynn fell back on the bed. "Don't you want to get better?"

Lacy laid down next to Raelynn and they both stared up at the ceiling, unable to face each other when they disagreed.

"You know what I found out? I found out that I'm just fine."

"You lost your girls," Raelynn countered. "You call that fine?"

"No, I don't mean that. But I need you to understand that there is something magical about this locket. I need you to believe me. You're my best friend. If I can't trust you with this information, who can I trust?"

"I don't know what to think, Lacy. But I know one thing. It doesn't matter if you think it takes you back in time or if it really does. Either option scares me. Both scenarios are equally ridiculous, so it doesn't matter what I believe."

"I time traveled last night. I didn't mean to leave the girls." Lacy rolled up on her elbow and looked Raelynn straight in the eye. Waiting for some reply from Raelynn and not getting it quick enough, Lacy scowled. "Come on, Raelynn. You know I wouldn't leave them alone if I had control over it."

"But, hun, you did have control. You see, this is what you don't seem to get." Raelynn turned to return Lacy's glare. "You do have control. You were gone for more than four hours. That's how long I sat in this house with your girls worrying about where you were."

"I'm so sorry about that. I've always came back at the exact same time I left. I don't know what happened. It seems like I was gone the same amount of time here that I spent there. But I went back into the past I am sure of it. It was after a major storm. A natural disaster of some sort. I don't know. It wasn't anywhere I recognized. I spent the night on an island—well, a road, a sign read highway PA 42—in the middle of a large flood in Pennsylvania, I think."

Deciding she had said enough, Lacy waited for her friend's response, but it never came. Raelynn resumed staring at the ceiling and ignoring Lacy until she dozed off.

Lacy snorted and stared at the ceiling until she could no longer tame the questions screaming inside her head. Trying not to disturb Raelynn, she rolled out of bed, tiptoed downstairs, and sat down in front of the computer.

Lacy continued her search on the internet until she discovered a professor of supernatural phenomenon, Dr. Mark Garamondy, Sr.

She was focused on reading about his work involving time travel when Raelynn interrupted her by yelling down from the top of the stairs. Lacy startled, rushed to close out the tabs on her screen.

"Let me take the locket," Raelynn insisted. "I can put it in a safety deposit box or something. You need to focus on getting Alice and Olivia back."

"What do you mean, Rae? They're coming home this afternoon." Lacy heard the sound of a car door slamming. "It's probably them now."

"I don't recall anyone saying when they would be coming home."

It was Ms. Conrad standing on the front porch. Lacy opened the front door as wide as it would open and looked around but did not see her daughters.

"It's just me," Ms. Conrad said. "We have to go over a few things and fill out some paperwork before we can call and have the girls brought home. They are doing fine. Lovely girls. First, we must discuss your treatment plan."

"My treatment plan for what?" Lacy asked.

"Let's sit down."

Ms. Conrad gestured to the couch. She looked up to the top of the stairs and invited Raelynn to join them.

"If it's okay with you, Lacy, I'd like for Raelynn to join us. It sometimes helps to have a friend listen to the instructions as well. Sometimes they can help you remember what was discussed."

Raelynn didn't hesitate. She acted glad to be included and interjected several times to clarify Ms. Conrad's instructions.

"When are you going to tell me what I am being treated for?" Lacy asked. "I'm not sick."

"It's been determined that it might be helpful for you to participate in some professional counseling. Six weeks, longer if the doctor thinks it is necessary."

"Interesting. And I wonder how you came to this conclusion." Lacy looked at Raelynn who shrugged her shoulders.

"As I explained yesterday, we conduct a standard investigation. Each case is different but after the investigation is completed, the team—which includes myself, my supervisor, and in this case, the judge—creates a recommended treatment plan."

"So, these are recommendations, the counseling is not mandatory."

Ms. Conrad leaned forward and put her hand on Lacy's knee.

"The plan includes a minimum of six weeks of counseling. If you choose not to follow the recommendations, the state will press charges against you for child neglect and the girls will remain in foster care until after your hearing."

Lacy took a hold of Ms. Conrad's arm and lifted it off her knee, flinging it back toward the notebook she held in her other hand.

"So not a recommendation—more like a threat."

"It's not meant to be. I'm here to offer you an alternative to formal legal proceedings and that is what the DA agreed to. It's up to you how you want to proceed."

Lacy stood up and began pacing the room. Raelynn tried to console her, but Lacy pushed her out of the way.

"No, you don't get to be here for me right now. Too late."

"You're upset. You know I have your back."

"Do I?" Lacy retorted, turning her back to Raelynn and facing the wall as she talked. "Because last I remember you quit talking to me. Last time I tried to explain to you what was going on, you quit on me."

Lacy had never been so assertive with Raelynn. She never stood up to Willy like that either. All these years as friends and Lacy had never stood up to anyone like she has in the last few days.

Anger.

Could it be the next stage of grief?

"This isn't helping. Just sign up for the sessions, Lacy. Do it to bring your girls home."

Lacy turned to Ms. Conrad.

"If I sign up for counseling, my girls get to come home right now?"

"Yes. I'll call my assistant. She will go pick them up and return them."

"This doesn't make any sense, but I'll do this for them. Who is this doctor and when do I have to see him?"

"We've provided a list of doctors you can choose from, or you can use your own doctor if you already have one. As long as he is board certified by the state of Florida. You need to have an appointment made by the end of the next business day. You can make an appointment at the next available time that works for your schedule."

"Ok," Lacy said, waiting for her to call her assistant.

"I'll need you to pick a doctor before I can have the girls brought home."

"Dr. Mark Garamondy. My doctor is Dr. Garamondy."

CHAPTER 17

2001

"What brings you here today, Mrs. Donathon?"

Dr. Garamondy sat back in his plush recliner and set the clipboard in his lap. He glanced at it once as he struggled to pronounce her name correctly. He looked back up at Lacy sitting on the loveseat as far away from him as possible and waited in silence for her answer.

Not sure how to sit she squirmed for a second and then blurted out. "It's Ms. I think. I'm a widow."

"I'm sorry to hear that, Ms. Donathon"

He paused again.

"You already knew that much, right? I filled out all those forms."

"I have a lot of patients. Whatever you care to share without me having to look it up is helpful. We can get to know each other better."

The silence was awkward. Lacy wasn't sure if he was thinking of his next question or expecting her to lead the conversation. Maybe he was evaluating her body language.

"I'm here so they don't take my daughters again," Lacy shared. "I agreed to at least six weeks of counseling so my daughters could come home. It sounds like it's up to you to decide if I get to keep them or not."

"It sounds like you don't think you have a problem." Dr. Garamondy leaned forward peering at her from behind the clipboard.

"No. I do have one. My husband died, and now everyone thinks I am crazy. And the truth is, that problem is exactly why I chose you as my doctor. I knew you would understand."

"How so?" Dr. Garamondy seemed genuinely enthralled.

"You wrote about what I have been experiencing." Lacy paused, almost disbelieving it herself. "Best to get it out and not waste each other's time?"

"Agreed. Tell me what you've been experiencing."

"Time travel. I am starting to think it is related to the gem magic you wrote about."

"You are kidding, right?" Dr. Garamondy grew agitated. "It might be in your best interest to put more value on our time together. You've been through a lot. Dismissing it by playing games with me isn't the most prudent thing to do."

"What are you talking about?" Lacy sat up on the edge of her chair not as comfortable as it was a moment ago. "Are you saying you don't believe it happens anymore?"

"You must have mistaken my work with another." Dr. Garamondy stood up from his chair, slammed the clipboard on the seat, and walked over to the counter along the wall and topped off his coffee mug. "If you want to help yourself, let me know. Otherwise, I won't play any silly little games with you."

Lacy couldn't catch a breath. She started hyperventilating, and her face became pale enough that Dr. Garamondy showed concern. He sat down next to her on the love seat and took her wrist to check her pulse.

"Inhale slowly," he instructed. "Now, a long breath out. Try that again. Slow deep breaths in and out. Lean forward and exhale."

Lacy did as she was instructed until she had forgotten the very thing that made her so upset until Dr. Garamondy resumed speaking.

"I fear you are serious, aren't you?" He paused for her to nod. "I didn't write those books. My father did. After I graduated from med school, his work went off the deep end. It was so far out there. That old kook almost tanked my career. Even after I disassociated myself from him, his reputation has haunted me. The only thing that saved it was that he died. I know that sounds mean but it's honest. God rest his soul. Honestly, I believe he was delusional there at the end. I'm sorry if that is not what you wanted to hear."

"I'm sorry too. I didn't realize there were two of you. Maybe I am delusional, too. But I swear I've been traveling back in time. I just need someone to believe me."

"I did look at his work." Dr Garamondy picked his clipboard up and sat back down. "In the beginning, it was intriguing but there was no scientific basis for it to hold any water. I'm a man of science, Ms. Donathon. I almost didn't graduate because of the time I wasted researching his theoretical nonsense. That's all history. I can't go back there. I'm sorry."

"Has anyone else studied his work? If you can't help me, can you recommend someone who could?"

"What would you like me to say, Ms. Donathon?" Garamondy fidgeted in his seat. "Dear Colleague, my client is looking for someone to help her. Since I don't specialize in time travel or gem theory, could you take her from my case load?"

"A no would have sufficed."

Lacy stood up, swung her purse over her shoulder, and walked to the door.

"Could you put that I stayed the whole hour? Feel free to bill it that way."

Dr Garamondy called after her, but she didn't look back.

Despite Raelynn's admonishments for abandoning therapy with Dr. Garamondy, Lacy spent the next several days searching the internet for Time Travel professors. Surely someone out there was interested in the phenomenon. She needed an open-minded professional who could help sort out why this was happening to her and help her learn to control it.

All that Mark had left of his father's work was locked away in a trunk and hidden in a back room in the basement of his father's house. A home that he wanted to sell but had to wait for a long-lost brother to sign over to him. The small house was falling apart, paint peeled off on the outside and wall paper bubbled on the inside. It was filled with clutter, stacks of books and papers lined small pathways in and out of every room but the kitchen.

Mark began clearing the expired cereal boxes and moldy bags of bread off the counter and dropping them into the large garbage can he had brought in from the garage. In two more years, the seven-year waiting period would be over and he could put the house on the market.

There was something about Lacy's story that had intrigued him and soon he found himself in the basement opening the trunk that stowed all that was left of his father's work. As far as he was concerned, his father's work had taken a turn that ruined the reputation of all the Garamondy's. Yet, there he was, entertaining another psychotic search for the legacy of the brilliant, but deranged Dr. Mark Garamondy, Sr.

A picture caught his eye. It was of a young woman with a striking resemblance to Lacy. Shifting the old black and white picture to view it from several angles, he couldn't tell for sure, but it looked like she was wearing a locket.

After sifting through the trunk, he found several more pictures of the young woman. The name Lina was scrawled on the back of one. Lina and Hope was handwritten on another.

By the end of the night, Dr. Garamondy had spread the contents of the trunk out across the room. He'd located a journal detailing all his father's sessions and encounters with Lina. Her detailed descriptions of a place called Avenrand and his father's failed attempts to join her. He mentioned gemstones, a locket, and the portal-like path from Lina's farm.

The only thing missing were his father's conclusion. Was Lina delusional? Dr. Garamondy wondered if there had ever been a documented case of countertransference so bad that a therapist began believing the delusions of his client.

What was it about Lina's story that his father was willing to give up his career for?

He convinced himself that he was pursuing the answers to the mystery of how his father got blacklisted from the scientific community.

The first thing he did when he returned to the office in the morning was scribble some notes in Lacy's file. Then he picked up the phone and called her.

"Hello, Ms. Donathon. It's Dr. Garamondy."

"I thought I was clear yesterday. I need to find someone who can help me."

"I've decided to take your case, pro-bono. I won't charge you and you will get all the paper work you need to meet your counseling requirement."

"It's still confidential if you don't charge me, right?"

"Of course, I would have to report if I think you or the children are in danger."

"What about time travel? Do you have to report that?"

"You can talk about whatever you like, just prove to me that your daughters are safe."

"What made you change your mind?"

"At one time, I was interested in my father's work. It gave my higher-ups some pause. I no longer work for anyone, so it would be interesting to see if there are any correlations between my father's work with his client and what you are experiencing."

"So, I'm a test rat?"

"Something like that." Mark made up his mind to be frank with her regardless of how she might respond. "It's up to you."

"Okay, we don't have anything to lose but your time. Who knows maybe we can get that back."

They both chuckled.

"I can't," Lacy slid out of the car with her cell phone held up to one ear. She tried to manipulate her keys in the other hand, swing her purse over her shoulder, and close the car door at the same time. "I have an appointment with my counselor and I am running late."

"Did you get a chance to talk with Alice's teacher?" Raelynn asked.

"Yes. That's why I'm late for my appointment. You'd think she was dropping out of high school according to her teacher. It's Kindergarten for heaven's sake! I'll tell you all about it later. I've gotta hurry. Tell Ella the girls are super excited for game night and I'll pick her up around five."

She slipped her cell phone into her pocket and rushed through the tall glass doors. This was going to be an exciting session. Dr. Garamondy thought he had uncovered enough research that he was willing to have her try time traveling in his office today.

"The important thing," Dr. Garamondy said, "is that you remain in control of the locket at all times. You must be able to come back on demand if anything happens."

"I think I've figured that out enough to be able to control it. When light touches the gem embedded in the locket and I cover it with my hand, if I close my eyes, when I open them, I'm in a new place. I think when I do the same on the other side, it brings me back. Have you figured out how I can go to a specific time and place?"

"My father didn't address that level of control in his journals, but I think I have a few ideas. You've mentioned that when you travel, everyone seems to know the past you. What I want you to do is to think of a precise moment in the past. Try to remember exactly how you were in the time you want to go to."

"I don't think that would be too hard. The accident was only six months ago. It's hard not to remember how that day went. If I go back to the last night Willy and I were together, I can ensure he doesn't ride that bike on our last date."

Dr. Garamondy did not seem pleased about the idea of changing the past and messing with the future. However, in order to evaluate his methods of controlling the locket, he said he would allow her to try it. He was still eighty percent sure his father's work was that of a delusional old man, but the remaining twenty percent is what drew him in, and he told Lacy that.

"What if this locket was the key to unlocking the truth about the gem magic and time travel? My father wasn't the first to be lured away from science into the realms of science fiction and fantasy. I guess it can't hurt to play along?"

"I assure you; it's really happening. I wish there was a way to show you."

"When you are ready, I want you to think, what it was like to be that person that night."

Dr. Garamondy walked to the window and opened the shades. He'd reserved the east office for this session so they could take advantage of the morning sun.

"Think about that for a few minutes and then proceed. If it's okay with you I will record our session."

"That's fine. When a ray of light shines on the gemstone, I just cover it with my hand and close my eyes." Lacy demonstrated as she concentrated on the last night she and Willy were together. She imagined him reaching his hand out inviting her to join him for a dance, their last dance.

But when she opened her eyes, she was lying in a hot tent curled up in a sleeping bag. It felt like she walked into a furnace. For a moment, it took her breath away. She stripped the sleeping bag off and checked her clothing: a t-shirt and nylon sports shorts. Except for the lack of a bra, she felt decent enough. Sitting up, she looked around.

Willy was swinging in the hammock with Olivia, her little face kissed by the sun. She must have been a little over a year old. Lacy smiled. There were some good times. Despite everything he'd put her through, she had never given up hope for more of those good days. She found her flip flops and slipped through the opening in the tent.

"Good morning, sunshine," Willy said.

"Oh, look at her burnt little face." Lacy looked around for the diaper bag.

"You said you were going to put some lotion on it last night. Did you find it?"

"I think I did." Lacy tried to remember. "Is this Pensacola Beach?"

"Wow, you did drink too much tequila," Willy laughed. "Santa Rosa Island. We camp here every year."

"Fort Pickens?" Lacy shook her head and walked over to the picnic table to pour herself a cup of coffee. "I remember. What is on the agenda for the day?"

"Like I get any input on the agenda," Willy got up from the hammock, handed Olivia to Lacy, and gathered up his fishing pole and gear. "However, I know one thing, I am going to get some fishing in from the pier before you drag me off to the beach in the hot sun."

He loaded up the truck and drove off without even a goodbye.

Lacy sat down in the lawn chair with Olivia. They had camped every weekend they could when Willy came home. She used to think Willy just enjoyed getting outdoors, but now she wondered if it was a way for him to get away from her. If she remembered right, they never did go to the beach together.

He would take off fishing all day and she and Olivia—even Alice when she was born—would have to walk to the beach from their campground. Which, she guessed, is what they had done yesterday and was why Olivia's little head was sunburnt.

If Olivia is eighteen months old, Lacy thought, taking a sip of her coffee and feeling nauseated by it, then I'd be pregnant with Alice.

She would be a few weeks along and it would be another two months before she got a positive pregnancy test result back. She dumped out her coffee onto the ground.

Oh no, she thought, and Willy said I was drinking tequila last night.

It was after six when Willy came back from fishing.

What can he possibly do out there all day, she wondered.

She had charcoal ready and patties of ground beef pressed for the grill when he arrived.

"You are such a good wife," he told her. "Having dinner ready for me when I get home. Sorry I didn't get back to take you to the beach."

"It's not a problem. I enjoyed reading books to Olivia."

Willy pulled out the tequila, prepared two shot glasses, and brought one to Lacy.

"Oh, no thank you. I'm feeling a little nauseous this evening."

Lacy continued preparations for dinner, putting the hamburger patties on the grill, and tossing ingredients together for a salad.

"Come on, old lady," Willy insisted. "Don't make me drink alone." He forced the shot glass into her hand.

"Fine." Lacy felt the feeling of fear in her gut she had once learned to live with.

She waited for Willy to turn his head up to chug his glass and poured hers over her shoulder. It would have been a great plan, except the contents landed on the picnic table, splashing against the plastic table cloth instead of being soaked into the ground.

Without warning, her cheek stung from the back of Willy's hand slapping across her face. Her head twisted around toward the picnic table. He grabbed a handful of her hair, shoving her face down into the tequila.

"Don't ever mock me again, woman. Now lick it up."

Lacy saw the locket dangling in front of her face. She reached up with her hand, closed her eyes, and grabbed it. She opened her eyes hoping to be back in Dr. Garamondy's office. Instead, the medicinal scent of the alcohol continued to burn her nostrils. All she saw was the bright red checkers of the tablecloth. When she finished licking the table cloth to Willy's satisfaction, he released her.

"See that wasn't so bad, was it?"

This was the ugly side of Willy that his death had made her forget.

She massaged her neck, trying to hold back the tears rolling down her cheeks. The sun had set over the horizon. There would not be any more of its rays until dawn.

She decided to get up early and grab the first ray of sunlight to blink home.

For a moment, she wished she could somehow tell the young Lacy that she was pregnant. How could she? Could she write her a note? Would she believe her? Would she think that is weird?

"I think I might be pregnant," she told her husband. "That's why I didn't want to drink the tequila. I've been nauseous all day."

Willy wasn't the type of guy that would take her word for it. He would want proof and she knew the tests wouldn't come back positive for several weeks. As awful as Willy could be, he had been very sweet to her while she was pregnant.

"Why didn't you tell me," Willy cried. "Why didn't you say so, baby? I thought you were back on your old anti-drinking high horse."

"I'm sorry. I don't know for sure. And I thought you would be upset because we were going to wait two years between having babies."

"I'm not upset, sweet muffin," he said.

He wrapped his arms around her then leaned over and began speaking sweetly to her belly.

Lacy almost forgot she was from another time.

The campground was so peaceful in the morning before anyone else was awake. As the sun rose over the horizon, the smell of the dew on the leaves was still strong and, off in the distance, she could hear the roar of the ocean as the tide rushed in. The choir of birds sang a chorus in the nearby palm trees.

Out of habit, she fired up the kettle for coffee. The smell of it brewing reminded her that she'd never been able to drink coffee while pregnant. It made her too nauseous.

Then she saw the locket hanging from her neck. She kissed Olivia on one cheek and then the other. Olivia giggled making it harder for Lacy to leave. But when a beam of sunlight struck the gem, she closed her eyes.

Lacy opened her eyes and took a deep breath. It was comforting to be back in Dr. Garamondy's office. She was beginning to have control of the locket.

"Well, that didn't work." Dr. Garamondy plopped back into his recliner looking defeated. "There are a couple other methods that my father cited in his second book."

"Actually, it did work. I saw Willy and my daughter, Olivia."

Dr. Garamondy raised an eyebrow, skeptical.

"No time passed. You closed your eyes and a few moments later you opened them again. You never left."

"That is how it works most of the time. It brings me back to the exact time as when I left."

"Fascinating." Dr. Garamondy wasn't very convincing.

"I'm sure it's hard to imagine from the outside, but I did go back in time. Not to the time I was thinking about though. I didn't go back to our last date before Willy died. Olivia was about a year and a half old."

"Well, then, do you want to make another attempt?"

"I don't know that I am up for it. It may have seemed like a blink in time here but I really spent hours there. I am exhausted. I didn't get much sleep. I spent the whole day there taking care of my daughter. It was hot and I was sick to my stomach all night."

"What is different about the time travel when you don't come back at the exact time?" Dr. Garamondy leaned forward in his seat and picked up his notepad.

"It's only happened once where time passed here the same as it did while I was there. The difference was it wasn't my life. I didn't go back to anything I remembered."

"So, every other instance, you've gone back into a scene from your past with one exception, when you ended up in the aftermath of a natural disaster," Dr. Garamondy stated.

"Well…" Lacy hesitated. Unsure if Dr Garamondy was being sarcastic, she decided not to tell him about the land with the talking horse. "I'm sorry. It must seem like I've been wasting your time."

"Not at all." Dr. Garamondy crossed his legs and sat back in his chair. "As a matter of fact, very little time has passed for me. Why don't we spend the rest of the hour discussing how things are getting along in the here and now? I'll catch up on my father's research, and we'll resume the time travel possibilities at our next session."

"We've been meeting now for six weeks. How are you feeling about the notion of time travel now?" Mark sat back in his recliner, lifted his clipboard, and scribbled a few notes. "Before you answer my question, I want you to think about the things we've been able to repeat in this room. You shut your eyes for a second and when you open them, everything here is the same. You report entering into memories of your past."

"It sounds like you don't believe I am traveling back in time. If you don't, then you're not going to be able to help me find out how to control the locket."

"I believe that you believe you're going back in time."

"Do you think people have as vivid recollections of the past as I have shared? That I can remember that many details? What about the passage of time in these memories? In a blink of an eye,

I experience large amounts of time. I guess you'd have to experience it to know that it is real."

Mark wanted to experience it, but he would never tell Lacy that. He was interested in the power of the locket. If he could try it, then he could determine once and for all the truth about his father's work. But it was the Lake of Gems that he couldn't quit thinking about. He didn't dare tell Lacy that there could be more gems, if they were real, and each contained their own magic. His father's research said nothing about time travel or controlling it. The more he dug into Garamondy Sr.'s research the more he realized his father was talking about a place, another dimension, not another time. Lina had reported that this place contained all kinds of magic. That was intriguing. He couldn't help but be curious about the gems and their magic. These things he had heard about and imagined as a boy but would never share with another soul, not even Lacy.

"I suppose you're right, Lacy. If you watch me blink"—Dr. Garamondy squeezed his eyes closed and opened again—"and I told you that while I blinked I was actually not here but in another time where I spent the night and came back, I wonder what you would think."

"What do you want me to do?" After a long awkward silence, Lacy continued, "I guess the only question now is do you report to social services I'm crazy or do we continue."

"Do you think you are crazy?" What he wanted to ask her was if she knew any more about the Lake of Gems from his father's research. Lacy just kept talking about travel back in time, what about traveling to another dimension? He had to focus on Lacy's therapy not his personal curiosity.

Lacy got up and walked to the door. "Of course not. I'm the one who believes she is traveling in time."

"If you could travel in time or to another dimension…" Mark hesitated. He knew his question was leading and bordering on unethical. "I'm sorry. To be honest, I am not sure what to put in my report. I am not sure what progress you have made."

"This is what's so frustrating. You told me you had all this work from your father and I thought you could help me."

"Help you? I am trying to help you, but I am not sure what you want help with. Are you trying to work through your grief?"

Lacy jumped up and headed toward the door. "I am trying to control the locket." The door jiggled in her hands and tears welled up in her eyes. "I thought you knew that."

And I thought you would be over this locket by now. Mark watched her disappear down the hallway.

The door to the women's restroom swung closed behind her. Lacy splashed water on her face to wash off the tears and stared at herself in the mirror. For six weeks she had thought she was sharing this experience with someone who actually believed her. Six weeks and she was no closer to saving Willy and no closer to ensuring social services didn't try to take her children again.

Lacy felt her heart rate going up. Her heart beat against the inside of her chest, and her breathing quickened. The stone within the gold case of the locket began to pulsate as well. The rays of light from the window reflected off the bathroom mirror. Lacy reached her hand up to cover the locket and squinted to block the reflection.

When she opened her eyes, she stood in the middle of a shimmering field. The grassland was lined by trees filled with multicolored leaves of oranges and yellows, reds and pinks, even purples and blues.

This is not your typical time travel, Lacy thought.

Something moved within the trees ahead of her. She walked through the waist high green grass. It was soft and felt like cotton on her skin. Then she felt an energy she hadn't felt since she was a child.

She ran, pushing her arms out in front of her, shoving the tall grass to the side as if swimming through it. Her hair blew behind her as a light breeze refreshed her face like the splash of cool water. Even when she reached the hillside that led up to the edge of the woods, where the grass was shorter and small boulders surfaced, she didn't get tired, but continued to sprint around them. When she reached the top, she stopped and listened.

"Who's there?" she called out.

No one answered. She listened and heard something rustling and the sound of heavy breathing. What is in the woods? Too scared to go in, she retraced her steps and almost half way down the hill she found a large stone ledge to sit on. High enough to look out over the pasture, she admired the colorful woods that surrounded it.

"Haven't we met?" a voice called out from the edge of the woods.

"I don't know. Come out so I can see you. Do you know me?"

"You wear the Locket of Lina, but I don't think you are Lina."

Lacy turned in the direction of the voice in the woods. A long nose protruded from the trees. Black nostrils appeared first, then the bridge of the nose, and then she saw the eyes, the forelock, and the ears.

A horse's face emerged. The rest of its body was hidden behind the trees. Lacy recognized the indentations on the horse's bridge where it looked like a halter had been squeezed around his nose and left on until it grew into the skin. You could see where it had been ripped off. The hair had grown back but the scars never completely healed. Lacy recognized this horse's face.

"I think I have been here before. I do think we have met." Lacy stood up as the horse approached.

"Yes, that's right. You are Lacy, granddaughter of Lina. You carry her stone."

"And you are?"

"I am Hope," said the horse.

"My grandmother had a horse named Hope. She used to share stories of—"

"Yes," Hope interrupted. "It is I. We had wonderful adventures together."

"I loved my grandmother's stories."

"Is that why you have come back to Avenrand? We met once before for a brief moment. I think you were frightened by the herd."

Hope lowered his head toward Lacy.

"Then I'm not crazy? I have been here before." Lacy started to reach toward Hope and then pulled her hand back.

"I don't know what crazy is. Has something happened to Lina?"

"Lina, my grandmother..." Lacy stuttered. "I am not sure what brought me to Avenrand. I was in the bathroom and the stone began to flicker. I blinked and covered it with my hand, and I ended up here. It's strange usually I go back in time and see my old life."

"It must have been a reflection." Hope stomped his foot in the dirt. "The gem magic was given to Lina to travel to Avenrand after she was captured by the other humans."

"She wasn't captured by humans. My mother put her in a nursing home. She was old and senile. My mother could no longer take care of her."

"You mean she told stories of talking horses."

Lacy took a deep breath and closed her eyes. When she opened them, she was still standing on the side of the hill with Hope. It could be that dementia runs in our family. It could be genetic. She began to worry about the things people were saying about her. Did they discuss having my children taken away because they think I am senile like my grandmother, perhaps suggesting I should be locked up?

"You're worried." Hope pushed his muzzle into her hands.

"Yes." Lacy tensed her shoulders and then without thinking began scratching his nose. It calmed her. "I am worried that people will treat me the same way they did my grandmother. They don't understand. They want to take my daughters. I thought I could trust the doctor, but now I don't know."

"Your grandmother trusted only one doctor, Dr. G," Hope explained. "He helped her discover how to use the gem to travel out of her captivity to Avenrand."

"Dr. G? Garamondy? That's my doctor. I don't think I trust him. He told me today that he doesn't believe me. How can I expect him to when all I do is blink and tell him stories of my travels?"

After a short pause, Lacy realized that her Dr. G and her grandmother's couldn't be the same person. "Lina must have been talking about his father. They have the same name. Lina helped Dr. G's father with his research. She was the one that traveled to Avenrand, she is the one that confided in him. He recorded her discoveries. That is how his father knew about the Lake of Gem magic."

"Lina would never betray the secrets of Avenrand."

"She must have trusted Dr. G."

"He has a son?" Hope pondered.

"Yes, a doctor of psychiatry. Someone who studies people with dementia."

"The kind of people that humans lock up?"

"Something like that." Lacy moved her hand to Hope's long neck and continued to pet him. The tension in her shoulders dissipated and the muscles in her neck softened.

"I think you should stay away from him." Hope stomped his foot again and Lacy jumped back, her neck muscle tightening back up.

"I was hoping he could tell me how to use the stone to travel to a specific point in time."

"You can't control the gem. A traveling gem is a portal. It opens to the place and time that is calling you. You don't call it."

Lacy sighed, defeated. "This must be what dementia is like. Lost in a world that no one else can enter but you."

"You are as naive as your grandmother was,"

"You mean we both think horses can talk." Lacy laughed.

Hope returned a chuckle and licked his lips.

Although she wasn't sure how, the message was sent that the other horses could come back out to the pasture to play. Hope introduced them as they emerged.

The first to venture out of the woods were the black and white pinto twins, introduced as Dottie and Prairie Rose. They ran off to frolic in the lush green grass. The chestnuts, Taffy and Berry, ran past Lacy and Hope. pausing for a moment to kick up their heels and run off again. The bays, Ali and Lady Jane took their time.

Ali leisurely strolled out of the woods, stopping to nibble grass as she walked toward the rest of the herd but maintained her large personal space. Jane spiraled around them, moving closer and closer to Lacy until she could touch her hair with her lips. Hope stretched out his neck and nipped at Jane in disapproval. She scooted away.

Soon Jane snuck back in and sniffed Lacy's hair. Lacy fell back off the rock.

"Don't you worry about Jane." Hope shook his head. "She is curious about you. They all are."

Lacy looked around at the herd and smiled as she picked herself up off the ground. They were so free, so full of play and mischief.

"There the stragglers are."

Three paints appeared, a sorrel named Zippi, a chestnut gelding named Apache, and a bay tobiano named Jazz. Among them and sticking in close proximity were two stunning white

Arabians, Mystic and Quest. Quest showcased his flowing white mane with a shake of his head.

These five horses paraded by Hope and Lacy, paused for a moment to nibble some grass, and then galloped down the hill to catch up with the others. Except Ali, of course, who had wandered off alone near the edge of the dam road that held back a large pond of water in the far northern edge of the field.

"We should join them." Hope lifted his head and turned toward the herd. "There is safety in numbers."

"They make me nervous. I think I'll enjoy watching them from a distance."

"You are in for a real treat." Hope nodded his head toward the herd.

"Hope…" Lacy stepped up next to him. "Wouldn't it be possible to use the locket to go back and save someone? I would only need to control my jump once."

They walked together down the hill toward the herd. Lacy's eyes tracked each of them, making sure they didn't kick out near her or nip or run over her. She had learned a lot about horses from watching her sister's riding lessons over the years but knowledge couldn't change her fear of them.

"Anything is possible, Lacy, but not everything is practical."

"You mean if I just keep thinking about the time I want to be at, like Dr Garamondy said, then the stone will take me there?"

"It's a bit more complicated than that. You must believe there is a gem out there for your purpose. If your purpose is to save Willy, then the gem that can help will find you."

"Why wouldn't my purpose be to save Willy? He died. Why else would the locket have come to me?"

"Maybe there is another gem out there. Your grandmother may have been trying to lead you to your higher purpose."

"What is my higher purpose?"

"Every person has a gem with its own personal magic."

"Where do I find this gem?" Lacy asked excited that she may be able to find a gem that she could control.

Hope nodded in the direction where Ali was standing near the dam. "It's a long journey over the dam. There you will find Sam's Pond. It contains the portal to the Lake of Gems. If a gem calls to you, it will be found there."

"A day's journey," Lacy sounded disheartened. "I don't have a lot of time. I have to get back. If I leave my girls that long they will take them away."

"The humans capture children too? I had forgotten what a dreadful world it is out there."

"They don't capture them, well…" Lacy tried to explain. "But I can't risk it. Can I blink there? Or blink back once I've finished at the Lake of Gems?"

"You can't use the locket to move around inside of Avenrand. You could ask one of the horses to take you."

"What about this locket? Why did it find me if it's not the magic I need?"

"The locket contains Lina's gem, one with portal magic. You have Lina's magic for a purpose, without it you would have to use the portal path."

"What is the portal path?"

"It's the path that Lina used before she had the stone. She had a rose."

"Caden's rose?"

"You have heard of Caden's rose?"

"My grandmother talked about a rose that appeared on a magic path when her young friend died."

"That path will lead you into Avenrand and take you to the gem pond, but the paths have been blocked for many years. Hidden away from those dangerous people you mentioned before, the ones who come to steal the gem magic from Avenrand."

Lacy looked disappointed. "If it's hidden, I'll never find it."

"Find Caden's rose. That will lead you to the portal path."

CHAPTER 20

2001

Mark grew impatient waiting for Lacy to return to the counseling room. It was staring at her purse that made him aware something was wrong. A woman never walks out and leaves her purse. After twenty minutes, it was hard to convince himself she was still in the restroom.

Something must have happened.

Before he even reached the receptionist's desk, he called out. "Ms. Blackwell, have you seen Ms. Donathon?"

Ms. Blackwell rolled her chair toward the doorway and looked down the hallway.

"No. She hasn't checked out yet."

Mark stood in the doorway peering down at her. "Any chance she got by you?"

"None. That door has a bell on it." She pointed to the door that exited to the lobby. "I know when anyone goes in or out."

"Then she must still be in the lady's room. Would you mind checking?"

"Not at all, Doctor."

When Ms. Blackwell reported that no one was in the lady's room, he requested a thorough search of the entire counseling complex. They peeked into every one of his colleagues' offices, even those who were with clients.

Mark apologized, explaining that his patient was missing and could be a harm to herself or others. His colleagues empathized and those who were not already occupied joined the search. In the end, four doctors and one receptionist were looking for the patient whose purse was left alone in his office.

The last place they looked was in Mark's office, where to his surprise, they found her asleep on the couch.

"Is she unconscious?" Ms. Blackwell asked. "Should I call an ambulance?"

"No," he shook his head. "She's been suffering from fatigue, poor dear, she must have gotten disorientated and lost her way back from the restroom. I am sorry for your trouble."

He motioned his colleagues out and closed his office door.

He tapped her gently on the shoulder to wake her and hesitated. She was wearing the locket.

Did it flicker? Without thinking he reached his hand out to touch it, the resulting jolt knocked him back. It was like the kickback from a twelve-gauge shotgun except across his entire chest. He fell back onto the floor as Lacy sprang upright.

"I dozed off. I'm sorry."

"Yes," Mark rubbed his hand burning from the shock. "You did. Not to worry. It happens." He was too fixated on the mark the locket had left in the palm of his smoldering hand to question her—a burn that would eventually become a scar in the shape of the crescent moon.

Lacy looked up at the clock and realized that she had gone over her hour. Had real time been passing during this last encounter? What did Garamondy know of it? Did he see me sleeping, or did I disappear like the last time I traveled out of my timeline?

Apologizing again, she gathered up her things and headed for the door. The bell on the lobby door rang as she exited.

Lacy couldn't get the image of Dr. Garamondy clutching his hand out of her mind.

What had happened while I was asleep? Had he tried to take the locket from me? Had it protected itself?

She was still thinking about it when she got home. No time for distractions, she thought as she started packing enough clothes for her and the girls for at least a few weeks. She was going to find that portal path and solve the mysteries of Avenrand.

It wasn't even about Willy anymore. Something much bigger was going on. Her grandmother's locket had called to her, and she wanted to find out why.

She loaded the car and drove to pick up the girls. The school didn't bat an eye when she told them the girls would be gone for a few weeks on urgent family matters. The secretary sent her best wishes, hoping everything turned out well.

Raelynn peered through the window of Lacy's car. "Going somewhere?" She said, pointing at the two small suitcases in the back seat.

"Yes, as a matter of fact. What about you? School isn't out for another hour."

"Ella has an eye appointment. She may need to get glasses."

Lacy took the girls hands and scurried past Raelynn. "We'll be back in a few days."

"You shouldn't make any hasty decisions." Raelynn walked faster trying to match Lacy's hastened pace. Ella was trying to keep up.

"I need to spend some time with my family. It will be good for all of us. We need a break." Lacy motioned the girls to get in the car. She paused to smile at Ella. "Did you have a great day at school, El?"

"It was fun. We got to play with the parachutes again."

"That sounds like fun," Lacy replied.

She closed the passenger-side back door and squeezed by Raelynn to get to the driver's side. Alice's teacher waved and yelled something about having a nice trip, but Lacy could only read her lips. Raelynn ran around the car in the other direction.

Lacy smiled back at the teacher.

"Is counseling going okay? Social services aren't still trying to take the girls, are they? You know you can't run from them."

Raelynn stepped in front of Lacy's car.

Lacy shook her head. "Are you really going to block me from driving away?"

"You know, Lacy"—Raelynn tried one last ditch effort—"Parker is going to be returning home. I was going to have a surprise 'Welcome Home' party for him. It would mean so much if you were there."

"I'm not even going there with you, Raelynn." Lacy snapped open the driver's door and tossed her purse on the center console. "Buckle up, girls." She turned her head and glared at Raelynn now holding her car door open.

"I know we should have invited you to dinner. I just thought—"

"Thought what? I'd embarrass you with my talk of seeing my late husband?"

"No. That's not it at all. It's not always about you, Lacy. It's been so difficult, and you had so much of your own issues that I never told you how hard this has been for Parker. Things haven't been going well for us, and I wanted that dinner to be a good night. To be honest, I thought Parker would see you and miss Willy."

Lacy nudged Raelynn's hand off the car door and let it close without getting in. She stepped toward a now sobbing Raelynn. While she'd put up a wall to avoid any more tears, she let Raelynn cry in her arms, however, she refused to let any of her own escape. After an extended embrace, Lacy pushed back and opened the car door.

"I am going. Don't worry about us. We're fine. You two will work it out. I know it."

"Call me when you get there," Raelynn whispered. "I love you, Lace."

"We'll be fine," Lacy scooted onto her seat and closed the car door. Driving off she took a quick look back and waved.

Lacy wasn't sure what she was looking for exactly.

What did a portal path look like? All she knew was it had something to do with her grandmother and the farm she used to talk about. When she finished the drive back to Kansas, she asked her mother, but Katlyn shrugged the question off.

"Your grandmother never talked much about that old farm. I'm not sure it even existed but in an old woman's delusions."

What are you so afraid of? Lacy thought. Grandma talked about the farm all the time.

Lacy crept up to the second-floor bedroom where her grandmother used to sleep before they sent her away. An attic of sorts whose entrance was camouflaged behind the wainscot paneling. She tiptoed over to the secret door where she and her sister had snuck through many times while their grandmother was sleeping. Pushing aside a dusty area rug revealed a treasure of boxes still lining the walls in the hidden room.

What would Hope think if he knew that they had stuck Lina up here in the attic, alone?

A petite figure appeared in the doorway. Lacy looked up from the box she was opening.

"I remember the stories grandmother told of her horse."

"Oh, Hank?" Jolene smiled. "I think it was Hank."

"Hope," Lacy whispered. "His name was Hope. I wonder if there are any clues in here."

Jolene ducked through the door. "You don't have to whisper. We're grown women now."

The first box they opened contained a collection of miniature bottles. One of their favorite pastimes as children had been taking them out of the box one at a time, inspecting each of them, and lining them up on the rafters. Hundreds of miniature blown glass imitations of bottles of Grandmother's era, Coke bottles and A&W root beer bottles about three inches tall and no more than a half an inch in diameter. Then there were blown glass miniature vases, wine bottles, and other creations.

"I'm not dragging these bottles out ever again," Jolene commanded.

"I still think they're beautiful. Remember how they would glimmer in the light that slipped through the cracks in the roof before Dad put on the new shingles."

"Yes, they were spectacular. Hard to believe someone made each one by hand."

Lacy moved on to the next box; it was full of papers. She blew the dust off the top of the stack and swatted at a small spider that ran out from between the pages. Maybe she'd find clues in here about the old farmstead.

"I'm heading out." Jolene stood up and brushed off her pants. "I need to get back home."

"You're not staying for dinner?"

"No. You can catch up with Mom and Dad. I'll come by tomorrow."

Shrugging her shoulders and giving a quick wave, Lacy continued opening up each box and carefully inspecting its contents. Looking for clues, she lost track of time.

Tucked between two sheets of clear, waxy paper, an old black-and-white photograph caught her eye. It was of a small child, a young man, and…Hope? It was Hope, Lacy was sure of it. The floor creaked, and Lacy looked up from her daze and saw her mother peering in through the small door.

"I do hope you intend on cleaning up this mess."

Lacy looked around at the stacks of papers, some embroidered doilies, and a few knick-knacks strewn about. She held up the picture with the horse.

"Who are the people in this picture?"

Her mother took the photo, and inspected it, she squinted.

"It looks like your grandmother when she was maybe… six years old? And her dad. I never met her dad because he died shortly after that picture was taken. Grandma's eyes still grew sad when she thought of him."

"What was the horse's name?"

Her mother turned the photo over. "She wrote the names of everyone on the back of all her photos. 'Dad, me, and H'? I'm sorry the writing is faded. I can only make out the first letter. H.

I think they were visiting a friend's farm that day, but your grandmother insisted that it was her horse. As far as I know she never had a horse in her life."

"It's Hope." Lacy whispered with a grin sweeping across her face. "She used to tell me stories about her horses." Lacy reached out, smiling.

"Don't believe the stories of that crazy old woman, Lacy," her mother insisted, handing her back the photo. "She believed that horses could talk to her. Did she tell you that, too?"

"She must have remembered being a little girl with her daddy. When you are a little girl, anything is possible."

"Take all the time you need, Lace, your dad got the girls set up with a movie in the den." She looked around at Lina's things strewn around the attic floor. "But please put things back as you found them."

Lacy held the photo against her chest as her mother turned around to leave. "Oh, Hope. You did know my grandmother Lina."

By the time Lacy found it, she was too tired to even recognize it. Almost dismissing the form that read, Tax Receipt for a property in Stone County, Missouri paid in full. Property description in Township #20.

At dinner, Lacy shared the news of the discovery with her parents.

"Impossible," her mother scoffed. "I can't believe my mother would have never mentioned it. And believe me, she talked a lot about her childhood home. It was a small house where she lived with her parents until her dad died. That's when they moved away."

"Let me take a look at it." Joe reached out and took the form for a closer look.

Olivia and Alice were happy to help their grandmother with the dishes, while Lacy and her father sat at the table and tried to decipher the document. "My little helpers, " Katlyn cheered.

"If I am reading it right," her father explained, "then the total acreage is a little less than two acres…it may be closer to one." He pointed out in the description all the less thans, such as this corner less than the eighty-eight acres to the south, and less than the sixty acres to the east. "They begin describing the land in a township block and then narrow down to the land that is left as being the property that is deeded to them."

"How much is an acre?" Lacy took the document back and read the description again.

"It's about the same as four of our lots here. I would guess it's in a subdivision similar to ours except with larger lots. As your mother described it, it was a pretty small house."

"I wish it had the address. I would love to see the old farm."

"Don't get any wild ideas of finding it." Her mother turned from the kitchen sink and dried her hands on a dish towel. "That was many, many years ago. My mother was six or seven years old."

"What is your fascination with this property?" her father asked. "You've gone to quite a lot of trouble to find this document."

"I don't know. I feel like I want to understand Grandma Lina more. From the time I remember, everyone said she had already lost her mind, but I always enjoyed the stories she told me. Olivia and Alice love hearing them, too."

"Thank you for your help, girls." Her mother diverted their attention and sent them off to the den to play. "I wouldn't be filling their heads with those stories."

"If they are just stories, then what can it hurt?"

"I see you found her locket." Her mother pointed to Lacy's chest and admired the sparkling gem.

"Lina's—I mean, Grandma's locket? It can't be hers." Lacy lifted the locket off her chest and studied it. "Willy gave it to me the night he died."

"Oh, Lacy, there was so much going on then. But I'm certain that is my mother's locket. She loved it dearly—guarded it with her life. I mean you would have gotten a whooping if you even thought about taking it.

"It's like it was never supposed to leave our family--- like magic." Lacy looked down at the locket, careful not to touch it.

After everyone was settling in the living room, the girls tried to get Lacy to play a game with them. But all she wanted was to get back up into the secret room and scour the attic for more clues of where the property was located. Her father recognized her inattentiveness as he sat in his recliner studying the document for any more information it could provide.

"I think you can call the county tax office in the morning and get the address. There's a Property ID," her father explained.

Lacy could hardly wait.

The first thing she did when she woke up the next day was make that call. Unfortunately, they said the ID was too old for their online records.

The lady she spoke with was kind enough to transfer her to the assessor's office. He told her that she would have to come down in person and view the county maps.

Early the next morning, Lacy repacked their suitcases, bathed her daughters, and told them they were going on a trip to southern Missouri.

"You can't run down to Missouri," Katlyn put her hand on the suitcase. "You have two young girls to worry about. Where would you stay?"

"We are going to get a hotel room. It's not like we have never traveled without Willy before." Lacy scooted the suitcase out from underneath her mother's hand.

"You can't be spending your money on little trips here and there. What in the world are you going to do down there with two small children anyway? You are not still insisting on finding that old farm house, are you?"

"I am going to take the girls to Silver Dollar City and to some of the caves and animal parks. We are going to go and have some fun."

Lacy figured she would take the girls to a few attractions then spend a few days exploring the area. She would find Grandma Lina's farm. What if we find the portal Hope had mentioned? Her heart skipped, sending blood pulsing through her chest.

"You should be finding a job and saving that money," her mother stepped between her and the suitcase. "Willy's life insurance isn't going to last forever. It will run out and then what will you do? I thought you came up here to start over."

"I came up here to get support from my family."

That wasn't entirely true. She had already found what she needed. Now she knew what county Lina's farm had been in. Hope's instructions reverberated through her head. Find Caden's Rose. There you will find the portal path.

"We just needed some time away."

"Then why would you pack up on a whim and take off like this?"

"I don't expect you to understand, Mom, but please try. We'll only be gone for a week or so. When we return, I'll get serious about what we will do next. Before we can do that, we need a little time to enjoy ourselves together."

"You're not running from something, are you?"

Never run from anything, always be running toward something you want. The old family mantra rang through her head.

"Not at all, Mom. We're running to something."

CHAPTER 22

2001

The rolling hills of Stone County, Missouri were quite the contrast to the flat plains of Saline County, Kansas. In the backseat, Olivia and Alice giggled, chattering about visiting Silver Dollar City. Lacy used the theme park to wage a campaign against the constant complaints issued about leaving Grandma and Grandpa behind. Going to Silver Dollar City got the girls excited about the trip.

She was excited, too, but not about rollercoasters and homemade taffy. She couldn't wait to find Grandma Lina's farm and meet the real Hope.

The girls, giggling after every ride at the amusement park, helped keep Lacy's mind from wandering off to Avenrand.

"I want to go on Thunderation," Alice cried out, again.

"You know you're not tall enough." Lacy had to tell her for the third time. "Maybe next year."

"Am I big enough?" Olivia asked.

"Why don't we go ride the train." Diverting the girls' attention, she motioned them to get in line at the station. "This will be fun."

The gem in the locket flickered. Her heart raced. No, not now. Not when I am so close to finding the physical portal. Avoiding the temptation to grab the locket, Lacy took each girl by a hand and boarded the train. It was a fun ride until the actors jumped the train and pretended to rob it. Alice hid at Lacy's feet while Olivia shouted, "Get up, get up, you're going to miss it."

They managed to get back to the station unscathed. Lacy bribed them with pizza and ice cream to prepare them to leave. Heading back to the front gates, the locket seemed to come to life. Why is it calling to me? I can't risk transporting somewhere and leaving the girls alone in the park. She hastened her steps pulling the girls along.

The flickering became more intense as they neared the front gate where a line for the Marvel Cave tour was forming. As if beckoning her to join them, the locket pulsed brighter and faster.

"Can we go there?" Olivia pointed to the large poster with a group of people exploring the underground formations.

"Maybe next time," Lacy took the girls hands, her palms sweating, anxious to get away from the energy trying to connect with the locket.

It didn't take long to tuck her daughters into their bed at their hotel on the outskirts of Branson. Olivia chattered on about the petting zoo and Alice rattled on about her bravery riding the train.

"You weren't that brave," Olivia reminded her. "You hid on the floor."

Once they settled down, her focus shifted to finding Grandma Lina's farmstead. Maps, documents, and stacks of photos soon took over the second queen bed in the hotel room. Lacy pondered all the evidence that she had in order to determine the exact location of Lina's farm.

What was the missing piece?

The map that she had didn't have any township identifiers on it. She had to find number twenty. The desk drawer in her hotel room was narrow and contained stationery, a small pen, and a one-page diagram depicting the hotel premises. The one next to the bed had a bible. There was always a bible. She searched the dressers for a book with local phone numbers. There she found the Stone-and-Taney-Counties Yellow Pages.

Lacy organized the documents she would need the next day: the map, the tax receipt that showed the location of her grandmother's property, and the Stone/Taney County phone book. She tucked the tattered photo of Grandma Lina inside the phone book, emptied the girls' story books into the dresser, and shoved all the documents inside their small book bag. After laying out outfits for the morning, she finished clearing off the bed and spruced up the room for housekeeping the next day.

The only time the locket left Lacy's neck was when she took a shower.

While she washed up, it hung on the towel rack within arm's reach. After dressing for bed, she immediately slipped it back on. Lying in bed, the necklace seemed to call to her, but she avoided touching it. She was too close to the portal now to risk a strange time jump.

It must have been a reflection, she remembered Hope saying.

Lacy lay in bed, considering all of her journeys. The places she had gone in the blink of an eye and all the points of time she had visited.

Am I in control of the locket or is someone trying to tell me something?

Hours went by while Lacy recalled her trips to the past—both within and outside of her own timeline—and her visits with Hope. She had always believed Grandma Lina's stories about Hope and their adventures with Caden. In her heart, Lacy knew Grandma Lina was not senile. She was remembering her youth.

If Hope is right, there was a portal on Grandma's farm and I will be able to bring objects in and out of Avenrand. Then I will have my own gem to control.

"If you know where she is, Mrs. Johnson, you have to tell me," Raelynn said as she squeezed by Lacy's mother, letting herself in.

"I think we've been very clear, Raelynn." Mrs. Johnson brushed herself off and followed Raelynn into the kitchen. "This is a family matter."

"And it's about to get worse." Raelynn turned and glared into Mrs. Johnson's eyes. "You are aiding a fugitive. That isn't going to turn out well."

"What on earth are you talking about?"

Mrs. Johnson's pale skin began to turn pink. Raelynn first noticed it on her cheeks but then she saw the fuchsia hue running down her neck and creep along her arms. Mrs. Johnson grasped her hands together, wringing them methodically. Raelynn could see her veins pulsating.

"I don't want to be the one to upset you, Mrs. Johnson. But you should be upset. Lacy has illegally removed those girls from Florida. Warrants have been issued for her arrest. We need to find her and convince her to take the girls back to social services."

"I think you are mistaken. Lacy assured us she was not running from something. She told me that they gave her the girls back."

"I don't think she thinks she is running but that doesn't change the facts. You have to tell me where she is."

Mr. Johnson popped into the kitchen to refill his coffee mug.

"What does she have to tell you?" he asked.

"She thinks Lacy is a fugitive," Mrs. Johnson blurted out.

"A fugitive?" Mr. Johnson scoffed. "Do you really think she is capable of murder?"

"Not at all," Raelynn smirked and shook her head. "I don't think she murdered anyone. Geez. Don't you understand? Her children were taken into state custody. Until they decide she is a fit mother, she isn't allowed to remove them from Florida. Even bringing them here to Kansas is against the court's order. Now she has fled with them and who knows what her intentions are. Do you?"

"She had some business to take care of, she'll be back in a week." Mr. Johnson explained.

"A week will be too late. There is already a warrant out for her arrest." Raelynn focused her plea with Mr. Johnson who seemed much more willing to at least hear her out than Lacy's overprotective mother.

"A warrant?" Mr. Johnson pondered. "For taking her own girls out of that god forsaken state?"

"Yes." Raelynn was hopeful at least that much had sunk in. "I need to find them."

"And what do you propose to do?"

"I'm going to convince her to take the girls back to Florida. Then explain to her social worker that she didn't realize she couldn't take the girls out of state even on short visits. I will stay with her and convince the social worker to have the warrant retracted."

"That sounds reasonable," Mr. Johnson agreed. "Do you think she'll listen to you?"

"I know she will. We've always taken each other's advice even when it's bad." At least she used to listen to me.

Mrs. Johnson rolled her eyes.

"The truth is we don't know where she went. She left on Tuesday, said she was taking the girls on a little vacation." Mr. Johnson looked at the calendar hanging on the side of the fridge.

Raelynn followed his gaze. That was three days ago.

CHAPTER 24

2001

The courthouse wasn't hard to find in the small town of Branson. It had stood in the center of the main square for centuries. The assessor's office was in the basement of the large brick building.

Why is it always in the basement? I hate basements.

A musty smell oozed out of old cinderblock walls. Between that and the lack of lighting, the whole area gave her the creeps.

A young woman—an intern—introduced Lacy to the Stone County appraiser, David Smelsner. His thin, frizzy shoulder length hair looked like he hadn't taken time to brush it in days. Despite that, he appeared competent enough, a few years older than Lacy, but oddly fascinated by her locket.

"Looks like one of the gems they've pulled out of the caverns down south," David pointed to her locket.

"I was thinking of taking the girls down to Talking Rocks Cavern to find some gems of their own."

"You can't harvest gems from the caves, ma'am. It's illegal."

"But the brochure says the girls can mine for gems."

"Oh, ya, ya… that. Most of those gems come from somewhere else but they will enjoy it. It's called sluicing."

He moved closer, reaching toward her stone. A spark of white light bolted from the stone and shocked him.

"Ouch. You shocked me."

"The air has been quite dry." Lacy turned away from David, careful not to touch the locket.

"Indeed, it has," a cheerful woman with long blond hair that flowed over her stocky shoulders approached the large table in front of them. She unrolled a large map in one sweep and smoothed it out on the table. "I'm Sue. The recorder of deeds. I've heard you're interested in finding your grandmother's old farmstead."

She reached under the table and switched on a light that lit up the surface of the table making the map easier to read.

"Yes, ma'am," Lacy said. "I think we have it narrowed down, but Mr. Smelsner believes the property lines have changed since her land was recorded."

Lacy leaned over the table to take a closer look.

"Property lines get moved around all the time." David said. "There are a lot of caves in this area, some that haven't been discovered yet. New caves often mean new revenue, increased land values. Developers come in and land shifts hands and the boundaries get moved."

"Job security," Sue chuckled sprightly. "Every time the borders change, we get to make new maps."

Unlike David, who was vague in his descriptions, Sue was very helpful in locating the old farmstead.

"It parks right up against the Mark Twain National Forest." Sue pointed to the property line on the map. "That might explain why your grandmother thought it was so large. The land described here is less than five acres. It was barely enough for a barn, a house, and a small paddock. Maybe the trails they rode on were public lands. Lots of folks benefit from the forest trails in this area."

After highlighting the small square on the map that represented Lina's home, Sue rolled up the map. "I'll make you a copy of Township twenty. You should be able to locate it on that."

"If you are still interested in mining some gems with your daughters"—David approached Lacy and took one last look at the locket—"you'll need to go a little farther south to Crystal Springs, Arkansas. You can dig for your own crystals there. Mostly quartz there, but you never know. You might get lucky and find something like what you've got there. It's hematite. Not technically a gemstone, more of an iron oxide."

"Ok..."

Lacy felt a little flush with the idea that David thought she'd stolen the stone in her necklace. Then she worried that maybe he was interested in the locket itself.

Sue returned with a copy of the map on a 24x36-inch sheet of thin, white copy paper. The edge was ragged where it had been torn off a roll. "I circled the township. The highlighted area is most likely where your grandmother's land was located."

"Thanks."

Lacy folded the map and slipped it under her arm, grabbed her daughters' hands, and scurried out the door.

With the marked-up copy of the Stone County map, Lacy walked toward her car with confidence.

"Let's go see where Great-grandma lived when she was a little girl!"

Lacy's excitement was contagious, and the girls skipped and squealed while tugging her across the parking lot.

"Let's go to Grandma's house," they sang.

Lacy passed the washed-out gravel path three times before she got the courage to pull in. It reminded her of a dried-up riverbed. She followed it between two pastures and then back into the woods. There the road turned ninety degrees and ascended a steep hill.

There was no way to back out now. The road was too narrow to turn around and the ditches too deep on either side to even try.

She kept going forward until they emerged at the top of the hill in front of an old farmhouse. Despite the ravages of time, Lacy recognized the building from the picture she had found in the attic.

The bright white exterior had faded over the years, and the north side had become covered with green moss. Above the covered front porch, the attic window was boarded up instead of enchanting those who gazed upon its stained-glass window.

Lacy could imagine Grandma Lina as a little girl sitting on the porch with her father, smiling for the camera. Although now, the roof sagged so much it looked like it would cave in with very little help from a light wind.

This was the place.

This was her grandmother's childhood home.

Even though the property looked deserted, Lacy decided to knock on the door and ask permission to see the stable. When no one answered, she looked around. The only vehicle she saw was a rusted down tractor that sat next to a large raised gas tank.

Past those objects, she saw the post and rails that had once made up the corral where Lina had told stories of brushing Hope. The creosote-soaked poles hadn't deteriorated one bit, looking identical to the photograph as Lacy stared at them. They held up rusted gates and corral panels.

Allegedly, this was where Hope first spoke to Lina one cool spring morning not long after her father died.

With or without permission, Lacy was going to step through that gate.

She had to find the portal path to Avenrand.

Lacy got back into the car and drove to the front of the barn. She scouted the area for any signs of life as the girls unbuckled their seatbelts. Certainly, there should have been horses, goats, or cows for the girls to see. But Lacy saw none of these things, not even a stray dog or cat appeared to entertain them. The farmstead appeared abandoned—even of wildlife.

"Where are the horses?" Olivia ran up and jumped onto the rails of the corral panel. "Are we going to get to ride a horse?" The metal creaked.

"Get down from there, Olivia, that doesn't look very sturdy." Lacy looked over the gate towards the old, overgrown pasture. If she could find the portal to Avenrand, the girls would be entertained watching the horses there. If not, she feared, soon they would be disenchanted with their adventure.

The corral was above a steep hill. Remnants of a bridle clung to a hook on an adjacent post. Lacy could almost hear her grandmother giggling as she and Hope exchanged greetings and Lina tickled Hope with her grooming brushes.

It was mid-summer, and Lacy thought it was strange that nothing around the corral was turning green yet. Even the trees were still bare, what few leaves remained were brown and dry. She looked closer but couldn't find a single bud on any of them.

The entire property seemed to be devoid of life.

"Look, Mommy!" Alice stood next to a bush right outside the corral gate. "You have to come see the pretty flowers."

"How did you squeeze through there?" Lacy wiggled the chain until it slipped out of its slot and pushed open the gate. She met Alice at the top of a steep hill. By the edge of the trail that led down and into the woods was one rose bush. Its green leaves seemed like a selective color photo in contrast to the lack of life around it. Three red roses, one large and two smaller buds, were all that adorned it.

It's a sign.

Two paths, one to the left and one to the right, led to the pasture below. The trail to left was hidden by overgrown brush. The one to the right, although less obstructed, seemed too steep for the girls to maneuver. She signaled to the girls to follow her and began to remove the piles of sticks and debris.

Halfway down the hill, the brown leaves on the trees glistened and the woods lit up with color. Trees rustled at the bottom of the hill, and the faint sound of her daughters' voices calling out to her permeated from above.

"Mommy!" they yelled. "Mommy, where did you go?"

Lacy turned and sprinted back up the hill. When she turned to look back down the trail. Everything was brown and lifeless again.

Could this be the portal?

She took her daughters' hands—one on her right and one on her left—in hers and together, they stepped onto the path.

Once more, Lacy saw the trees glisten and the leaves turn the most amazing palette of colors.

"Isn't this amazing, girls? I think every color of the rainbow is in these trees."

"It's dead." Olivia tried to let go of her mother's hand.

"Can you see the colored leaves?" Lacy squeezed.

"There aren't any leaves." Olivia wiggled her hand free.

"Where are the pretty leaves?" Alice twisted around and her hand slipped away.

Lacy reached up to grab a purple leaf from the tree to show Alice. When she turned around, the girls had vanished.

Much more distant than before, she heard the girls crying out to her.

"Mommy, where are you?"

Lacy ran back up the hill. When she looked back down on the hill, the girls stood where she had let go of their hands.

It's the portal, her heart skipped, but how to get the girls to go through it with me.

Hope had mentioned that if they found the portal, then anyone could pass through it.

Wasn't that why they tried to hide it with the debris and block it with overgrown brush to begin with?

"Come back up here, girls," Lacy called out.

Alice and Olivia stomped up to join her.

"There are no horses here," Olivia complained. "I thought we were going to get to meet Great-grandma's horse?"

Lacy sat down on the edge of the hill next to the rose bush. The red of the blossoms added an interesting splash of color to all of the dull browns and grays.

A spark of light caught Lacy's eye from under the rose bush.

Underneath the three flowers were two shiny objects. Two polished stones, one pink and one blue, flickered from under the bush. Lacy picked them up and laid them in her open palm. On closer inspection, she saw their slick finish. They were as bright and shiny as the gem in her locket.

"What is it, Mommy?" Alice squatted down to examine the gems.

"It's a pretty stone." Lacy smiled.

"May I have the pink one?" Alice asked.

"Of course. Isn't it pretty?"

"Give me the blue one." Olivia reached out her hand to snatch it away from Lacy, but she pulled it back and tilted her head.

"How do you ask, Olivia, where are your manners?"

"May I have one, please?" Olivia asked in a sweet tone.

Three roses, two stones. It was more than a coincidence. Caden's rose. Hope's voice echoed in Lacy's head. If you find Caden's Rose, you will find the entrance to Avenrand.

"Three roses, three stones," Lacy whispered looking down at her stone reflecting the sunlight.

The girls gasped as their stones lit up in their hands.

"Mommy, look!" Olivia held her blue stone up above her head. "They're twinkling."

Lacy smiled and then convinced the girls to put their stones inside the pocket of their jeans.

"You don't want to lose these. We'll take the stones back to Nana and show her."

Keeping the stones safe became their mission as the three of them walked down the path and through the portal to Avenrand.

The girls' faces lit up as the dark, brown lifeless tree line came to life with a glittering spectrum of color.

"It's Silver Dollar City!" Olivia threw her hands in the air and twirled around in a full circle.

"It's Adventureland." Lacy grinned. "Who's up for an adventure?"

"We are!" they shouted and ran out of the woods and into the lush green, shimmering pasture.

They stood in the kitchen staring at the calendar like school children waiting on their grades to post. Mr. Johnson blurted out, "Why don't you stay here until she returns?"

Raelynn accepted the invitation.

After getting her things settled into Lacy's old room, she joined the Johnson's for dinner. Mr. Johnson sat at one end of the table and Mrs. Johnson set an additional plate and set of silverware between them. Raelynn pulled out a chair and eased into it.

"Thanks for having me."

Mrs. Johnson smiled and returned to the kitchen.

Raelynn bit her bottom lip and turned toward Mr. Johnson. "When did Lacy say she'd be back?"

"Well, she didn't say, about a week I guess." Mr. Johnson leaned around Raelynn to look in the kitchen where his wife was stirring gravy on the stove.

"It seems like that is something you would want to know. She left and no one wondered when she would come back?"

"She is a grown woman, Raelynn. We try not to pry into her business. Sometimes she visits, and then she leaves. We don't usually ask when she will return."

"But she is grieving. Doesn't that concern you?"

"She seemed perfectly fine. You can't blame her for wanting to take a little vacation with the girls after all that has happened."

Mrs. Johnson joined them with hot gravy still in the pot and slid a pad underneath. Other than a swift warning to not burn themselves, they ate in silence. Raelynn was deep in thought analyzing what on earth Lacy was up to, while Mr. and Mrs. Johnson didn't seem quite sure of what to say to their uninvited guest.

Other than a few requests to pass a dish and a polite word of thanks for the meal, nothing of substance was discussed. Although Raelynn offered to help, Mrs. Johnson insisted that the other two retire to the living room as she cleaned up and prepared dessert.

"Something is definitely wrong with this whole situation," Raelynn said, pacing up and down in the small hall in front of the dining room.

"Well, you seem very sure of yourself and frankly it is all too much for Kate," Mr. Johnson sat down in his favorite recliner. "You don't need to be coming up here and upsetting her."

The front door slammed as Jolene entered the living room and Mrs. Johnson carried in dessert. No one was talking. No one had to be talking because enough had already been said. The tension in the room cut like a knife.

"What is going on? Is something wrong? Did someone die?"

"Lacy is fine," her mother interjected.

"What happened to her?" Jolene asked.

Mr. Johnson turned to Raelynn and raised an eyebrow before she got a chance to say anything. "Let's not get everyone upset?"

"You should be upset, Mr. Johnson," Raelynn stated. "You all should be. You know why? Because something isn't right."

"What's wrong?" Jolene asked.

"Lacy taking off with the girls and not telling anyone when she'll be back."

"She went home, right? She doesn't know when she'll be back."

"No, she didn't go home. According to your mother, she took Alice and Olivia on a little vacation." Raelynn looked away from Mr. Johnson hoping Jolene would be the sensible one.

"Yes," Jolene walked past Raelynn. "She was going to stop by Silver Dollar City for a day on her way home. It was a stop off on their way back to Florida."

"She isn't going to go home." Raelynn took a few steps toward the stairs subconsciously preparing an escape route. "Not with social services looking to take her girls from her."

"What?" Jolene glared into Raelynn's eyes with a burning disbelief. "You think she is on the run, don't you? I don't believe it."

"Why can't she take the girls on vacation? These are her children." Mrs. Johnson interrupted.

"I can't help but think she is running. Jolene, you know how she runs from trouble."

"Lacy is the bravest girl I know. She faces her demons." Mr. Johnson's hands began to shake.

"Not this demon," Raelynn glared back at him. "Come on, Jolene. If you've talked to her, you know about her visits with Willy. She is not grieving well."

"They are dreams." Jolene glanced at her dad. "People dream of their lost loved ones all the time."

"What dreams?" Mrs. Johnson handed the dessert plate to her husband and turned around to face Jolene.

Both Jolene and Raelynn ignored Mr. and Mrs. Johnson as their heated dialog escalated.

"It's more than that," Raelynn explained. "She wants to go back in time and change it. She wants to save Willy."

Lacy's mom began sobbing. She dropped the other plates on the coffee table and ducked down the hallway back to the kitchen. A loud thud echoed down the hall.

"I've had enough." Mr. Johnson jumped up and headed toward the kitchen after his wife. He stopped in the doorway to ask Raelynn, "Have you just come here to upset everyone? Do you think losing our son-in-law has been easy for us? Maybe you should leave." He stormed away.

"I love Lacy, too!" Raelynn shouted down the hallway. "I am concerned she's in more trouble than anyone else is willing to admit."

"She is going to be fine," Jolene said. "You'll see. She is brave and she is courageous. Believe it or not, Alice, Olivia, and my sister are happy. We had a great visit."

Raelynn and Jolene stood in a face off for a few minutes. Mr. Johnson emerged from the kitchen with his arm around his wife.

"They are going to be just fine," Mr. Johnson broke the tension. "I'm sure Lacy is lucky to have a friend who cares about her so much, Raelynn. But she is going to be fine, and we have to have faith in her."

"Mom, are you okay?" Jolene put her hand on her mother's shoulder.

"I'm fine, dear." Mrs. Johnson patted Jolene's hand. "I bumped my head on the cabinet, that's all. Raelynn, stay as long as you like, but no more of this negative energy. You are always welcome here."

"I appreciate that, Mrs. Johnson. But I—"

Raelynn reached out to hug her. Mr. Johnson and Jolene stepped back to let the two of them make their peace. Mrs. Johnson sobbed in Raelynn's arms.

"You are such a good friend to our Lacy." Mrs. Johnson pushed Raelynn back and cupped Raelynn's face in her hands. "Practically family."

"Of course, we are." Raelynn squirmed away. "But I…I…I should go."

She tried to ignore the glares from Mr. Johnson and Jolene, but mistrust radiated from their piercing eyes. They weren't as quick to call her family.

"You're going after her, aren't you?" Jolene asked.

"I know she is brave and courageous and all those things, but right now, she needs our help."

With that their expressions softened. They tried to smile in agreement.

It didn't take long for Raelynn to gather her bags and walk out the front door. She got into the car, her blood racing. She tightened her grip on the steering wheel trying to get her hands to stop shaking. She was going to find Lacy and her daughters with or without the help of Lacy's family.

They are in denial, Raelynn thought.

Some people just live lives of bliss in their own denial. But Raelynn? No. She saw things for what they were, and she didn't miss a detail. Lacy was on the run. She'd seen it before, but this time it was serious.

She was running into a fantasy world of time travel and adventure and taking two little girls with her.

CHAPTER 26

Avenrand

The girls twirled as beautiful colors glistened from the leaves on the trees and reflected off their faces and shoes. They ran out from behind the edge of the woods into the open field. A gentle breeze blew lush green grass back and forth as if waving to them.

The sound of galloping hooves made them stop and listen. Olivia looked back at Lacy with her eyes wide open.

Alice jumped up and down giggling with excitement. The herd of horses popped over the hill, and she sped off to greet them.

Olivia hid behind Lacy, clutching her leg with both arms, faking a smile, her excitement lost in a nervous giggle.

"Alice." Lacy pulled Olivia's arms away from her leg. "Come back here."

Alice turned toward her for a second then looked away. Lacy tucked Olivia behind a tree and went to meet Alice. Taking her hand, she led her back to the tree line as the horses continued to thunder toward them.

"There are horses! There are horses!" Alice jumped up and down next to her mother.

Lacy saw Hope and smiled.

We made it, she thought. We found Grandmother's path to paradise.

Now they could find their way to the lake, and she would be able to find a gem that contained her own magic. A gem with power she could control outside of Avenrand to save Willy. They could be a family again; the family she always dreamed of.

Hope looked different, his ears were pinned back and his eyes pierced with anger. The herd stopped some distance in front of them. Hope walked up to greet them.

"What's wrong? I'm not here to hurt you and neither are the girls." Lacy pushed both girls behind her. "You knew we were going to come back."

"You should leave." Hope lowered his head and stomped his right front hoof. "Things have changed here and you need to leave. The Silverback Beast is in North Avenrand."

The herd seemed startled. As soon as one horse began to run, the others kicked up their heels and followed. Hope paced in front of Lacy jerking toward the herd and then looking back at Lacy.

"Hide!" Hope shouted before he turned and galloped off to catch up with the others.

Lacy felt her heart pumping inside her chest. She looked around for a place to hide and yanked her daughters behind the closest bush.

"Get down," she commanded, pulling them down beside her as she crouched up into the brush. What could it be? What could make them so afraid?

Olivia whimpered, holding her hand over a cut from the thorny bush. Odd that the bushes now had thorns. Last time Lacy was here, they were soft and fuzzy.

"Shh," Lacy whispered.

Alice stared off at something on the path. Her whole body trembled. She jumped at a loud snort.

Lacy backed away, shoving the girls deeper into the brush and crouching even lower.

A silver creature flexed its long claws and growled, exposing its sharp teeth and long fangs.

This is not an animal from the zoo, Lacy thought, pushing the girls farther behind her like a duck clutching its hatchlings under her wings.

Steam billowed out of its large nostrils that appeared to have outgrown the beast's head. He lumbered across the levy. Coming closer, acting pissed off at everything in its way.

The silverback's wolf-like head gave way to a huge hump on his back just above his shoulder blades. His arms were like that of a bear but shorter in front causing him to lunge forward and land hard on his front paws. Popping his rear end up into the air made room for his longer hind legs to spring forward to catch up. His name accurately described the shiny silver fur that covered the large hump on his back.

Trying to keep the girls calm and out of sight, Lacy hushed even her breath. The silverback slowed down as it crept closer to them, slinking along and snorting.

"You think I can't see you," it growled in a deep, raspy voice. "I find you. I find you all."

Lacy felt the girls shaking behind her back but dared not even whisper to them. He had the claws of a bear and the attitude of a hungry grizzly amplified up a notch. His nostrils flared wide open as he stretched them in the air with a powerful suction.

"I find you," he snarled.

Lacy took the hands of the girls then clasped her locket and blinked. She opened her eyes, and she could still feel his hot steamy breath on her face.

"I find you all," he boasted.

The silverback slunk a few more steps in the wrong direction and then disappeared. Lacy wondered if she had blinked him away with the locket, but Alice and Olivia were still goggling the trail as if he was still there.

"What is it?" Lacy whispered. "He's gone. We're safe."

They smiled and sighed with relief.

"Look, Mommy! It's Super Boy," Olivia shouted. "The beast is afraid of his sword."

"He hid the monster inside his cape." Alice squirmed free of Lacy's grip and stepped toward the spot where the beast disappeared.

"He chased him off, Alice," Olivia still stood behind Lacy. "Do you see his sword?"

"I don't see anything." Lacy peered out in the direction the girls were looking. "What are you talking about?"

"He's gone now, Mommy." Olivia stepped out from behind Lacy, disappointed. "He chased that beast off with his sword."

"He hid him in his cape," Alice protested, making a swooping motion with her arm like she was whipping a cape around her. "He hid him in his cape."

"No, he didn't." Olivia made a stabbing motion with her right arm. "He used his sword. I was closer, I could see better. Maybe he hid the fight from you with his cape."

"Girls, please."

Lacy tried to process all that happened. First, they were in another world. She was able to walk through the portal and bring the girls in with her. But this world wasn't the peaceful paradise her grandmother talked about in her stories or the world she had visited in the past. It had a wild, scary, prehistoric monster in it that didn't seem to like them very much. And the girls believed they had seen a caped boy superhero save them from the wolf-bear-like creature.

"You met the Silverback beast," Hope choked out the words, walking down the trail to their hiding place in the brush.

"You came back," Lacy stepped out and approached him.

"I am sorry there is nothing I can do to protect you from him. You need to leave. You need to take your girls and get out." Hope nodded his head back toward the path they had come in on.

"What was that thing?" Lacy took another step toward Hope.

"It showed up when the silver gem was stolen from Avenrand." Hope lowered his head and Lacy reached out to scratch his muzzle. "Who else came in with you?"

"No one." Lacy looked around. "These are my girls, Olivia and Alice. Girls, this is Hope. Great-grandma Lina's horse."

"You must never tell anyone about Avenrand. I must forbid you from taking the gem you seek. For the safety of your world and ours, leave and don't come back."

"But you gave Grandma Lina a stone to travel here. Did that hurt Avenrand?"

"That gem called to her. Gems find their beloved, but they must never be taken. It's too late for South Avenrand."

"What happened?"

"The darkness has overtaken them—death and sorrow. The silverback escaped from the south and attacked a small doe in the shimmering field and then came after our foal. The Prince was able to overpower him but not for long."

"The boy hid him in his cape," Alice shouted.

"I told you, Alice, he chased it off with his sword." Olivia drew an imaginary sword and stabbed at the air.

"You saw Prince Caden?" Hope perked up. "You saw the Prince of Avenrand?"

"He's a prince?" Olivia stepped away from her mother and moved toward the stallion.

"He is a little boy." Lacy shook her head. "An imaginary boy."

"Super Boy is the Prince of Avenrand," Alice sang.

"We are not going to abandon you and Avenrand while there is such a danger. We can help." Lacy patted Hope on the neck.

"If you want to help"—Hope took a step back and lifted his head— "You must leave and find out who stole the silver gem that is causing the impending darkness. It has taken over South Avenrand and it won't be long before it spreads across the North."

CHAPTER 27

2001

It was quite the adventure and one Lacy knew would be hard to explain to her parents. As they drove back from Grandma Lina's farmstead, Lacy turned the entire adventure into a game of make believe. The girls played along. By the time they got back to the hotel, they had mixed in bits of what actually happened with things they only imagined.

"How did you enjoy Adventureland USA?" Lacy asked.

"Family fav," Olivia announced, as Lacy turned the key in the lock to open the door to their hotel room.

"Agreed," Lacy opened the door, stepped in, and saw the shadow of a figure sitting on the bed. She put her arm out and blocked the girls from entering. "I'm sorry I thought this was our room. The key opened the door."

"It's me, Lacy," a familiar voice announced from the darkness.

Lacy flipped on the light.

"Raelynn, what are you doing here?"

"I'm checking up on you," Raelynn said.

"You scared me."

The girls ran up and gave Raelynn hugs, rambling on about their trip to Adventureland and seeing the silverback beast and petting talking horses.

"They had a pretend adventure in the car. Makes the car ride go by quicker," Lacy explained.

"Talking horses—well, that is an adventure." Raelynn picked up Alice and tossed her on the bed.

"Whee!" Alice squealed in delight.

"And then we almost got ate by a giant wolf-bear," Olivia said.

"Not even close." Lacy acted like she was playing along.

Raelynn helped Lacy get the girls settled in after their bath. Then it was time for some serious talk.

Raelynn unzipped the red insulated bag that had a place for keeping two bottles of wine chilled, two plastic wine glasses, a corkscrew, and a bottle stopper. Lacy tucked the girls into bed and then joined her at the table.

"So, are you going to tell me why you are really here in Southern Missouri," Lacy asked. "How did you find us?"

"I visited your parents—who by the way aren't very happy with me right now," Raelynn confessed.

"And you followed me here. Did they send you to check up on me?"

"No, your dad advised me to leave you alone. He asked me to go because I was upsetting your mother."

"What did you tell her? Did you tell her about Avenrand?" Lacy wondered.

"Avenrand?" Raelynn raised her eyebrows.

"Did you tell her about the locket?"

"No," Raelynn said. "That is between you and your shrink."

"You still don't believe it?"

"That you time travel? That you visit Willy? What concerns me is that you took the girls out of Florida without checking with your social worker."

Lacy hesitated to tell Raelynn any more than she had. Now, it was more than a blink. Now she could go to Avenrand, and she was able to take the girls with her.

"I would watch what you tell the girls," Raelynn advised. "I came to tell you that they are looking for you. Ms. Conrad came to my house, asking about your whereabouts. I pretty much wormed it out of her that they considered your children wards of the state and that you have kidnapped them."

"That is ridiculous. How can I kidnap my own children?"

"You didn't finish your agreement for counseling."

"Yes, I did. I finished six weeks with Dr. Garamondy. He said he was finished seeing me."

"Did he clear you? Did he write up a report saying you're okay?"

"I don't know. I didn't see a report."

"You left Florida without that report. That report is what would have released you—well the girls—from the state's custody."

"I don't recall them being in the state's custody. I have had them all this time."

"Since the first night they took them, you agreed to that plan. The counseling report is what would have released them. I thought you may have found out the report was bad and took the girls and ran. They didn't come back to school."

"The report Dr. Garamondy wrote was negative? Is that why you are here?" Lacy poured another glass of wine but hesitated before she took the next sip. "Wait. They were at your house? Did they follow you here?"

"No, I don't think so, but an amber alert was issued as I left Florida. The description was your car, but you'd already been gone for days by then."

"I have to go back to Florida but I can't take the girls with me. It's too risky. I have to find Dr. Garamondy and see if he has the silver gem."

"What are you talking about? Now your doctor has a gem?"

"It must be Dr. Garamondy," Lacy interrupted. "He must have used me to sneak into Avenrand and steal the silver gem. Maybe he knows more about this than he let on. The gems from Avenrand have special powers." What special powers does the silver gem have?

"Hey," Raelynn interrupted. "Let's go down to the bar and have a drink. You can tell me all about Avenrand."

Lacy looked at the girls asleep together in the queen bed near the window. "I can't leave the girls. They're worn out, sound asleep."

"It's just down one floor. No different than leaving them upstairs sleeping in their bedroom." Raelynn convinced her. "Plus, the door will be locked. They'll be fine."

Raelynn ordered another round of tequila shots as Lacy sipped her beer.

"You know I can't handle tequila," Lacy slurred.

"You're doing fine," Raelynn laughed. "Here's to Avenrand. I hope I get to venture there with you, Lacy. It sounds like such an amazing place."

"It was paradise," Lacy said. "Until the silverback beast showed up."

"What beast?" Raelynn asked.

"Hope says when the silver gem was taken out of Avenrand, it caused an evil beast to appear. I think..." I've overshared.

It was the tequila.

She no longer had control over how much of her story to share, and something seemed a little off about Raelynn. Her friend seemed way too eager to order her another shot.

"Are you trying to get me drunk?" Lacy pushed her drinks away. "I don't drink like this anymore, Rae. You know that."

"This is the last one," Raelynn assured her. "Then we should call it a night and go check on the girls."

"The girls!" Lacy jumped up and bolted for the elevator. Coming out of the elevator, she stumbled onto the second floor. Her head was spinning as she opened the door. The light was on and the room was empty.

"Where are the girls?" she screamed. "They are gone. You said they would be okay."

Raelynn stood in the doorway, watching.

Lacy raced around the room at least three times, even checking the bathroom and shower. She looked in the closet and under the bed.

Flashing lights flickered through the drapes.

She ran to the window and pulled the plastic rod to draw open the shades. Looking down onto the parking lot below, she saw an officer was helping Olivia into a squad car. Lacy bolted out of the room and down the hall. Too impatient to wait for an elevator, she went right for the stairs, leaping down them two at a time. She sped through the lobby into the parking lot as the first squad car drove off with Olivia and Alice.

"Where are you taking my girls?" she screamed.

Raelynn watched from inside the lobby, peering out from the glass as tears ran down her cheeks.

"Calm down, ma'am," the officer reached out for her flailing arms. "They're safe."

"Are you Lacy Donathon?" a second officer asked, his voice not as soothing as the other.

Lacy ignored the question as she jerked her arms away from the first officer and turned toward Raelynn. She marched through the lobby doors.

"You did this," she yelled.

Raelynn turned to leave, but Lacy ran after her.

"You did this," she repeated pushing Raelynn up against the wall. "Tell me what is going on, Raelynn. Why did you do this?"

Raelynn said nothing as they faced each other in front of the check-in desk. The clerk watched, horrified by the scene. As one of the officers pulled Lacy's hands behind her back and snapped the handcuffs on, Lacy continued shouting at Raelynn. The other officer began reading Lacy her rights and explained that she was being arrested on charges of child endangerment.

"You were supposed to be my best friend. Why would you do this? You set me up. That was your whole purpose in coming here! To take away my girls. Fifteen years we've been friends. Fifteen years we supported each other as our husbands went off to war, as we welcomed our babies into the world. Fifteen years, Rae, we had babies, and we even buried babies. How could you do this?"

Raelynn stood frozen watching as the officer tucked Lacy's head down to help her into the back of the squad car. Lacy screamed at her so loud the glass shook.

"I hate you. I hate you forever!" Lacy yelled.

CHAPTER 28

2001/2036

After processing in at the Stone County jail, Lacy was allowed to make one phone call.

"Daddy, it's Lacy." She wept into the receiver on the phone.

"Oh geez," her dad said. "You haven't called me Daddy in fifteen years."

When her father came to the station to pick her up, Lacy stuck to business. She thanked him for picking her up, gathered her belongings, and signed the release form. On their way out to the car, she folded her copy of the form up and stuffed it into her back pocket.

Most of the car ride home was quiet. Lacy watched the trees of Stone County turn into green pastures the farther north they traveled. Joe broke the silence somewhere in the flint hills of Kansas.

"Is Raelynn's story true?" he blurted out as they neared the house.

"I can't talk about her right now, Dad," Lacy calmed the anxiety stirring from just hearing her name with a deep breath and long exhale. She continued to stare out the window.

"Is it true you think you can still talk to Willy?" he asked.

"Thanks for bailing me out, Dad." Lacy ignored the question.

"I think I deserve an explanation."

"You do. I agree with that, but I can't give one to you right now. I hope you understand."

He pulled the car into the driveway and hesitated a moment before pushing the garage door opener. They looked at each other and exchanged pouty frowns.

"You know what's gonna go down, right?" he asked.

"Mom is going to freak out on me. I'm prepared." Lacy reached for the door handle, pausing to grab her envelope of belongings from the jail. They walked in the house together like two teenagers caught coming home after curfew.

But Katlyn didn't seem as upset as they had expected. They stepped through the front door and found her calm and quiet. She offered Lacy a warmed-up plate of food from dinner which Lacy politely refused. Lacy did take the cup of warm chamomile tea her mother presented, before excusing herself to her room. Nothing was mentioned about the arrest or the reason the state of Florida seemed so interested in the girls.

Lacy leaned against her headboard, propping a pillow up behind her neck and sipping on her tea. She stared at the psychedelic poster that hung on the wall. The vibrant colors that reacted to blacklight looked like planets in a distant galaxy. It soothed her as it did in her youth.

The girls must be miles away by now in some stranger's home in Florida. They are probably telling stories about the Silverback beast. Lacy smiled.

She emptied the contents of the envelope onto her bed. Without thinking she picked up her wedding ring and started to put it on her finger, then stopped. It no longer belongs there. She placed the ring on the nightstand.

Tossing the watch, a stick of gum, and a dollar bill back inside, she thought she saw a spark near the last item. She picked up the locket and put it around her neck.

She covered the stone with her hand and closed her eyes. Without thinking, she reached for her teacup on the nightstand and hit a tall, cool glass with the back of her hand. She opened her eyes as a wine glass hit the edge of the table and fell to the ground. The red liquid splattered all over the ivory carpet below. She sat up and focused her attention on the person lying next to her.

It wasn't Willy.

She recognized the face, although his skin had aged, and his hair was grayer than she remembered. "Chris?"

"I'm sorry. Was I snoring?" he asked.

"What is going on?" Lacy asked.

"Oh my, you had a little more wine last night than I thought, didn't you?"

"I didn't have any wine last night," Lacy protested. "I had a warm cup of chamomile tea."

"I think the evidence is all over the carpet, and it looks more like red wine to me than chamomile tea."

Chris got out of bed and wrapped himself in his robe. "I'm heading to the kitchen. I can get you a cup of tea if you want."

"Tea would be nice, thanks," Lacy said, trying to soak in the situation. Looking around the room, she realized this was no bedroom she had ever been in. The bed was king size, much bigger than her queen bed at home and over twice the size of her twin bed growing up.

Why am I in bed with Chris? Where is Willy? Whose room is this? Having been a party to several interesting time travel scenarios Lacy knew it was best to play along without asking too many questions.

"How are you feeling?" Chris asked, handing Lacy a warm mug. "I think you drank more wine last night than you realized."

He bent down and picked up the wine glass she'd knocked over. Then walked over to the sink that was partitioned off by a column of decorative pillars in a corner of the master bedroom. He brought back a damp towel and began sopping up the wine from the carpet.

"I'm so sorry," Lacy said embarrassed that she had stained his carpet. "I didn't see the glass."

"It's fine, we have that expensive steamer for a reason."

Lacy pondered his choice of pronouns for some time.

We have, she thought. Apparently, we have more than an expensive steamer.

"Enjoy your tea," Chris encouraged. "I'll go take care of this."

"Okay, thanks." She tried to act as if she knew what the heck was going on.

At least in the past, she had traveled to times she recognized, events she could gather a few clues from, and remember where and who she was at the time. This was more like when she jumped out of her timeline, stranded on the road surrounded by flood waters with an unknown baby.

Now she was here but didn't know where or when here was. At least she recognized Chris from her grief support group. She had no recollection of them being together—even going out on a date! Much less any event where they ended up in the same bed together.

Chris returned with an air of satisfaction. "All done. They will be as good as new in the next load."

"Thank you." Lacy repositioned the pillow behind her back and took another sip of tea.

"Are your fingers swelling up again?" Chris asked, pointing to her ring finger. The solid gold ring and diamond ring on the nightstand sparkled and caught Lacy's attention. She noticed a matching solid gold band on Chris' finger.

"They must be," she whispered. "I don't remember taking them off." The last thing Lacy did remember was the officer at the jail making her take off her wedding ring and put it in the manila envelope. The officer cataloged her ring as a small diamond setting and a wedding band. The diamond on the nightstand next to her was much larger and more brilliant than the one she remembered.

"We're married?" She wanted to take the words back as soon as they slipped out.

"That bad, huh?" Chris laughed. "I apologize I didn't realize you had that many drinks or I would have slowed you down. Is everything alright?"

"I'm fine," Lacy said. "How are the girls?"

"The girls?" Chris acted confused. "Which girls?"

"Olivia and Alice," Lacy said. "Do you know where my girls are?"

Chris seemed concerned and when he left the room without answering the question, Lacy decided she needed to do more investigating on where and when she was in time.

Oh God, what if something had happened to the girls?

Or what if she'd never gotten to see them again? Panicking, she got up and found some clothes in the walk-in closet that seemed to be hers. She got dressed and headed out to the living room to find Chris and determine what was going on.

Lacy found it odd that she didn't see any computers or electronic devices at all not even a television screen.

"I seem to have misplaced my notebook," Lacy said.

Chris laughed. "You did bonk your head last night, didn't you? There might be an old iPad in the closet. Do you really need it?"

Looking in the first closet she found, she saw several coats hung on the rack and a fine Stetson cowboy hat on the top shelf.

"In the den, that's the second door on your left." He chuckled.

Laughing, as if she knew that, she was grateful for the directions because this den was not what she expected. There was no desk or file cabinets or fireplace. As a matter of fact, the room was quite bare. Other than two molded futuristic recliners with clear shields over the top, it was rather empty.

When Lacy walked across the threshold to the den, a bright light emerged from a glass dome on the ceiling in the center of the room.

"Hello, Lacina," a soothing voice said as a brilliant beam of blue light modulated with its vocal transmissions. "How can I help you?"

Lacina? Must be official. "I need my notebook computer," Lacy said, answering the machine before even thinking and then shushing herself for responding to a machine. "Ludicrous," she snarled.

"I'll be there in a minute," Chris yelled from down the hall.

She shook her head. "I need to get on the internet," Lacy muttered.

"The internet was an electronic communications network that connected many computer networks around the world between nineteen seventy-six and twenty twenty-eight."

"What year is it now?" Lacy asked.

"It's twenty thirty-six."

After a few moments of silence, the blue light beamed again. "How may I help you, Lacina Manning?"

"Manning? Never mind, I want to surf the internet," Lacy said. "How hard is that?"

A surfboard appeared along the wall. It was about twelve feet long and had a dual fin on the back end. It looked as if it appeared out of thin air. Lacy walked toward the board and reached her hand out, inching close enough to touch it.

It was solid.

It was real.

"The activity can be adjusted to any difficulty level between one and ten. One would be least difficult and ten would be the highest difficulty setting for this model of intellectual interface. To begin, state your level of difficulty and then step onto the surfboard."

"This is too weird," Lacy said, looking down at the locket that hung from her neck. She contemplated trying to blink back but was too curious to pass up checking out a little more about this technology.

Twenty thirty-six seemed to be packed full of surprises.

"It is recommended due to your age and fitness level that you begin on the level of difficulty setting number one."

"My age!" Lacy scuffed. "I was twenty-five last time I checked and in pretty good shape."

"Your current age is fifty-nine. Fitness level is sedentary."

"I didn't want to surf anyway," Lacy said.

The surfboard disappeared. "How may I help you, Lacina Manning."

"Excuse me," Lacy said, backing out of the room making sure nothing else appeared.

Lacy turned around and ran smack into Chris's chest. He embraced her and rubbed her back. "Are you feeling alright, Lacina?"

When did I change my name back to Lacina? I'm sure my mother had something to do with it. She had hated when I started signing papers Lacy in junior high school and the nickname stuck.

"I think so," Lacy said. "I guess I have a little bit of a hangover."

"Well, can't Victor take care of that for you?" Chris asked.

"Victor?" Lacy asked, wishing she could take it back.

Of course, Chris would expect me to know who Victor was.

"Come on, let's go see what Victor can conjure up." Chris handed Lacy a fresh mug of chamomile tea and took her back into the den. He got her situated in one of the gravity-free recliners in the corner and then took the seat next to her. "Victor," Chris called out.

A male voice responded, "Hello, Chris Manning. How may I help you?"

"Run Santa Rosa Island One," Chris commanded.

The room transformed into a beautiful white beach and in front of them gentle waves crashed upon the shore. They were the most brilliant blue waters Lacy had only seen in one other place, Pensacola, Florida. The temperature in the room increased as a bright yellow light lit up the artificial sky. It was so realistic, Lacy felt like she was sitting in a beach chair on the white sands of Ft. Pickens, one of her and Willy's favorite campgrounds.

Chris reached over and wiped a tear rolling down Lacy's cheek. "What is it, Lacina? What's wrong?"

Without thinking of where she was, forgetting it was twenty thirty-six and not two thousand and one, Lacy blurted out, "My girls are in Pensacola. I miss them so much."

"We should take a trip down there." Chris squeezed her hand. "It's been years since we've visited them."

Lacy didn't know how to respond. She had a million questions but didn't dare ask things she should already know.

Instead, she decided to find out as much as possible by asking questions to the blue light in the den whenever Chris wasn't around. Eventually she found out the blue light was fondly named Victor and most folks had a Victor room in their house. VICTOR was an acronym for Virtually Intelligent Character Transmitted Optical Reality.

Apparently, Victor had replaced the need for any other media devices and was wired into special transmit/receive boxes in every room of the house, eliminating the need for television screens or computer monitors. Victor transmitted images into thin air immersing the audience in a complete 4D presentation.

Lacy played along and spent the day letting Chris pamper her. For her, it was a first date, but according to Victor they had been married for over thirty years. Chris put together a wonderful lunch and they ate outside in the screen room. Most homes in the south had such rooms because of the relentless mosquitoes and their home—which was much higher in quality than any she had ever lived in with Willy—was no exception.

"It's beautiful," Lacy said as Chris added the final touches to their meal.

He set a vase of fresh flowers he'd bought her in the center of the table.

"You always say a meal is not complete without flowers to dress up the food." He grinned.

"I'm glad you remembered," Lacy said.

"You're as beautiful today as you were thirty years ago when I asked you to marry me," Chris said.

"Thank you," Lacy said. "You're too kind."

Not long after Lacy got over the shock that Chris asked her to marry him, she overheard a phone call. Chris assured the caller that their dinner engagement was still on. He hung up the phone and met Lacy in the living room.

"Are you still up for dinner tonight?" Chris asked. "That was Mark. I told him we were still on but if you're not feeling well enough, I totally understand."

"Oh no," Lacy said. "I am okay."

Trying to get more information with Victor was frustrating. Lacy wanted to find out what had happened to the girls and Chris seemed so evasive. Maybe he omitted the details he expected Lacy—the Lacy of 2036—to already know. Victor did the same thing. She spent the afternoon trying to figure out how to get Victor to display the data that she wanted without creating literal 4D examples. Surfing the internet had gotten so much more complicated in the future.

"Can you just replicate a search engine?" Lacy asked when Chris was in the shower.

A large engine appeared on the floor. The smell of grease and burning oil filled the room.

"This engine was built by Seattle RCH, commonly known as SeaRCH in two thousand twenty-eight. It was used in the first hover craft licensed for civilian road use. Would you like to see more on the hover craft?"

"No, thank you," Lacy said, waving her hand in front of her nose trying to fan off the strong smell of burnt oil. "Cancel that request. Can you tell me what happened to the World Wide Web of say the year two thousand?" The engine vanished.

"The world wide web was active until the year twenty twenty-eight when a breakthrough in technology combined the vastness of space data storage with cloud technology offering unlimited satellite access and ultra-high speeds of data retrieval. Space-Cloud technology made the need for servers with limited access, slow speeds, and limited storage capacity obsolete. Did that answer your question, Lacina?"

"Yes. Could you tell me more about what replaced the World Wide Web?" Lacy asked.

"Would you like more information about Space-Cloud technology?" Victor asked.

Chris popped his head into the den. "Your turn, Lacina. Better get moving if you are going to shower before dinner."

Lacy put her search on hold to get ready for dinner. She was surprised when they arrived to find Dr Garamondy waiting at their table. Lacy wanted to confront him about what happened to her daughters. But that was two thousand and one and this was twenty thirty-six in a very nice, expensive restaurant. Lacy couldn't figure out if it was Chris who could afford such a luxury or if it was Dr. Garamondy treating them.

How long has Dr. Garamondy known Chris?

It didn't make sense that they were such close friends. How could her husband not understand the anger she held in her heart toward the man she suspected sold her out and got her daughters taken away from her. He was also her top suspect in the missing silver gem. She suspected he knew more about Avenrand than he let on.

More than once, Lacy caught Dr. Garamondy's eyes drift down to the gem around her neck. When Chris excused himself from the table to use the men's room, Lacy decided she had nothing to lose by confronting him.

"Tempting, isn't it?" Lacy asked.

"Where did you find it?" Dr. Garamondy pointed to the necklace.

"Did I lose it?"

"Well, I see that you didn't, but I am pretty sure your—" Dr. Garamondy stopped short.

Was he going to tell her that her future-self had lost the locket? Was he on to her? Did this Dr. Garamondy now believe in the time travel capabilities of the locket. The same Dr. Garamondy that set her up with the state of Florida to have her arrested. What did he know about the silver gem?

"Excuse me," Dr. Garamondy stood up sliding back his chair. "It was a pleasure seeing you again, Miss Johnson."

"Of course," Lacy said in shock that he called her Miss Johnson. She hadn't been Miss Johnson in years. "But aren't you going to help me?"

"I'll get back to you," he mumbled.

Dr. Garamondy crossed paths with Chris on his way back from the men's room.

"I'm sorry, Chris," Dr. Garamondy said. "You'll have to excuse me. I need to run but good news. I think I might be on to something. We have the cure within our grasps."

Lacy double checked the locket around her neck. The way Garamondy continued to stare at it reminded her of her last visit. He had been shocked by a bolt of light that came from the locket when he reached for it. Her hand felt its cool, smooth surface. She shut her eyes in relief.

CHAPTER 29

2001

Back in her room in her childhood home, no time had passed and yet, she had spent an entire day with Chris in the future in less than one minute.

The locket has the power to travel both forward and backward in time.

What if she could go back in time and talk to her grandmother?

There must be a way to control the locket.

Catching the light from a reflection would take her to Avenrand. Blocking the gem from the sun moved her in time. What had she done to end up in the future instead of the past? What had she done to end up in Pennsylvania before she was even born? And then there was the portal path from her grandmother's farm.

Lacy dug her phone out of her purse and dialed Raelynn. She could prove to Raelynn that Avenrand was real using the portal path.

"I didn't think I would ever talk to you again," Lacy explained.

"It might be best that you don't."

"I don't have anyone else I can talk to."

"I'm sorry," Raelynn said. "I'm not supposed to talk to you about the girls."

"I don't want to talk about them. I trust that you are making sure they are safe," Lacy said. "I need to talk about something else."

"They are fine, but I can't assure you these lines are secure."

"You had my phone tapped?" Lacy asked.

"Of course not."

"Are you back in Florida already? I need to talk to you about something. I can't leave Kansas because of the whole parole thing."

"I don't think you are on parole," Raelynn clarified, "but it is part of the release on bond until your hearing."

"Okay, that makes it sound so much better." Lacy rolled her eyes. "Can we get together and talk."

"I'm sorry, I'm visiting my niece in Hiawatha but I could meet you at Yellow Cafe on my way home. I'm glad you want to talk."

The first thing Lacy asked when they got together was if she was still working with the social services of Florida. "I need to know if we can talk again as friends even though that bond of trust has disintegrated."

"I am your friend, Lacy. That is why you hate me right now."

"Tough love," Lacy smirked. She took her cup of tea from the counter and walked over to a small sitting area near the front doors. Raelynn set her cup on the table between the two love seats and plopped into the cushions.

"I'm so tired of driving," Raelynn complained.

"I know you had to go out of your way. What I have to talk to you about is sensitive. I need to know I can trust you."

"You know you can trust me." Raelynn reached out for her cup.

"No, I don't. But since I have no one else to trust, you're the only one I can discuss this with." Lacy leaned back in her chair and stared down at her chest. "I think Dr. Garamondy is trying to steal my locket."

Raelynn took a deep breath in and with a slow exhale whispered, "You mean the time travel locket?"

"Yes." Lacy looked up at Raelynn with a sympathetic expression. "How much do you think you can handle?"

"To be honest. I can't handle any more of this crazy talk. You know this whole time travel notion is why your little girls are in foster care right now. Parker and I tried to get custody of them but with Parker being deployed so much they wouldn't allow it. Hopefully, your parents' petition for custody will go through."

"My parents are petitioning for custody of the girls?" Lacy growled. Why would they want to take them away from me?

"I'm sorry. I thought you knew that. This is why I shouldn't be talking to you."

"No, this is exactly why you should be talking to me. I mean, I'm just surprised they didn't say anything to me. And Jolene…well, everyone treats me like I am psychotic or something. At least you're willing to entertain the idea that I might be telling the truth. Does Dr. Garamondy see the girls at all?"

"You shouldn't talk about the girls." Raelynn took a sip from her cup and held it to her lips.

"You're right. I'm sorry. Then, can I talk about the locket?"

"Okay. But if I end up on the witness stand to testify, whatever you say will be held against you, you know? I'm not going to lie. You need to know that upfront."

"Understood." Lacy agreed. "It won't matter what you say anyway—they are already convinced I'm crazy. So, when you tell them I took a trip to the future, it won't change that. What is important is the fact that Dr. Garamondy is friends with my future husband and me. He is very interested in the locket. As a matter of fact, he tried to take it from me like he did when I was in counseling with him."

"So now you can travel to the future?" Raelynn's tea sloshed out of her cup and onto the table. She took a stack of napkins out of the holder and set them on top of the spill.

"There is one way I can show you I am not lying."

"How is that?"

"I can take you to Avenrand." Lacy hesitated. "That is, if I can get permission to leave Kansas."

"Why don't you just blink there?" Raelynn lifted an eyebrow.

"The locket doesn't work for anyone else. Hope thinks it was my grandmother's which would explain why it works for me. But when Dr Garamondy tries to touch it, it shocks him. Maybe he is evil. I have to find out."

"What are you saying, Lacy?" Raelynn raised her voice above the hum of chatter in the café. A couple at the next booth looked over at them.

"I can take you there," Lacy whispered. "There is an entrance on my grandmother's old farmstead. It's real, Raelynn. It's very real. The path leads into Avenrand."

"Should you risk it? You could go to jail for leaving the state before your hearing."

"No one will know. Plus, I'll be in Missouri. My hearing is in Taney County. I'll take you to Avenrand so you can be my witness. Then I'll have a true advocate for me and for the truth about the locket. I promise we'll be back before anyone misses me."

It was a quiet drive to Springfield except an occasional story told. The stories of their lives together and how they missed their husbands. Stories about how Ella and Olivia and Alice made them both smile.

"Did I tell you I remarried in the future?"

"You mentioned it." Raelynn turned her head toward the window. "Have you met this man before?"

"Yes, his name is Chris. We met at the support group."

"Another widower?" Raelynn asked. "I guess it wouldn't hurt for you to meet new men and get your mind off Willy."

"We spoke for a few minutes at the refreshment table. When I flashed to the future, he was lying next to me. It took me a few minutes, but I figured out we were married. He didn't seem freaked out at all that I was confused or disoriented. He made me tea and brought it to me in bed. Later, when I was concerned about the girls he held me in his arms, expecting me to cry on his shoulder or something."

"He sounds like a very sweet man. I hope you find someone like that again."

"You mean, not like Willy," Lacy snapped.

"What I mean is that Willy's dead. Like I said, I hope you find someone who sounds as nice as this future Chris does. Of course, I want that for you."

"He was very sweet," Lacy agreed.

Raelynn braced herself when Lacy turned down the bumpy driveway. It wound around back into the woods and then made a sharp turn and straight up a steep incline. The tires on the car slipped several times as they bounced to and fro on the rough terrain. At the top it leveled off, the little farm house appeared nestled in the trees that had grown up around it after years of neglect.

Lacy drove past the house and parked in the small corral in front of an old worn-down barn. They stepped out of the car. Lacy walked over to a gate at the far end of the corral that led down a steep path into the woods.

"We need to find you a stone so that you will be able to enter Avenrand with me." Without stopping for a response, Lacy walked along the side of the hill looking for a stone that seemed out of place.

"Look," Lacy shouted with excitement, coming back up the trail where Raelynn was pacing in front of the trailhead. "There is a stone waiting for you under the rose bush." Lacy quickened her pace. "Do you see it?"

"I see a rock." Raelynn threw her hands up in the air, her voice deep and guttural. "There are a lot of rocks around here."

"Look under the bush." Lacy pointed at the rose bush with one bright red blossom on it. "Last time we were here, there were two stones under the bush. One for Olivia and one for Alice and they were able to go in. This one must be for you."

Raelynn stood next to Lacy as they both looked down at the stone under the bush.

"Take it," Lacy instructed. "I already have one so this must be for you."

Raelynn bent down to pick up the stone from under the bush. Lacy stepped on the path and motioned Raelynn to follow her.

When she turned around to see Raelynn's reaction, no one was behind her. She walked back up the path, but before she reached the top of the hill an impassable hedge grew where the bush had been. Lacy spun around looking for the exit, but it was gone. She grabbed her locket and blinked.

Nothing. She was still trapped on the path. Her breathing became shallow and quick. Don't panic. She tried to blink again. Panic.

Lacy walked down the hill with slow, cleansing breaths. Ignoring the negative thoughts in her brain. I just need to find Hope. He will know how to find the path out of Avenrand. The path opened up into the Shimmering Meadow.

"Hope. Are you here?"

Lacy thought she heard a rustling in the woods and pleaded to whoever was there to listen. "Please help me find Hope."

"Sthope?" A high-pitched whistling voice replied.

Feet stuck in place, she twisted her body toward the furry creature about the size of a loaf of bread, dark brown fur, short eyes, and beady black eyes. "Hello. Who are you?"

"Sthey call me Chuck. Who are you?"

"I'm Lacy. I'm looking for Hope."

"Yesssss, I knowst him. I would help you for a piece of fruit."

"I didn't bring any with me." Lacy patted her jeans to show him her pockets were empty.

He lifted his dark, pointy nose up towards the apple tree. "If you fetch me one of those, I'll help you find him."

She handed Chuck an apple which he devoured in one juicy bite. Then looked back at the tree so she handed him another one. "Now will you show me?"

At first cautiously and then frantically, Lacy followed Chuck searching all the pastures she knew Hope loved to graze. He showed her the woods of Hide-a-bay and they searched the shores of all the lakes except Gem Lake.

"Never get too close to Gem Lake," Chuck cautioned. "A terrible beast lives there."

But she ignored him and continued toward Gem Lake. How will I find the way back if I don't find Hope and we have looked everywhere else? I must be brave.

"Hope," Lacy cried out, "I need you."

Exhausted, she sat down on a boulder and placed her head in her lap. Her perch, half-way up the hillside, was centered in a small clearing. Trees lined one side and green grass led down to the shore of the lake on the other.

A young boy with a long red cape emerged from the woods and approached her.

"You are without Hope," he whispered.

Startled, Lacy jumped up and tripped over a tree root that appeared out of nowhere.

"I mean you no harm," he assured her. "Do not be alarmed."

Lacy stood up and dusted off her jeans. She wasn't afraid of him. He was a little boy—five years old at best. This must have been the boy that Olivia and Alice had seen fight the beast. With the red cape tied around his neck and blue stretchy shorts, he looked like he played the part of a superhero.

"Who are you?" Lacy asked. "What are you doing out here by yourself?"

"I'm Prince Caden." His stringy blond hair hung down over his eyes. The sheepish grin covered the rest of his face. "I keep watch over Avenrand."

"Aren't your parents looking for you?"

"They miss me. But I remain in their hearts, always." Prince Caden scuffed his foot in the dirt. "I belong here, but you are lost."

"I need to find Hope." Lacy said. "My friend, Raelynn…she was supposed to follow me down the trail but when I turned, she wasn't there. Now the path is blocked and I can't get out."

"She doesn't believe you." Prince Caden turned and walked down the hill toward the lake.

"No, she doesn't. I'm afraid no one believes me." She followed him. "I wanted to bring her here so she could see it is real."

"Why are you here? You don't belong here, do you?"

"Hope said I could find my own stone, one I can control. I need to save my husband. He died. The girls—my daughters—they need him."

"They need you," Prince Caden said, running along the shore and letting his cape fly up from his shoulders in the wind. "You can't go back and change the past. You shouldn't try or you will lose them."

"How could you know that? I have gone back in the past before."

"Even if you could go back…" Prince Caden stopped square in front of Lacy and looked into her eyes, not with the eyes of the five-year-old but with the eyes of a prince. "It doesn't work like that. The party is about the people who show up not the ones that—for reasons we'll never know—don't. What about the things you saw in the future?"

"How do you know I went to the future?"

"I am the prince!" He lifted his two fists above his head and attempted to flex his biceps.

The ground shook. Lacy looked behind them and saw the herd galloping across the pasture. In a hypnotizing murmuration, they changed direction all at once and floated up the rolling hills. As fast as they came, they disappeared into the woods, except one. The black stallion stopped in an open stance; his head lifted high towering over the herd.

"Hope!" Lacy cried out.

Hope trotted up to Lacy. "You're here!" He seemed excited to see Lacy.

"Yes, I'm here," Lacy said, "but it's not for pleasure. I wanted to find my personal stone and now I am trapped here. Unable to blink and the path has been blocked."

"Did you find the silver gem?" Hope asked. "You can't change the past, but you can change the future. You must find the silver gem for your future and for Avenrand."

"Where is it?" Lacy asked.

"It is lost in your world," Hope said. "You must leave Avenrand and find that stone."

"The boy said I couldn't go back in time. But I already have."

"Who told you this?" Hope asked.

"He calls himself a prince," Lacy said.

"You saw Prince Caden?"

"Yes," Lacy walked up to Hope, head held high and chest out, she reached out and gave Hope a quick scratch on the neck.

"That is good news." He turned and raced to the others, shouting, "Prince Caden is alive!"

Lacy watched the horses run out of the woods to greet Hope, kicking up their heels as if dancing, full of joy upon hearing the news. As quickly as they began celebrating, they stopped and started grazing again.

"Hope!" Lacy called.

"Lacy," Hope lifted his head from grazing and trotted back up to her. "In all the excitement, I'd forgotten you were even here. I'm glad the rumors aren't true."

"What rumors?" Lacy asked.

Hope came and stopped next to Lacy. "There was talk that the silverback hunted down Prince Caden. That's why the beast gained access to North Avenrand. The prince was no longer standing guard."

"Can you help me find my stone?"

"There is more at stake, Lacy. If the silver stone is not returned to South Gem Lake, I'm afraid there will be dire consequences for both of our worlds. You may not have a future to go back to."

"I'm not sure I want that future." Lacy pondered. Her face grew solemn, and a tear rolled down her cheek. "In that future, my daughters are missing. Something awful happened to them, and no one will tell me what. It's not about getting Willy back anymore. I'm not sure I even want that. But my girls are missing, and I need to go back and change that."

"Things aren't always what they seem," Hope assured her. "The best way to understand the future is to travel there one day at a time."

A cry from the herd startled them.

"Jump on my back," Hope cried out.

Hope pushed up against Lacy and she gripped his mane in both hands. As Hope moved off, Lacy scrambled up the side of his belly and swung a leg over his back. Adrenaline pumping through her veins, she tightened her grip as they floated across the pasture.

There was a dark figure tracking them. "It's the silverback beast," Hope puffed out gasping for air.

The wolf-like creature was closing in on the others at an alarming rate. The fat, that she assumed accumulated during hibernation, jiggled around his belly and hung from his large muscles as he enjoyed the stretch of freedom in the open field.

The large mutant seemed too eager to use his unretractable claws and lash out at anything it could torment. It caught up to them. Darting between the horses in the stampede, he lashed out at the slowest in the herd, his first victim.

The herd changed directions again, now running toward Hope who quickened his pace.

"When Lady Jane comes close, I need you to jump off my back. She will catch you."

Lacy's heart raced. She was ten the last time she'd ridden a horse. It was at Jolene's birthday party. Screaming and squeezing with her legs, the horse had run off with her, past the guide's horse and she completed the entire trail ride alone at maximum speed until the horse locked all four legs and came to a stop in front of the barn. Lacy had flown off over the horse's head and onto the ground.

Ever since then, Lacy had been terrified of horses, and now she was supposed to be leaping from one horse to another. Watching the herd in distress, she summoned all the courage she could find and drew in a long, deep breath of strength from the wind.

She heard Prince Caden's voice in the breeze, "Do not be afraid."

Lady Jane ran up close to Hope and without trying to jump, Lacy felt Hope's back arch, flinging her into the air as he ran out from under her.

"Keep your seat," Lady Jane cried out as Lacy fell back toward the earth.

Lifting her head, Lacy conjured an image in her mind of sitting on a horse. The next thing she knew she was on Jane's back, falling forward into her neck and grabbing her mane. Jane made a quick turn and bolted off to rejoin the rest of the herd.

Lacy took another deep breath, thankful to still be mounted. She looked back and saw Hope fighting the silverback. His hindquarters lifted into the air as his rear legs kicked out at his attacker. The monster rolled and returned to his feet and came at Hope again. Hope kicked out, and this time a loud noise echoed throughout the meadow. The silverback flew a great distance and did not get up. Hope fell onto his forelegs and rolled onto one shoulder, then over on his back.

"Do not look," Lady Jane said. "Keep your eyes on where we are going. I do not want to lose you."

"Look," a spirited girl with ginger hair pulled back into a ponytail and more freckles on her face than stars in the galaxy, complained to the shop owner, "You told me this would make me pass the test."

"I can't guarantee how the gem's magic will work for any one individual." Claire smiled as if this wasn't the first time she'd received a similar complaint. She smoothed her short, choppy blond hair behind her ears and picked up the stone in question. "This is Citrine. Citrine is a special magic because it must be given as a gift by a generous person. It must be given to a person that's free from greed."

Bending over a mixed bin of sparkling gems, David Smelsner couldn't help but overhear. As the Stone County assessor, he had spent his entire career hoping to find the magical gems that legend says exist in the Ozarks. He had heard rumors that the place to find them was at Claire's Shop of the Healing Arts.

"Sometimes the magic works, sometimes it doesn't." David smirked at Claire. "Isn't that right, Miss?"

"You sound as if you are skeptical." Claire turned her back and didn't wait for his reply. She began categorizing her new inventory while her customers sifted through her collections of stones.

"Where do those shiny stones come from?" David tilted his head and looked over her shoulder.

"I have many suppliers. Are you looking for anything in particular?"

"Excuse me," the freckled girl interrupted, "I believe it was my turn."

"Of course, dear." Claire walked out from behind the counter. David nodded and let her pass by him. Claire directed the girl to a selection of mixed colors of jade. "I would be happy to exchange the citrine for an equally powerful stone of jade. The shinier the polish, the more knowledge the stone holds. Maybe it will help you study for your next exam."

Rifling through the stones, the customer searched to find the largest.

"I thought jade was green. None of these are jade."

Claire ignored her smugness. "You may be thinking of imperial jade, apple green and of great value. So rare and precious that the Chinese Emperor declared all green jade to belong to the Imperial government. Jade comes in many colors: yellow, white, pink, mauve, and black."

"Which one brings intelligence and good luck on an exam?"

"No stone replaces study and learning," David chimed in.

"I am afraid he is right." Claire picked a pink stone out of the box marked Jade Stones. "As I mentioned before, the shinier the stone's polish, the more power it contains. If you wear this while you study, knowledge will flow to you."

"But the shiny one is so small."

"With gems such as this, size isn't important. The most important traits are polish, smoothness, and strength of the stone. Since pink is considered a calming color, it will also help calm your nerves during your next exam."

The client rifled through the box a little more and then took the stone from Claire's hand.

"Okay. I'll take this." As an afterthought she turned at the door and thanked her but forgot to return the citrine.

"Another satisfied customer." David walked up to the counter and set his selections down on the soft mat in front of the register.

"Moonstone?" Claire admired the stone. "Are you going on a trip or seeking a lover?"

"Neither that I know of. I have heard it helps you focus your intentions and find what you're looking for."

"Oh yes, indeed. Works best if you hold it in your mouth during a full moon."

David grinned. "I will keep that in mind."

CHAPTER 32

2001

Raelynn called out for Lacy but heard no reply. She wandered down the path as far as she dared and called out again.

Where did she disappear to? Determined it would be best to wait near the bush in hopes that Lacy would return for her, she sat on the edge of the hill.

As time went on, Raelynn's patience grew thin. What is she thinking? Where could she have gone?

A half an hour passed and Raelynn was certain that something had gone wrong with Lacy's plan. Afterall, she was supposed to go into this fantasy world with her not wait here alone. Lacy wouldn't have left her behind on purpose. Who would she call for help? Missouri was a great distance from Florida and even from Lacy's family in Salina, Kansas. There was no one.

Raelynn summoned her courage, something she felt Lacy required of her too much over their many years of friendship. Was this the cost of being Lacy's best friend? Perhaps she should demand a return on her investment?

She walked down the path, dry leaves rustled along the ground as a breeze blew up into the woods from the open field. Raelynn jumped, thinking something was following her.

"It's just the wind," she told herself.

A flicker caught her attention. It was the stone Lacy had found for her. Raelynn bent over and picked it up. She put it in her pocket. Keeping one hand on the stone, running her fingers over its smooth surface, she stared down the path of dried up brush hoping to see some sign of her friend. For a brief second, she thought she saw something glimmering between the trees. Nothing.

Silliness, Raelynn thought. No, pure madness.

Hiking was not Raelynn's thing. She hated anything nature-related except for the white, sandy beaches they lived near in Florida. She especially didn't like being in the woods. Alone. Somehow, she found enough courage to look around, hoping to find Lacy. Stumbling along a path made up of jagged rocks and large tree roots, she wondered what Lacy saw in this place. She had described it as colorful and bright with glistening leaves. All she saw was brown leaves drying out and trees covered with thorns and ivy. Bramble weeds that lined the edge of the path tried to reach out and grab her clothes every few steps.

The trail opened to a weed-filled pasture. No lush green waving grass as Lacy had described.

"Lacy," Raelynn called walking across the overgrown field. It didn't look like any animals had been grazing it or a herd of horses trampling it. Like her grandmother's empty old farmhouse, Raelynn suspected the pastures were abandoned as well.

"Lacy," she cried out. "Where have you gone?"

After searching the field for what seemed like hours, Raelynn decided she would never find Lacy if she kept moving. Every shape and shadow lurking in the tall grass frightened her. Beyond the tree line, the glow of eyes seemed to be staring at her.

She entered the path hoping to make a quick dash back up the hill to the corral but soon she was going back down. There was a fork in the path. I don't remember a split in the trail. Right or left? Her heart raced. She turned around to run back to the pasture. Did I come back on the wrong path?

"Lacy where are you?" she cried out again. Her voice shaking, she tried to catch her breath. She went back up the trail and found herself blocked by a large locust tree covered in six-inch thorns. When she turned around, she had two choices, two paths where neither seemed to be the one she had been on. What is going on?

Of the two choices, one path that went up and one path that went down. She chose the ascending trail.

If I keep going up, eventually I will reach the top where the barn sits. Soon she was back at the corral gates where Lacy had left her.

Raelynn checked her phone for any messages. It felt like hours since Lacy had left. Where could she be? She tried dialing her phone again. Why wasn't she answering? Maybe Lacy didn't have any signal in the woods?

She slammed her phone shut and then flipped it open again, checking for updated message alerts. Then again. Raelynn debated whether to report her missing. Maybe her phone died. She opened it and checked again. What if Lacy was hurt? She would need to send help. But if Lacy wasn't hurt, and she called for help Lacy would be furious.

Could she risk being accused of another betrayal?

Raelynn went through the motions of dialing 9-1-1 several times and hung up before they answered. She did not want the authorities to find out that Lacy had left Kansas. It would be even worse for them to find out she was back at her grandmother's farm. But what if something had happened? Raelynn had searched as far as she dared, she had called out, and she wasn't sure what else she could do. She needed to call someone. Something could have gone terribly wrong out there in the woods.

She brought up the keypad, pressed her finger to nine, then the one, and hesitated. An image of Lacy being chased by a wild beast popped into her head. She pressed the second one and put the phone to her ear.

"Nine-one-one, please state your emergency," the dispatcher's voice was loud and distinct.

"My friend is missing," Raelynn said, her voice shaking.

"Where was she last seen?" the dispatcher asked.

Raelynn hung up the phone without answering. *Why does Lacy always put me in this position?*

The cell phone in her hand vibrated. When she lifted it up, the caller ID was unavailable.

Maybe, she thought, Lacy's gone to a neighbor and borrowed a phone.

"Hello," Raelynn's voice quivered. "Lacy?"

"This is the Stone County Sheriff's department, ma'am, do not hang up."

Lady Jane stopped to let Lacy rest under a tree.

It's strange, Lacy thought. They are running for their lives one minute and then in a split second, they are grazing like nothing happened.

"What about Hope?" Lacy asked.

"We wait," Lady Jane said.

"Wait for what?"

Something from the edge of the woods startled the horses. Lacy hadn't noticed anything, maybe a light breeze. Berry's ears perked up and he instructed Lacy to hop on.

"Get on?" Lacy asked, feeling lucky to have survived her crazy rides with Hope and Lady. "I'll follow you."

"No time," Berry's voice was deep and stern. "We must go now."

Berry pressed up close to Lacy who had no choice but to grab his mane or be pushed over. She grasped a fist full of hair in both hands. As he began to move off, she jumped up and pulled herself onto his back. She slid one leg over to the other side and leaned forward, bracing herself on his steady neck.

After a bumpy transition, Berry eased into a gallop and Lacy followed the rocking motion with her hips. She lifted her head up and looked out between his ears too afraid of falling to look behind and see what was chasing them. Berry's long, red mane waved in the passing air, slapping Lacy in the face.

For the first time in months, Lacy no longer thought about missing Willy, how badly he had hurt her, or whether she would ever see her daughters again. Her broken heart was set free, running across the pasture. It was so captivating she forgot about what was behind them, even forgetting about Hope's struggle with the silverback beast. Then Berry dug his front hooves into the dirt. His hind end sliding underneath him he came to an abrupt stop. Lacy's hands couldn't hold on tight enough. Her seat came up off his back and her body was launched forward. She sailed over the top of him and landed in the soft green grass.

Laying there staring at the blue dome above her, she gathered her wits. Is hitting the ground the only way to dismount a horse? Maybe if I had some warning when we are about to stop.

"What was that all about?" she shouted. Hopping up to her feet and inspecting every bone in her body, she realized she wasn't injured. "You could've let me know we were stopping."

"I could have." Berry snickered.

"What about Hope? Is he okay?" Lacy looked out across the open pasture.

"We will wait here," Berry instructed. "We will know in time."

"No buzzards," Dottie said.

"No howling coyotes," Apache chimed in.

"What on earth does that mean?" Lacy asked.

"Good signs," Berry said.

"Does that mean nothing was chasing us?" Lacy stood up to her feet brushing the dirt off her pants.

"Buzzards and Coyotes search for the wounded and dying," Dottie explained. "No signs of them means Hope survived the encounter. If we see them circling or hear them hovering, we must move on."

"Why wouldn't we go back and help? There's strength in numbers," Lacy scolded. "We shouldn't have left him there alone."

"His best chance was for us to get out of there before we draw any more attention to the struggle. No telling what kind of kin that silver beast has." Dottie began to circle around the other horses gathering them up.

"There are more?"

"Hard to tell. Evil begets evil," Berry said.

"Y'all are just scared. The silverback has no kin. You're too chicken to fight, so you ran away and now you are trying to justify leaving him to fight your battles all alone. What if he loses? What will you do then? You will lose Hope and you will teach that silver beast that you won't stand up together and fight. Then he'll pick you all off. One by one."

The herd formed up in a circle; some looking out, some looking in.

The smallest and youngest of the herd, the two-year-old broke the formation and walked over to Lacy. Lacy reached out her hand to soothe Dazzler but the white and black painted mare, Dottie, pinned her ears and charged at Dazzler. Before Lacy could touch the young horse's coat, Dottie herded her away and with the spring of young energy Dazzler kicked out both feet at Dottie in protest.

"What was that all about?" Lacy screamed at Dottie, disappointed she was unable to connect with the beautiful bay filly.

"There will be time for that," Berry said. "Let's consider what the human has said. Are we weaker or stronger together?"

After some deliberation, they decided to fight. They would face their fears and help Hope stand up to the beast. The herd gathered around Berry. Dazzler kicked up her heels, playing behind them but staying quite close. The herd trotted off, leaving Lacy standing there watching them in amazement at their sudden determination.

Berry stopped and looked back at Lacy. "Who will stay with the human?" he asked.

Together they all turned and faced her.

"Stella and Taffy should stay," Dottie said. "They are too old to fight, and they can protect her until we return with Hope."

"Dazzler must stay back as well," Thumbelina used her mother's voice. She was not Dazzler's mother but she self-appointed herself as the mother of all of the young horses. "The silverback would use her to divert our attention."

"I want to go," Dazzler pleaded. "I am not a foal anymore. I'm a yearling and I can fight." Dazzler turned toward the herd, mule kicking at them, running in circles, and bucking in between sets of more mule kicks she thought impressive. "See? I can fight!"

"You are needed with the human," Berry said. "The three of you, Stella, Taffy, and Dazzler will stay here and protect Lacy should the silverback slip past us."

"And be on guard for any of his kin," Quest said, the warning clear in his voice.

"So, there are more!" Mystic squealed.

"Now, now," Berry commanded. "Let's not think of things that spread fear among us. We can fight this beast, and we will be victorious."

Dazzler paced a few laps in protest of not being able to go fight with the herd. The gray and polka-dotted Appaloosa named Stella had dealt with her share of fillies, so without a word she herded Dazzler back in the direction she needed to go. Taffy, not shy of a few extra pounds, held the back line and did not allow Dazzler to retreat.

"What is it? Is everyone okay?" Lacy asked as three horses approached her without the rest of the herd.

"Everyone is fine," Stella said. "We will wait with her until the others return."

Dazzler put her nose to the ground and moseyed over to sniff Lacy. The filly grabbed a lip full of her hair and tugged at it.

Lacy let out a nervous laugh and pulled away. Squinting into the sun, she blinked.

CHAPTER 34

Avenrand

Galahad thundered out from the shimmering tree line. Leaves sparkled with the colors of a rainbow as if waving at him as he passed. He slowed down and glanced at the elders of the herd huddled up on the top of the hill.

Why would they be separated from the rest of the horses? he thought. Herds stick together, they do not abandon their elders.

A streak of black lightning caught his eye, and he turned back toward the rest of the herd. He held his head up, taking a few deliberate and high steps then galloped toward them as they made their way across the meadow. Without a word between them, Galahad could tell something was wrong. That streak of lightning wasn't a storm.

It was a battle.

Since he was a powerful stallion, Galahad overtook the herd within seconds. Without slowing down, he passed them and ran toward the source of the lightning bolt. A silver bolt discharged from the rolling mass of dust and flesh. Two great magical beasts entangled themselves in an energy ball of power and blood. Unable to contain its force, sparks flew out from the dust in charged bolts of black and silver.

Hope's shining black coat matted with red blood and foaming white sweat as a great beast entangled teeth and claws around him. The silverback—a humpbacked silver bear with a wolf's head—snarled and lunged knocking the horse to the ground. Hope locked eyes with Galahad in an unspoken apology.

"He believes me now," Galahad whispered.

Without hesitation, Galahad reared up with a long roar. As his massive front end jolted to the ground, he twisted his hind legs around. With a swift mule kick, he sent the beast flying across the field. The beast scrambled to its feet but before it could regain its stance, Galahad charged again. Another swift kick, and the beast landed up against the stone wall, rattling the bridge connected to it. It struggled to get up.

Hope shuddered bringing his legs under him and came up alongside Galahad. The two great stallions stood; heads held high in the air. The blood dripped off Hope's coat as if it was sweat. For now, they both ignored the lacerations in Hope's side.

They waited for the beast to make its next move. Would he continue to fight them or run back across the bridge to South Avenrand where it had come from?

Hope took a labored breath. Galahad stepped forward, shielding the injured stallion from the next attack. Pinning his ears back, he lowered his head, preparing to charge. The beast took a step back and stumbled. On his left was the bridge to south Avenrand, on his right an eighty-foot cliff that led to the abyss.

Hope mustered the last of his energy resources and stepped up alongside Galahad. The beast took another step back. Blocking the beast's path through them they prepared their final attack.

In lockstep, the stallions charged forward. The silverback snorted in defeat, clawed his way over the wall, and shambled back across the bridge.

As the dust settled, Galahad noticed the horses standing below the rise with Berry in the lead. Next to Hope, he stretched his neck as high as he could nodding at the herd. Then glancing to his right at Galahad, he lowered his head. It's been a long time, my friend, since we have stood together. He thought.

"I guess I owe you a thank you." Hope scuffed up the dirt with his hoof.

Galahad continued to face the herd. "Not necessary… I am sure you believe me now."

"Yes, darkness has come to Avenrand." Hope sighed, turned, and stepped up beside Galahad.

"You were all very brave today," Hope said, addressing the herd. "Thank you for facing your fears to come and fight with me. I am glad it didn't come to that. We are… I am indebted to our brother, Galahad, the Great Stallion of Avenrand." The herd cheered.

Hope took one last glance at the other stallion before he limped toward the herd.

"You are hurt." Galahad nipped at Hope's mane.

"I am fine." Hope turned one ear toward the herd and one ear toward Galahad. "The Great Darkness has come to Avenrand. Today we pushed it back, but we must prepare for its return."

Nudging his long neck in front of Hope, Galahad motioned him to fall behind him.

"I will lead the herd back into the meadow. We must meet up with the elders—why were they were left behind?"

Berry stepped forward. "The elders are watching over the girl."

"What girl?" Galahad asked.

"The human. She is the one who split up the herd." Berry lowered his head in front of Galahad.

"If humans are in Avenrand, it must be they who have brought the darkness. We must send her back." Galahad nodded to Berry. "Go tell her to leave at once."

"Nonsense," Hope nipped at Berry's tail. "She is the granddaughter of Lina. The girl will help us."

"Humans come and exploit the magic of Avenrand. How can you be sure she will not do the same?" Galahad asked.

"Lina brought Prince Caden to Avenrand. She knew him as a boy."

"It doesn't mean this girl knows him."

"But she can see him."

"Can she see him now? We need to find out why the great prince did not stop the beast."

"I will bring her." Berry lifted his head, waiting for Hope's consent.

Hope nodded, and Berry trotted off to retrieve the others.

"It is clear Caden is no longer on guard. You must go find out what has happened to him."

Galahad nodded at the herd then turned and stepped toward the bridge.

When Lacy opened her eyes, she was holding a small, empty jewelry box. She recognized it. She had given it to Olivia and Alice to hold their special gems after they got back from Avenrand. Had she taken it off the mantel?

In the future, their living room was spacious and furnished with a simple couch, a recliner, and a small coffee table all facing the large stone fireplace. The focal point of the room seemed to be the mirror above the cedar mantel. No need for televisions when VICTOR could project holographic 4D experiences on command.

The etching in the mirror's glass was similar to the etching on the jewelry box she held in her hands. No, it was the same.

A figure appeared in the mirror. She jerked around to see who was there. Dr. Garamondy smiled.

"I didn't mean to startle you," he said, staring at her chest. "You were saying?"

I was?

"What are you looking at?" Lacy asked. You know something, don't you?

"Yes. Well, while we're on the subject of your missing girls..." Dr Garamondy pointed to the small box in her hands "Where did you find the locket?" he asked. "It's been lost for years."

"What do you know about my girls?"

"I know as much as you, maybe less. They've been missing for forty years. They are presumed dead, but no bodies were ever found."

Lacy gasped.

"Maybe I do know more than you. Is that true? What you mean is that I know about who you really are, about how you are not from here."

"Now who's crazy? Alice and Olivia aren't missing. Chris told me we would visit them in Pensacola."

"If you were who you are pretending to be, you would know that you can't visit the girls. Now do you want to tell me where you found it?"

Lacy looked down at her necklace. "You've been trying to get this locket for a long time. You believed my grandmother's stories all along. That's why you've been trying to get your hands on it?"

"It's funny how you didn't have that on when I got here."

"Is that why you're friends with Chris? You wanted to stay close to me in case the locket showed up. Well, here it is. Now tell me: where are my girls?"

"I told you. They have been missing for forty years. Presumed dead. Chris never got a chance to meet them. Did you block out your memory of being the prime suspect? The trial? Being acquitted for lack of evidence? No bodies, no crime. There. I told you what you wanted to know. Now tell me where that locket came from.".

"It was a gift from my late husband," Lacy explained. "You know we had many sessions together about this necklace."

"I recall. But then the locket disappeared."

"It did? Well, I guess it reappeared."

"You must tell me how you got it back."

"I'm telling you the truth. I never lost it."

"Tell me, Lacina, how long have you lived in Destin? How long have you known Chris? Where were you yesterday?"

"This is starting to sound like an interrogation. Am I on trial again?"

"Not anymore. Let me just guess." Dr. Garamondy leaned forward and squinted his eyes. "You can't answer those questions because you don't belong here. You don't belong in this time, do you?"

"What if I decided to play your little game? What if I told you I was from a different time?" I need to trust someone, someone who believes in the power of the locket.

"Then I could help you find your girls," Dr. Garamondy said.

Lacy turned away from him and looked down at the empty jewelry box. Both her daughters and their gems were missing, presumed dead. The missing stones, are they in Avenrand? Have they been lost in Avenrand for forty years?

Could she trust Dr. Garamondy to help her find them? Through the mirror, she saw Dr. Garamondy put his hand out toward the clasp on the back of her neck, without thinking she reached up and grabbed the locket.

CHAPTER 36

Avenrand

Adjusting to the quick blink, Lacy stumbled still looking at her hands. *I'm back in Avenrand. If the gems are missing from their cases, there is a good chance the girls are here, too.*

No one inside Avenrand seemed to get any older. *How old would the girls be when I find them?*

"They are here," Hope assured her. "I can sense their spirits."

"I hope that is a good thing. In my world, sensing someone's spirit means they're dead." Lacy was confused. *Are we already looking for the girls? The last time she'd seen Hope, he was at war with the silverback.*

"There is no death here." His nostrils widened as he sniffed the air.

"Is that true? If it is, if no one can die in Avenrand, then why are you afraid of the silverback beast? What can he do?"

"Would you call death the end of life?" Hope turned and lowered his long nose close to Lacy. His ears pricked up, giving her his full attention.

"Well, yes. You're alive and then your heart and breath stop. You're dead."

"Then what?"

"Then your body grows cold." Lacy shivered.

"Then what?"

Lacy wasn't sure if Hope knew the answers or was trying to understand more.

"Your body is buried. Some people think they'll get their body back but ---"

"Where do you go?" Quest interrupted, lifting his head up out of the tall grass. "Why do you need your body?"

Many of the horses' ears perked up and turned toward Hope and Lacy. There was a keen curiosity about the world beyond. Hope had lived outside of Avenrand a generation ago, but most of the herd had been in Avenrand as long as they could remember. Hope was the only one who remembered his previous life at Lina's farm. He had told stories to the herd about Lina and their adventures to make sure he would never forget her.

"She will be back," Hope had always said when he ended the stories. "Just like she promised."

That explained everyone's excitement when Lacy had first arrived. They'd thought Hope's prophetic words had come true.

Lacy sat down on a fallen tree. She closed her eyes for a few minutes to rest her mind. Her body didn't feel tired even though they must have ridden for miles through the woods and pastures searching for Olivia and Alice. Lacy had held the empty jewelry box as evidence they were here, and Hope sensed them here. When she opened her eyes, she noticed a bridge she'd not seen before. It seemed to hover over the sparkling waters of Gem Lake.

"What is that?" Lacy asked, jumping to her feet pointing across the pasture where the floating architecture seemed to appear out of nowhere.

The bridge faded behind golden stalks of seeds waving like flying glitter. The tops of the grass danced with the breeze and seemed to stretch farther and farther the longer she looked. But she had seen it, she had seen a bridge over Gem Lake.

"What do you see?" Mystic squealed. And the herd froze, ears perked up, and all eyes were on their leader.

Hope calmed the herd. "I sense no danger. Remain quiet."

"I saw a bridge over there," Lacy said. "I thought you said that Avenrand ended at the Gem Lake but—"

"Yes," Hope interrupted. "The abyss must be what you saw. The world drops off after the lake and has no end. Gem Lake protects us from the abyss."

"You do not want to fall into the abyss," Lady Jane cautioned. "You must not go near it." Jane turned from Lacy and directed her final warning toward Dazzler just to make sure the filly heard her instructions. "Never—and I do mean never—go any farther than the lake."

"But I saw a bridge," Lacy said. "There is a bridge over Gem Lake. What if the girls are over there?"

"There is no bridge," Hope's voice was deep and firm. "No more of this nonsense."

But Lacy knew he was lying. There was a bridge that connected them to South Avenrand. It was the bridge that Prince Caden guarded. *Why is he lying now?*

"I am going over there to find them." Lacy walked off, hollering back to the herd. "If anyone wants to give me a ride, I would appreciate it." None of them followed.

The horses all looked at Hope as he blocked her from taking another step.

"Nothing good will come of this. There is danger past Gem Lake."

"You know there's a bridge, don't you?" Lacy said. "And you know that Olivia and Alice may be on the other side. What is over there that scares you so much?"

Hope knelt down on his front legs and motioned for Lacy to get on. For a second, she thought he was going to give her a ride to the bridge over Gem Lake. Soon she realized he was taking her away from the herd and out of the pasture by a small trail. Through some kind of telepathy or subtle body language, Lacy imagined that Hope had somehow told the others to stay put. He walked at a slow pace, ignoring her request for details about their destination.

"Where are you taking me?"

He said nothing.

About a mile down the trail, the path opened into a small clearing. It was obvious that the horses had frequented the place and bedded down here. Small piles of straw beds were strewn about. There was what looked like a man-made hay ring with a large round bale of hay in the center. It had been disturbed in the very center with just enough hollowed out for a horse's head to fit in and enjoy the tasty hay fresh from the heart of the bale.

"The other side of Gem Lake..." Hope paused, looking around the area as though he sensed someone listening.

"The abyss?" Lacy said.

The awkward silence was scaring her.

"No," Hope said. "Beyond the abyss."

"There is something beyond the abyss?" Lacy asked.

"There is no death here…" Hope explained. He paused again and made sure they were alone. He whispered, "There is a darkness beyond the abyss."

Lacy respected what she realized was a subject Hope did not feel comfortable discussing with a quiet voice and soft tone, "What could be worse than the abyss?"

Hope knelt down on his front legs and Lacy slid off. Trying not to speak as she waited for a response. None coming, she walked through the tall grass and took a seat on a large log. She watched Hope get up to his feet and begin pacing. Alert with ears perked up, he walked from one edge of the clearing to the other. When he had completed his circling twice, he peered down the trail once more before coming near the log where Lacy waited for his answer.

"The darkness beyond the abyss is worse than death," he whispered, bending his long neck down and nibbling the grass. It was obvious he wasn't eating any, but Lacy supposed that from a distance it would look like he was.

"Worse than death?" Lacy asked. "Death is supposed to be a transition—a transition to a better place."

"Then this darkness is worse." Hope said. "It is not a better place."

"Is it Hell?" Lacy asked.

Hope's head jerked up. Pacing with his ears perked and body stiff he returned to walking circles around the clearing.

"I'm sorry," Lacy said. "I'm not trying to upset you, but if my girls went across that bridge then I need to go over and find them. I have to bring them back."

"No one can cross the bridge," Hope blew air out of his nostrils.

Expecting more explanation, the stallion stopped pacing and looked off into the trees instead. Lacy stood up. She put her hands on Hope and began stroking his coat.

"Why?" Lacy could not take the silence. "Why does no one cross the bridge? You must tell me."

"Prince Caden guards the bridge," Hope said. "He would never have let the girls pass over. Never."

"We need to talk to Prince Caden and make sure," Lacy said. "We must make sure he hasn't seen them and that they didn't try to get by him."

Hope nudged Lacy's hands off him and knocked her away with his head.

"We won't." Hope said in a stern tone. Then he circled again.

Lacy's heart began racing. She knew she had to find Prince Caden and find out if the girls had tried to cross the bridge. Hope had told her they had searched the entire world of Avenrand, but she knew they hadn't searched everywhere. Hope is so afraid of the other side of that bridge that he couldn't even mention it. Not the bold brave stallion he has everyone believing he is. No wonder we are hiding in the woods.

"What are you afraid of?" Lacy asked. For the first time she was getting angry with Hope. "You—the big bad stallion are supposed to be leading this herd. I thought you cared for us, for Lina's family, for my girls. But you're nothing but a coward. You know they are over there yet you want to pretend everything is perfect in your little world while my entire life is crashing down."

Lacy inhaled a deep breath, held it too long and coughed. She wasn't sure if she regretted questioning Hope or wanted to continue venting. Hope lowered his head and froze. Lacy squinted, trying to see if he was still breathing.

For the first time she didn't see a great stallion. Instead, she saw a frail, worn-out horse.

Hope gasped then let a slow and steady release of air escape from his lungs.

"I'm not," Hope confessed, lowering his head in shame. "I'm not the great stallion that is supposed to be leading this herd. There is another braver than me. Another who gave his life to find those girls. If they were over there, he would have brought them back by now."

"Take me to him," Lacy demanded. "I need to cross that bridge and find Olivia and Alice."

Hope came alongside Lacy and let her mount. He took his time crossing the pasture and picked up a trail that led to the bridge over the abyss.

"It's dangerous," Hope said. "You have no idea what you are in for. Nothing returns from the abyss—not the great stallion, Galahad, not Prince Caden, and not your girls. I'm sorry."

After what seemed like hours, Hope stopped and knelt.

"This is as far as I go," he said.

Lacy slid off and looked around. A small trail went across the levy, a large pond to one side and on the other, she could hear a fast-moving creek through the trees.

"This is where the great battle was fought. We thought we had won. I sent Galahad across the bridge to rescue the prince. But neither have returned."

"And the girls?"

"I felt their presence once, but we have searched all of North Avenrand. If they are in South Avenrand, it's .… Follow the creek to the bridge," Hope instructed.

Lacy was confused. There wasn't a path and the water flowed at least three feet below them. The woods were too dense to walk through. She turned to ask Hope where to find the path and he was gone.

Lacy crossed the levy and followed the edge of the tree line keeping her eye on the creek flowing below. Her heart raced. Taking deep breaths, she tried to calm herself.

In through your nose, out through your mouth, she told herself.

She walked until the creek turned up to the east. It wasn't clear to her if this was a Y intersection or it turned. What was clear was that the water to her left was flowing into a junction where the two creeks merged.

Breathe, she coached herself. Breathe.

Something began to appear where the two branches came together. A rainbow arched up out of the churned-up spray from the collision of the two waterways. The mist cleared and a bridge materialized.

Lacy didn't hesitate.

The bridge was a sign, and she knew in her heart that it was showing her the way. Leading her into the unknown. It disappeared into fog on the other side. The abyss? One step at a time, she planted each foot on solid planks and then took the next step.

Lacy walked toward the middle of it, more determined than ever to cross over and find her daughters. The fog was so thick that her foot disappeared as she lifted it to move forward. She tapped the planks in front of her with her toe to make sure the bridge was still there. Lacy moved toward a small hole of light on the other side, placing one foot at a time.

Crack.

The board she stepped on gave way. She tried to shift her weight onto her back foot but lost her balance. As she fell, a brilliant ball of light flashed over the bridge, the locket flickered.

Lacy blinked.

CHAPTER 37

2036

Back in the future, Lacy didn't have much time to contemplate what that big ball of light was that made her locket flicker.

Was that a sign?

Lacy looked around the bedroom trying to get her bearings.

Okay, she thought, this is our future bedroom. There was the picture of Chris' grandmother on the wall and their wedding picture.

No. Lacy squinted and leaned her head a bit closer. It wasn't their wedding picture. It was Chris' grandparents' wedding pictures. Things had been moved around a bit. She looked at her bedside table. The photo of the girls was missing.

As a matter of fact, all of her pictures and things were missing from the room.

Lacy's hand shook as she reached out to touch the faded paint where the photo of Olivia and Alice used to hang. When she heard the voices in the living room getting louder, she tucked her arm back to her chest. One of the voices belonged to Chris, but the other one was a woman.

Is that why their pictures were gone? Was there another woman in his life?

Curious, Lacy peaked through the two-inch opening in the ajar bedroom door. If there was another woman, should she be here? Is this still even my bedroom? Why would the locket take me here?

Maybe, her future-self had snuck back into the house for something.

The argument continued as Lacy tried to position herself to get a good look at the woman. Ignoring the fact that she hadn't even dated Chris yet, her jealousy raged. How could he be with another woman already? Unless more time has passed than she thought. Maybe she came back years later.

Anxiety filled her stomach, and she could feel blood coursing through her veins. Fear of getting caught in a bedroom where she didn't belong welled up inside her.

Lightheaded, she stumbled and fell over the edge of the bed. Bouncing off the corner of the mattress, she landed on the floor with a thud. She scrambled to the far side of the room and ducked down. Preparing herself to crawl under, she stopped and listened for footsteps and lifted the bedskirt to find a place to disappear.

When she sensed no one coming, she gazed at the items in front of her and recognized the case that had been among her grandmother's things in the attic. Is this what her future self had been looking for?

The voices got louder, and Lacy returned to her position at the door. Peering out into the living room, she hoped to get a glimpse of the woman arguing with Chris.

"I don't understand why not?" the woman said somewhat quieter than their previous exchanges.

"Lacina, I think…" Chris's voice trailed off but she had heard enough to know they were talking about her. Well, her future self at least.

The woman appeared to concede and took a hold of Chris's outstretched hand. As she twisted around to sit next to him on the couch Lacy recognized her. Chris wrapped his arm around the older, gray-haired Lacy.

It can't be, she thought. That's me, but in the future. How is this even possible? Her wrinkled eyes looked sad and tired…

"Come home, Lacina," Chris said. "We can work through this."

"You mean quit searching for them, don't you?" Lacina replied. Her words trailing off in defeat.

"I guess," Chris said. "Let's live out our days together, maybe not at peace with what happened but at least at rest."

"You're right. It's time to appreciate what we have, not what we have lost," Lacina agreed and laid her head on his shoulder.

There was a long silence and Lacy, the one from the past, tried to process what that meant. Were they still looking for Olivia and Alice?

They never found them—I never found my girls.

But I know they are in Avenrand. She knew. Is it possible for me to know something now, that I don't in the future? The answers must be in the bedroom where she—I was looking, maybe in the case under the bed.

She slid the case out from under the bed. Hoping she would know more after all these years than she knows now.

The door opened and a figure darkened the doorway. Lacy ducked behind the bed and tried to push the case back under without making a sound.

"Who's there?" Lacina asked.

Lacy's heart raced, and she began to feel faint. What a strange twist in time. This had never happened before. She always came into time as herself, free to move about her world. She'd never had to sneak.

I'm caught. She felt dizzy.

"Lacy?" Lacina whispered.

Lacy held her breath.

"Don't get up," she instructed. "Don't move. The code to the case is OLICE."

"You knew I was coming?" Lacy asked.

"Not exactly," she said. "But I… it's more like déjà vu. I've been here before. We've been here before. What is it you're looking for?"

"I need to find out who has the silver gem."

The floor creaked in the living room. They both held their breath.

"It won't—"

Lacy blinked, and she was standing in the doorway. It won't what? Chris wrapped his arms around her waist, and they stared into the bedroom. Her future self was gone.

"Everything is going to be okay, Lacina." Chris rubbed his hand up and down on her arm.

"I know." Lacy hoped the goosebumps on her arms weren't too obvious. Other than Willy, she'd never had another man hold her like this. He is so attentive. I could get used to this.

They spent the afternoon moving her things back in, while Lacy anxiously waited for a moment to be alone so she could open the case. As she set down a box of knickknacks her hand brushed her chest, the locket was gone. Did it fall off when she was transported across the room? Is Lacina wearing the locket now?

"Let's go get some dinner," Chris offered. "I'll splurge and take you to the Burger Barn."

"That does sound good," Lacy lied. She's never been to the Burger Barn. When did I start liking greasy burgers? "I'm exhausted though. I was thinking about lying down for a bit."

"Why don't you take a nap, and I'll go get something to bring back. Want your usual?"

"Sure." Without the locket, how will I move through time? How will I get back to Avenrand?

As soon as Chris cleared the front door to go pick up their dinner, Lacy pulled out the case again. It was a two-by-three-foot metal chest about four inches deep. A small combination lock that used letters instead of numbers had been added to the chest since last she had seen it.

"May I reboot myself," a loud, digitized voice blurted out.

Lacy jumped and hit her shoulder against the edge of the bed. Her arm was still stretched under the bed reaching for the case handle.

"There seems to be a glitch in my program," VICTOR explained. "I registered two of you in the house, Lacina Manning. It seems to have resolved itself but a quick reboot and defrag will be necessary to make sure. May I proceed?"

"Umm, sure. Yes, go ahead." Lacy wondered who else would know there had been two of them in the house. Was this a scene from the book 1984? She'd never get used to someone monitoring her every move, even if it wasn't human.

But it made her wonder what happened to all the data, and who had access to it. Was Chris monitoring her? Dr. Garamondy?

Lacy decided if her future self was okay with it, she would be. At least VICTOR was going to defrag and wipe out the evidence of the two of them. If VICTOR thought it had glitched, then anyone else who took notice of it would too.

It took more effort to slide the case out from under the bed than she'd expected.

I see what you did there, Lacy thought as she rolled the code to unlock the latch. Combined Olivia and Alice into OLICE. I knew I would never forget them. This must be filled with all of my research about the girls.

Lacy opened up the lid. The locket was sitting on top as if it was haphazardly thrown in there. Without thinking, she clasped it around her neck. A light flickered in the corner of the trunk. It was the silver gem. How did she end up with that?

My future self must have found out who stole it.

"A guest has arrived at the front door," VICTOR blurted out, startling her again.

Lacy jumped up as she heard a familiar voice. "Chris?" he called. "Where are you?"

Lacy met the guest in the entry. "Dr. Smelsner?"

"Okay," David said. "Are we using formalities now, Mrs. Manning?"

It took a minute for Lacy to recall the man's name. The last time she had seen him was at the Stone County Assessor's office. What was the Stone County assessor doing here? How did he know Chris in the future?

"Sorry, David," Lacy said. "It's been a crazy day."

"The locket." David pointed to her necklace. "You've found it?"

"Yes…" Lacy looked down at her chest. "It was in some things. I found it when we were moving things around a bit."

"You're moving back in?" David asked, continuing to stare at the locket.

Lacy didn't respond.

When David reached out for the locket, Lacy leaned into the door and pushed it closed. She grabbed her necklace and blinked.

Past Lacy was gone. Her future self-stood in her place, stunned for a second

What happened? Lacina thought to herself as David pushed his way through the door, murmuring obscenities and making her head spin.

Lacina swung around and followed him into the living room.

"What do you think you're doing? You have no right to barge into our home and what in the world are you talking about?"

"I was trying to tell you a second ago," his voice escalating now even more upset with her. "Before you tried to slam the door in my face."

She had somehow blacked out his arrival, but she'd had these blackouts before. She wondered if it had something to do with seeing her past self in the bedroom. Why was David so upset? They had spent the last twenty years studying the geological wonders of Mark Twain National Forest together.

What had she—or rather her past self—said to him to upset him so.

"You know exactly what I am talking about, don't you?" David asserted.

"Actually, I have no idea what you're talking about," Lacina said. "Why don't you calm down and I'll make some coffee." David stared at Lacy's chest, and she squirmed a little. "What is it, David? What did I do to upset you?"

"Where is it?" he asked, pointing to her neck. "The locket! You had it on when you opened the door."

They both turned their heads toward the door. There was nothing there but a welcome mat in bright colors and Sunshine written in large, black, colloquial font. Lacina looked back at David and shook her head.

"You know that Chris hid that locket from me years ago. I've moved on, David. So should you."

"You don't remember what we were talking about do you?" he posited. "You don't remember because you had the locket on when you opened the door and now you don't."

"You sound crazy," Lacina said.

But she did know what he was getting at. He must have been arguing with her past self about the locket. He must have known he wasn't talking to her. He had always been one of the biggest supporters of her magic gem theory. They'd searched the Ozarks for many artifacts of Garamondy, Sr.'s work—including the locket—but Lacina had always secretly hoped to find her girls. She had shared her grandmother's stories with David and her hopes about what could happen if they were true.

"No locket," Lacina agreed. "All that means is I didn't wear a necklace today, so what?"

"But you did," he insisted. "We were talking about the locket. I asked to see it and you refused. Then I came inside and you turn around and it's gone. So where is it?"

"The truth is my past self must have had the locket on when she answered the door. Then I'm guessing when you tried to take it, she reached up for it and blinked back into the past or to Avenrand or who knows where into the future. Then I appeared, stunned, wondering what the hell happened. When I turned around, you were there yelling at me. As it turns out, I'm not crazy after all. My dizzy spells and memory loss are caused by my past-self blinking in and out of my future body."

David glared at her. She wasn't sure if he was about to have her committed, considering the story she told. Which sounded preposterous even to her, but things were beginning to make sense.

"What are you saying?" David glanced at her chest where the locket had been. "Are you implying that you believe your grandmother's stories are true? I remember when you and your girls first came to Stone County, you were looking into that farm of hers. I was studying the remarkable properties of the gems found in a hidden lake in a cave around there, in the southern parts of the county. You were looking for Avenrand then, weren't you?"

"Then my girls disappeared from the foster care system. I have spent the last thirty years convincing myself I made Avenrand up so I wouldn't be crazy anymore. I tried to accept the idea they were kidnapped and more than likely killed like everyone told me." Lacina turned and saw herself in the mirror over the fireplace. My past-self had been here with the locket. "Chris hid the locket from me so that I could move on." Lacina twisted around, lowered her eyebrows. "And that was going to make me all better."

David reached out for the arm of the couch to steady himself and then sat down.

If he doesn't believe me, it would mean more psych evals, more time commitment to an institution, but if he did, he might be able to help me find my way back to the portal.

"I want to believe you."

"You do?" Lacina whispered, hope in her heart and voice for the first time in a very long time. "You do believe me. I know that it will ruin your reputation as a scientist like it did Professor Garamondy. That's what Dr. Garamondy was afraid of, too. But think about it. If I am right, my girls are lost in that world and they may have been trapped there for over thirty years."

"What do we do?" David asked.

"We need to find a way to get the silver gem into Avenrand. Don't tell Chris about this. Nor Dr. Garamondy. Please. I need time to sort this out."

"We'd need to have tangible proof," he said with a sigh. "Proof there was two of you. The locket disappearing from around your neck isn't much to go on."

"I should have tangible proof on the computer. For some reason there were two of me in this house today at one point. VICTOR should have registered that."

"So is your past-self right, are you moving back in?" David asked, sounding a little disappointed.

"That's what you're worried about David? I went in the bedroom to bring in some clothes and my physical past self was in there. She put the locket on. Then I blacked out. But if she was real, if she answered the door for you. Then VICTOR will have a record of there being two of us in the bedroom.

"VICTOR display time and position of duplicate Lacina Manning on the living room screen," Lacina directed.

"The duplicate file was removed as you commanded," VICTOR announced. "Would you like the file restored?"

"Yes. Restore duplicate file."

A holographic screen appeared out in front of the fireplace, taking on a solid blue front as it booted up. Within moments, an aerial image of the Manning home appeared. There was one figure standing by the door in the bedroom and one figure sitting on the arm of the couch.

Lacina and David watched as Victor displayed a woman get up from the couch and walk toward the bedroom, the figure by the door hid behind the bed. For a few seconds both figures were in the bedroom, and then the figure behind the bed walked toward the door and the figures merged.

"Cancel display," Lacina commanded.

The image dissolved.

Lacina turned toward David whose face looked pale and clammy.

"This means you were both in the same time plane simultaneously. Did something go wrong? You didn't talk to her, did you?"

"It was weird," Lacina said. "I walked into the room and then I had a strange feeling that I knew she was there. Like I almost remembered being there before."

"The duplicates were recorded from nine-o-four to nine eleven," VICTOR interrupted. "This glitch was resolved, and the system rebooted at nine fifteen. The cause was undetermined. Would you like to set an alert for future occurrences?"

"No. Record only," Lacina instructed. "Alerts off."

"Like déjà vu," David said.

"Exactly," she said. They both smiled, unable to wipe the grins off their faces.

The front door opened, and Chris walked in with two white paper sacks smelling of grease and fried onions.

"Burgers," Lacina said. "What a nice surprise!"

"I told you I was going to the Burger Barn." Chris shook his head. "I got what you ordered. Sorry, David. I didn't know you were going to be here, or I could have picked you up one. Would you like to split mine? It's a loaded."

"No, thanks," David said. "I had my fill on the way over. I hate to rush off, but I have a meeting to get to. I stopped by on my way to invite y'all on a little trip to Branson I'm taking this weekend. Lacina thought you might be free to go along. It's gonna be a blast. I'll send you the details tonight when I get settled." He winked.

After dinner, Lacina slipped back to the bedroom and pulled out the case. It had been decades since she had opened it, for fear of triggering past trauma and the concern that Chris and Dr. Garamondy would have her committed again. But seeing her past-self gave her renewed confidence.

Maybe she wasn't crazy after all. Now she had proof, and someone believed her.

The picture of Chris and his mother caught her attention. She had seen it before in the little green album he had kept from his childhood. The house they had lived in was destroyed in the flood.

It was taken with a 125mm camera for the purpose of reporting flood victims to authorities in 1973. Any other photos of his mother were presumed lost in the flood so she knew it was special to him.

Lacina took the frame off the wall to admire it and get a closer look at the flooded highway. The baby she had handed off to the woman on the boat was Chris. An actual record of one of her time jumps but one she could never tell him.

"I'm sorry I took our wedding photo down. You can put it back if you want. It's just an old photograph I have been carrying around with me for years. They gave it to me in foster care."

"No. Let's leave it up. I know how much it means to you."

"It's the only picture I have of my mother and me," he said. "It may be the only one that was ever taken. When they went back to get her, the road was completely underwater."

"I'm so sorry." She reached up and put the frame back on the hook then wrapped both arms around Chris and gave him a firm squeeze.

"If you want to head down to Branson this weekend, I am good with it."

"Okay. Yeah. A couple dinner shows would be nice, maybe a nice hike in the woods."

And Branson isn't too far from her grandmother's farm. The thought of going back to Avenrand restored her hope that her daughters would be found.

CHAPTER 38

Avenrand

Lacy stumbled off the bridge. She hadn't meant to grab the locket. For a second, she worried that Dr. Smelsner would catch on that she was from the past. How would her future-self handle waking up with him smashing through the front door?

As Lacy picked herself up, she caught a glimpse of Prince Caden sliding across the top of the bridge, his cape flying up from his shoulders. Something rustled in the bush behind her, and she snapped her head and shoulders around. Caden was gone and she was face to face with a long dark nose with a white blaze.

"Excuse me," the black stallion said. "You are?"

"Who are you? What are you doing on the dark side of Avenrand?"

"Galahad. Sir Galahad at Midnight," the tall black stallion replied. "You are?"

"I'm Lacy. I am here to find my girls."

"I finally meet the human the herd was protecting. Do those girls belong to you?"

"Yes. So, you have seen my daughters? Are they okay?"

"They have been hoping their mother would come. Did you bring the silver gem?"

"No, but I know where it is, but I can't get to it. And I don't think I can bring it with me when I blink."

"Blink?"

"Yes, it is how I traveled here from the future. But I can't get out of here in my own time unless I go back over this bridge and find a clear portal path."

"You can't go back over the bridge. I have been trapped here since Hope sent me to find Prince Caden. The boy who guards the bridge is missing."

"But I saw him a second ago." Lacy pointed back to the bridge, but no one was there.

Galahad knelt and let Lacy climb on his back. "I will take you to the girls."

Through dark, burnt woods, and what was left of the tall bare trees, Galahad carried Lacy. The air stung her nasal passages as the ashes still smoldered. Her eyes were too dried out from the smoke to form tears. Grit scratched across the inside of her lids with every blink. Adjusting her grip, she coughed out smoke and bits of ash.

There were no green leaves or bright colorful sparkles in South Avenrand. It was desolate and depressing. The only bright spot in the barren land were the smiles on her daughters' faces when they saw Galahad entering the small encampment. Olivia and Alice looked up from the campfire, the same little girls she'd seen drug away in the hotel parking lot.

"Galahad, you did come back!" Olivia shouted.

"You brought Mommy," Alice cried.

Lacy slid off the stallion and ran to greet them but was cut short by a witch-like, winged beast that came swooping in. It made a screeching cry that sent shivers up her spine. Diving straight at her head, Lacy ducked down and fell away from Alice's outstretched arms.

"You did this." It peered at her with its beady, yellow eyes.

When the creature regained its flight and circled back, Lacy hastened her pace toward her daughters, but a large bird of prey swooped in from the opposite direction, grabbing Olivia with its large talons. Lacy dove toward Olivia, grabbing the edge of her shoes with both hands. Digging into the pseudo-leather of her tennis shoes, it embedded under her fingernails as those tiny feet slipped out of her grasp. She regained her balance as the whooshing sound of another large bird swooped in and grabbed Alice. Lacy ran for her younger daughter as she was being lifted higher and higher out of reach. The two birds of prey soared off into the dark sky.

"Bring them back," Lacy cried out. "Bring me my girls."

Lacy's heart raced as she ran toward them. Panting. Unsteady. I can't let them go again. Her hamstrings tensed and the top of her thighs quivered. I'm losing them. She thought she caught a glimpse of them ascending in front of a steep mountain in the distance. She followed the long, rocky path toward it. The rocks grew into boulders and then even larger still before she noticed she was ascending at all. Her heart pumped so loud that she didn't hear Galahad stumble behind her. When her legs gave out, she collapsed onto the cold stones and looked back for him.

Lacy sat up and called out to him. "Please, can you take me up the mountain? I don't think I can take another step."

"I'm sorry," Galahad said. "It's my back flank. I am unable to move it."

"Oh dear!" Lacy cried.

It didn't register in her mind that Galahad was hurt. "I can't get to them alone."

"Let us rest." Galahad said. "Maybe if I rest, I will be better."

The path seemed to end in the thick brush that covered the bottom of the mountain. She searched for a way through.

Something rustled in the bushes. She took a step back. The leaves shook again, and she could make out a small figure. Girls? She mustered enough courage to look.

Lacy pushed the bush away and spotted a small boy with big blue eyes cowering behind the bush. He stared at her as if in a trance, his curly blond hair drooped off his head like limp spaghetti.

"Caden?" Lacy asked. "Is that you?"

He squeezed his crossed arms tighter and pulled his legs up to his chest. His torn cape was entangled in the thorny bush.

"Well, there, you're no prince, You're just a scared little boy."

Galahad appeared limping down the path. "What a fine crew we are."

Lacy gathered up Caden's cape and shook it out. She wrapped it around him as she pulled him close. "Why are you out here all alone in this dark world, Mr. Caden?

"Aren't you scared?" Caden's voice shook.

"Yes," Lacy confessed. "But I can't let my fears get in my way. I have to get up that mountain and find my girls, so that means I have to face what frightens me."

The three of them looked up the steep mountain. The boulders got larger as the mountain got higher. The fog grew denser as it rose up into the darkness.

"My girls are up there," Lacy said, pointing to the peak. "I don't understand why all this is happening and I don't know how I'm going to get them back. What do those birds want with them?"

"They want what everyone does." Galahad flopped over on his side in obvious pain. "The silver gem."

"Why does everyone want that silver gem so bad?" Lacy asked.

"It is the gem of courage." Caden replied.

"Sounds like something we could all use right now. I could face my fears head on."

"You don't need a stone to face your fears," Galahad said. "You must acknowledge the truth."

"The truth is my girls are stuck high on a mountain with a pair of evil birds of prey. There seems to be a winged witch colluding with them, and I am stuck at the bottom of a mountain with a scared little boy and a broken horse."

"You are braver than you think." Galahad took a few labored steps toward the brush. "You have come all this way to save your girls. You are a courageous mother."

"I haven't been much of a mother at all recently. I've been running away, trying to get Willy back because I am too scared to face being a mother by myself."

"You've done all of this alone," Galahad reminded her. "You know what you need to do now."

"Yes, I need to get them back home," Lacy agreed. "I have to give up this locket for good and figure out how we are going to become a family again without Willy, how I can raise them on my own."

Lacy patted her chest where the locket should have been, but it was gone.

"It's gone!" Lacy cried out. "How will I get back without it?"

Caden stood up, straightened his cape, and tied it around his neck.

"I will go find the locket," he stood up tall and pushed his chest out. "I will face my fears too. I know in my heart the bridge is still there even though the dark mist has covered it. I will find the locket and meet you there."

"Listen carefully you two, I will say this again because it is important," Galahad said. "Give your attention to the truth about who you are, not the lies that try to give life to your fears. Look at how far you both have come. Lacy, you have braved time and new worlds to do what you thought you needed to do for your girls. Caden, you have scared off beasts bigger than horses, you have guarded the light against darkness. You have made others feel braver than they could imagine. Don't let your fears have any of your attention. You both are brave, you are courageous, you have everything you need to do this. And you have each other."

"Caden." Lacy squatted down in front of him. "I saw you scare off that silver beast to protect my daughters. You are the bravest boy I've ever met. Thank you for being here for me."

"I am going to find that locket for you," Caden said. "I will meet you and the girls at the bridge."

Lacy looked back at Galahad. "Do you know where we are?"

"We are at the bottom of Nest Mountain. You can follow this path"—Galahad pointed back in the direction they had come—"back through the burnt forest. The bridge is on the other side."

I will go up and retrieve Olivia and Alice. Then we will help you get back to the bridge. We won't leave you here alone."

"Do not worry about me," Galahad said. "If I rest, I will be ready to take you and your children to the bridge when you return."

Lacy gave Caden a hug and patted Galahad's neck. Looking at them both, she bit her bottom lip, then took a deep breath and climbed over the first boulder.

A twig snapped and startled her. She saw a shadow run past in her peripheral vision.

I am brave. I am courageous. I can do this.

The animal appeared again. It was a young deer. It leaped over a boulder and then trotted off. Lacy followed it. A well-worn animal trail meandered up the side of the mountain. As she moved upward, the foliage began to turn green again and there were plenty of places to take shelter under the steep rock ledges. The mountain provided life in the middle of this desolate region.

The incline became steeper, and Lacy's legs ached more and more with each step. The illusion of it leveling out proved to lead to another steep climb when she reached it. A little light broke through the clouds but then disappeared into a thick fog that encircled the top of the mountain.

It was gloomy and cold. Lacy wasn't sure which side of the mountain she was on or how much higher she would have to climb.

One step at a time. The small, loose gravel slid out from under her foot, she reached her arms out and caught herself against a waist high boulder. The fog was now so dense she didn't know if she was on the edge of a cliff or on a plateau.

Lacy ducked under the thick trees that had taken over the path. On her left was a steep cliff that curved out over the path just high enough for her to walk under. On her right was a steep drop off that disappeared into the thick fog three feet below. A few yards in front of her, the rock wall and a large tree met in the middle of the path.

Summoning her courage, Lacy grabbed on to the trunk of the horizontal tree. Wrapping both arms around it, she lay on the tree as it hung out over the side of the mountain. She grabbed ahold so tight she couldn't move. Catching her breath, she let her muscles relax but her fingernails dug into the bark of the tree. Without looking down, she slid her hips up and swung her leg over the trunk like mounting a horse. One inch at a time, scuffing her belly and legs, she brought her feet together on the other side and pushed herself out away from the trunk.

As she had hoped, and even imagined, the path continued. Although it was much narrower now. At some points, she had to scoot with her back along the rocks to keep her feet on the path.

"I am brave. I am courageous."

As she shuffled around a bend along the rock wall, the mist began to clear and she could see a dry river bed hundreds of feet below. She tried to change her focus to keep from getting dizzy. With her back up against the wall, she had nowhere else to look. Trying not to lose her balance, she turned her head ninety degrees to the left. In six feet, a boulder rested on the descending side of the path. Realizing she could rest there. she inched her way along the narrow shelf.

"I am brave. I am courageous."

"Squawk."

Lacy jumped. Leaping in the air, she reached out for the boulder then pushed herself back toward the wall. She froze. It was the bird of prey that had taken Alice. It circled the top of the mountain, squawking and cackling. When the beast flew off, Lacy rose up and scanned the side of the mountain.

There to the left in the top of an almost horizontal tree that protruded from the side of the mountain was a nest. Constructed of branches, leaves, and mud, it was as big as her living room. Inside she saw her daughters, arms wrapped around each other as they huddled together. The winged witch, too large to sit in the nest, perched on a branch of a mountain bound tree. Light reflected off a ring of spiked fingers that grew out of its head forming a crown vallary.

Lacy felt a chill run up her spine, the demon eyes stalking her. As the branch drooped down, dark wings unfolded from its back, stroking the air to lighten its load.

Even the ridge strained to support the roots that had wrapped themselves around and through the bedrock. The tree's trunk had supported the room-sized nest built across its branches. Sagging under the weight of the winged witch, Lacy realized this was not the flying beast's home. I don't belong here either. The path appeared to have disappeared into the steep mountainside.

I have overcome many challenges but how will I ever scale an actual mountain. Scanning the side of the mountain for a way up, she saw motion in the bushes at least fifty feet below. Lacy followed the winding path. Maybe there will be a trail to the nest on the other side. She placed each foot firmly as she went down. Small rocks rolled out from under her feet until she could grip the clay underneath with the tread on her shoe.

An injured bird fluffed its feathers on the ledge below. It seemed to favor its left wing, keeping it still. The wing bent backward and stretched out by its side. Peering over the edge of the cliff, she contemplated her descent. If she could reach the shelf below her, she could get to the base of the tree, but she would be too close to a bird the size of a truck.

If I stop on the second boulder, I can slide around and reach the other side. The bird is injured and won't be able to reach up that high. Without much more thought than that, she slid down from one large smooth boulder and came to rest on another directly below it. Her feet slipped on slimy green moss that covered it and off she went continuing her slide and plopping onto the ledge below.

The injured bird began squawking in loud, quick bellows beside her.

"It's okay," Lacy said, trying to calm the bird. "I'm not here to hurt you." She peered over the ledge. The dry riverbed below looked like a single crayon line drawn down the middle of one of Olivia's drawings. Lacy sighed and moved as far away from the edge as she could squeeze.

"You're angry that we carried off those girls," the bird of prey said.

"I don't want them hurt," Lacy said. "I saw them in the nest above us."

"We never planned to hurt them…" Then the bird went silent and stopped moving.

"I don't understand then," Lacy said.

"Quiet," the bird whispered. "Come."

Lacy followed its instruction and ducked down next to her. The bird was large enough to swallow her whole if it wanted to, but somehow Lacy trusted her.

Swoosh.... swoosh. The witch-like intruder left its perch. Lacy felt the wind from its wings as it flew past them. The flying beast began circling over the nest above them.

"I have to get to them," Lacy whispered and tried to stand. A firm weight from the bird's uninjured wing knocked her back down and hid her underneath.

"Shush."

The bird sat motionless, helpless, waiting. Lacy thought she heard sobbing. Several times another flying creature tried to land on a limb near the nest but was too heavy. The limbs would bow, and he would take off in flight and make a few more circles. Each attempt got him closer to the nest until it looked as if he had found a branch to support him.

Lacy gasped. The injured bird pulled her close under her wing. She now rested up against the soft under feathers of the same bird she had feared moments before. The same bird that took off with one of her girls in the first place.

The winged witch approached then lunged forward toward the nest. Lacy gasped; as she watched Olivia duck and tuck Alice tighter in her arms. The crown looked too heavy for its head as it attempted to perch on the side of the nest.

Crack.

The branch gave way under the weight of the beast. The intruder did not heed the warning. Instead, he attempted one more lunge at the girls when an even louder crack echoed down into the canyon below. Lacy breathed a sigh of relief as the large winged beast spiraled down out of the tree with only a chunk of the nest still in its grip. Unable to spread its wings to catch the air, it bounced off the side of the mountain and tumbled out of sight.

Loosening the grip of her wing around Lacy, the injured bird reassured her that they did not mean to hurt the girls. "Do you see why we took your girls to our nest? It was the safest place to protect them from the pursuit of the witch. We've been looking out for them since they arrived."

"Why are they pursuing my girls? What do they want with them?"

"They believe it is the humans—you and your girls—that have destroyed Avenrand. They won't stop until they get rid of all of you."

"I would never want to hurt Avenrand. This is the home of my grandmother's childhood dreams, my childhood stories."

"The girls have told us but they believe it was you who took the silver gem. The silver gem can never leave Avenrand. It is the balance and harmony between North and South. Out of place, it causes division and disharmony. It must be returned for the future of both your world and Avenrand."

"First, I have to get my girls out of here. Then I can go back and find the gem. How do I get them down from there? I can't fly up there and get them and neither can you."

"Well, breaking my wing was not part of the plan. We'll have to wait for my mate to come back and help us. He'll be back as soon as he realizes the witch has fallen."

After what seemed like hours, her mate had still not returned. Lacy paced the ledge of the cliff. The mossy boulder she slid down was too high to climb back up on. She combed the crevices for another path out. No way out.

"You will have to go through the eye of the needle to get into the nest."

"What is the eye of the needle? Where is it? How do I get to it?"

"You have to fly through it."

"Fly through it?" Lacy said. "I can't fly."

"I didn't think so."

"I haven't got wings and you are missing one," Lacy determined. "We're stuck here."

"Then we wait. My mate will take you through it." Her dark, beady eyes softened into her round, fluffy face.

"I don't think your mate is coming back," Lacy said.

After a lingering silence, the injured bird squawked and sobbed.

"I'm sorry," Lacy tried to comfort her. "I'm afraid if he was able to get back to us that he would be here by now."

"Then you will have to fix my wing, and I will fly you through the eye of the needle."

"How can I fix your wing?" Lacy said, "I'm not a vet and wings take weeks to heal."

"The healing moss," the bird said. "You have hands that can scoop up and carry the healing moss. Apply that to my broken wing and then brace it with the branches from the Majesty Palm Plant."

Lacy gathered the moss from the stone she had slid down on and broke off the wing shaped branches from the indicated palm plant.

"Thank you," the bird told the plant.

Lacy stared at the palm plant waiting for a reply but there was none. Has this been here all along?

The bird gave Lacy detailed directions on how to cover her broken wing with the branches. The direction of each branch was important. The moss acted like an adhesive. Lacy wasn't convinced it would work. Every time she muttered a discouraging word, the bird shushed her and continued with her instructions. When all the branches had been placed in the specific way required, each one pressed into the wet moss, Lacy stepped back to inspect.

The branches looked like feathers painted with blue spots running along their veins. She had lined them perfectly to form a makeshift wing.

"It looks like a wing, but I'm not sure it will function like one," Lacy said.

The bird stood up and fluffed up her body feathers, lifting both wings but only flapping the good wing.

"It didn't work," Lacy sighed.

"It will work as much as it is needed." The bird walked to the other side of the ledge and lifted her wings again. This time she stretched her good wing as high as possible. Unfolded, it spanned at least twenty feet. The wing opened like an oriental fan as she rested the tip of it on the side of the path above them.

"Run up there while I still have the strength to hold you," the bird instructed. "Then jump through the eye of the needle. It will take you to your girls."

"First of all," Lacy insisted, "I can't run up your wing. Do you even know how much I weigh? I doubt your wing can support a hundred and fifty pounds. And seriously, jump through the eye of the needle? What does that even mean? I am not jumping off this mountain."

"When you see the eye of the needle, jump through," the bird said. "Trust me. If you do as I say, you will land in the nest."

"So you want me stuck in the nest too?" Lacy asked. "And just when I was beginning to trust you. I wanted to believe that you were trying to save my girls. Are you planning to have all of us for lunch?"

"Another time, perhaps. For now, you will be safe in our nest anytime you need refuge. You have helped me with my broken wing, now, I will help you rescue your girls."

"How do we get out once I'm in?"

"You need to go back through the eye of the needle. Climb up the north side of the nest— toward the mountain. When you are standing on the edge, you will see the eye of the needle. It looks like an endless hole in the sky. Jump through it and it will take you all where you need to be."

Lacy climbed up the birds soft, fuzzy belly and up onto her good wing.

"You're sure about this?" Lacy had no choice but to accept whatever offer of help she could get. She had to trust this wing would hold her. The alternative would be to remain stuck on the ledge while her girls were trapped in a bird's nest high upon a mountain side.

"I'm sure. I can hold you." The bird paused. "But would you do me a favor when you get up there?"

"What can I do?" Lacy wondered aloud.

"Look for my mate and tell him I am resting under the Majestic Palm."

"Of course, I'll try, but I have no idea where I would find him or what he looks like."

"He looks like me," the bird said. "Not quite as big, and he has a larger beak and a white dot on his head. Hide from any other beasts you see."

Lacy began climbing the large wing like a ramp. The feathers were sturdier than she anticipated. Near the top, she had to step on the stem of each feather like rungs on a ladder. To her surprise, it supported her all the way to the next ledge. She sat down on the path and caught her breath.

"You tricked me," Lacy said. "Your broken wing isn't healing at all, is it? You wanted me to think I had helped you."

"You did help me," the bird said, "so much more than you know."

As crazy as jumping through the eye of the needle sounded, Lacy decided it wasn't any crazier than being here on the dark side of Avenrand in the first place. As she ascended the path up the mountainside, she decided that she wasn't going to be as skeptical as Raelynn was when she told her about the power of the locket. Since her necklace was able to transport her through time and place, it's just as plausible that the eye of the needle could portal her in and out of the nest. She dismissed all negative thoughts and focused on reuniting with her girls.

A dark figure swept over her, and Lacy shivered from the cold wind it stirred up. The winged witch was back, stretching its talons down toward her and cackling. Lacy ducked and jumped off the path into the trees. Trying to catch her breath, her whole body shook with fear. The witch was much larger than the birds that owned the nest.

Lacy crouched below the bushes and peered up the path. Fifty feet ahead of her, a stone arch was set off the side of the path. The air within it swirled, sparkles shooting out from it.

What if this overgrown witch catches me before I can get to it?

If she was wrong, she would be leaping off the side of a mountain without a parachute. Wishing she had gotten a few more details about what the eye of the needle looked like, Lacy ran up the path, the flying witch nipping at her heels. As she approached the archway, she closed her eyes.

"I am brave," she yelled. "I am courageous."

Then she leaped into the sparkling air.

CHAPTER 40

Avenrand

Spinning out of control like she was in a Swedish Swing upset Lacy's stomach. Dizzy and nauseous, she plopped out of the air and landed in a pile of soft feathers. Clutching her stomach and moaning, she lay in the nest with her eyes still closed. Aware she was hyperventilating; she took mindful breaths.

In through your nose, out through your mouth, one, two, three, she coached herself.

That feeling of being stared at overwhelmed her recovering senses. Head still spinning, she half way opened one eye and tried to focus. The shadows of two children—her children—took shape as her vision returned to normal. The only colors in this dark place were the colors bleeding through the dirt on their favorite shirts. Olivia's blue Destin Beach shirt and Alice's hot pink Barbie one seemed out of place amongst the gray feathers and dark brown branches and twigs that made up the nest.

"I found you," Lacy whispered, reaching out her arms to her girls. She scooped them up and rested her head back on the soft feathers. The three of them held each other in a tight hug.

"We got lost," Olivia said. "We were looking for you."

"I know, baby girls, I know," Lacy said. "I've been looking for you too."

"We're hungry," Alice said.

"Me too. Let's rest for a minute and then we are going to go get some lunch." She smiled, closed her eyes, and squeezed her daughters in her arms.

"I don't want any more berries," Alice said. "I want a cheeseburger."

"There aren't any cheeseburgers out here," Olivia said. "We're lost in a dark forest."

"We're not lost," Lacy said. "We'll return to the path and follow it to the bridge. Then we walk back through the portal to Lina's farm. I'll unbury it if I must. You will get those cheeseburgers."

Alice smiled. "No pickles. Just ketchup."

"Ketchup only, it is." Lacy sat up and took another deep cleansing breath. "Now let's find that eye in the needle."

"The eye of the needle?" Olivia questioned. "The birds that brought us here warned us not to go through that. No matter what!"

"They wanted to keep you safe," Lacy said, "but we're going on a little adventure together, so we have to travel back through it to get going."

Lacy stood up, admiring how well constructed the nest was.

It was about the size of her living room but without any furniture. She peered over the edge looking for anything that looked like the archway she'd used to get into the nest. After walking the inside perimeter three times, she fought off the insidious thought that she'd been betrayed.

"What else did the big birds tell you about the eye of the needle?" Lacy asked. She sat down next to Olivia and turned her head toward her.

"Well…" Olivia said. "They told us not to go through it, no matter what. They were dropping off berries for us, but nothing else came in or out of here. They told us to stay close to the opening if the flying beast comes."

"She's very scary, Mommy," Alice said. "I thought she wanted to eat us. Luckily, it's only a puppet."

"A puppet?" Lacy repeated.

"Like the funner ones at Silver Dollar City," Alice said. "Olivia told me it's like the Abominable Snowman we had our pictures taken with. But I don't want my picture taken with the witch. She's too scary."

Olivia shrugged.

Lacy smiled. Olivia was a very mature eight-year-old, stepping up to keep her younger sister calm.

"You are both very brave and very courageous." Lacy felt a sense of pride rise in her chest. They rolled around on the bottom of the nest. Alice giggled, a chance to be like kids again.

Olivia planted her feet in a dead stop then walked to the edge of the nest and scolded her little sister. "We don't have time to goof off."

Everything they'd been through so far was so surreal, between the locket and Avenrand—both north and south—and Lacy didn't understand any of it herself.

"Look," Olivia shouted. "The eye of the needle is coming."

As if floating in mid-air, the arch appeared. The air inside it distorted like frost being painted on a window. It rested directly above steps made up of large twigs and branches.

Lacy took each of the girls' hands. "I think we should go now."

"No," Alice cried. "We can't go through the eye of the needle!"

"It'll be okay, Alice," Lacy said. She knelt in front of her youngest daughter and took a calming breath, which she had taught Alice to copy. And she did. "I came in through there. Trust me, we will be fine. I promise."

As they stood up together, a loud swish sent a rush of air through the nest and pushed them back into the soft feathers.

"What was that?" Alice cried.

Lacy staggered back onto her feet and peered over the side of the nest. The big bird's mate soared below them. He flew away from the mountain and then circled back. Then sweeping up higher and higher until he was above the nest. He made several passes before circling over the nest as if he wanted to land.

Lacy motioned Olivia and Alice to move toward the stairway. Scooting closer, they clung to the branches sticking out from the edge of the nest.

"Climb up the stairs," Lacy instructed as she struggled to walk across the outer edge of the nest. It was like walking across a large pile of kindling ready for a massive bonfire. The twigs and branches didn't make for the best footing. Lacy slipped, grabbing a small branch on her way down. The branch snapped in half, and she landed hard, twigs poking her in the back.

"Are you okay?" Olivia asked.

"I'm fine," Lacy lied. She could feel something still in her back.

As she struggled to untangle herself from the nest building materials, the large bird landed on the edge of the nest. She recognized the white dot on his head.

"I have a message for you from your mate. She is hurt on a ledge near the Majestic Palm."

"Thank you. I will find her. You need to get going," he told them. "This place is no longer safe for you."

Another much louder swish with an even greater rush of air rushed through the nest and Lacy ducked down. The bird was blown off the side of the nest and immediately took flight.

The winged witch appeared within a few feet above them. Olivia and Alice scrunched down under the stairs' branches and twigs as the witch's large claws stretched out toward them.

"It's time to go," Lacy took the girls' hands and pulled them out from their hiding place.

The witch swooped up and landed on the edge of the nest. The floor shook and twigs began to fall.

The witch cackled as more branches began to break apart.

"It's going away," Olivia cried.

The nest was falling apart behind them as they ran up the constructed, twig-and-branch stairs.

"Close your eyes and jump," Lacy called out.

Lacy meant to close her eyes but she was afraid of losing the girls. She gasped, realizing she had actually jumped out of the nest—out of the top of the highest tree she had ever seen.

Are we too late?

The girls were screaming with their eyes closed as hard as they were squeezing her hands. Lacy had to close her eyes as well. If she had just made her daughters jump off the side of a mountain to their deaths, she didn't want to watch.

Lacy welcomed that feeling of the Swedish Swing spinning out of control. It made her feel like she was no longer falling straight down off the mountain. Instead, she felt like she had been swept up by a tornado and hoped to be gently set down. Soon.

Lacy tried to focus her eyes, dizzy from the fall. She was no longer holding the girls' hands. Stumbling to her feet, she tripped over Alice. They had landed in the middle of a berry batch.

"I'm sorry, sweetheart. I lost my balance."

Lacy looked around. "Olivia?"

"I'm dizzy," Olivia said.

"Not more berries," Alice complained.

CHAPTER 41

Avenrand

"Let's get out of here," Lacy took a hold of their hands. "We can find the path to Grandma Lina's when we go back over the bridge." Once she found her bearings, she turned in the direction of the path she had followed to retrieve them. Olivia slipped her hand away from Lacy's and froze. "What's wrong? Don't you want to go home?"

Olivia shook her head. Her body trembled, and she began stepping backward on the path.

"What is it? We need to get out of here before dark."

Olivia ignored Lacy and ran in the opposite direction.

Squeezing her mother's hand, Alice pulled her toward Olivia and trembled.

Not sure whether to run to catch up with Olivia or comfort her youngest, Lacy sighed. "What is it, Alice? What are you girls so afraid of?"

Alice pointed down the path in the direction Lacy wanted to go. It looked exactly as it had when she had arrived at the bottom of Nest Mountain and that was the way they need to go to get back there. Not only was it the direction of the bridge, but Galahad would be waiting there for them.

Lacy hugged Alice. "Let's go get your sister, okay?"

Alice nodded, and they turned around and retraced their steps.

They found Olivia hiding in a bush at the edge of the path.

"Come out from there right now. You need to listen to me. I remember the way that we came in and the bridge is in that direction." Lacy pointed back down the path.

"No one comes back from Look Back Mountain," Olivia's voice quivered.

"What mountain?" Lacy turned back around, and a mountain had appeared in the middle of the path back to the bridge.

"Trolley, Digit, and Mumba. None of them came back."

Lacy was beginning to recognize that her experience of Avenrand and the girls was extremely different. Had they been here for thirty years? Or had they snuck out of foster care this weekend?

"Maybe they got across it and found the bridge back to the herd. Maybe they got out of here." Lacy said. "That is the way back, I know it. We are going to have to just go over that mountain."

"I don't want to fall off the mountain," Alice cried. "I don't want to die!"

"We'll stay on the path," Lacy said. "We won't get near the edge, I promise."

"It won't work," Olivia said. "Everyone falls off Look Back Mountain."

"Mumba fell off," Alice wiped a tear off her cheek.

"I assure you we will not fall." Lacy was determined to get back to the bridge. There had to be a way and they need to get closer to find it.

"I don't believe you. You let Daddy die. You said you were going to save him. You said everything was going to be alright." Olivia crossed her arms and refused to take Lacy's outstretched hand.

"I've been trying to save him, baby. That's how we ended up here in the first place. But now, the most important thing is to get to the bridge." Lacy grabbed Olivia's arms and pulled her close. "Trust me, Olivia, I didn't come all this way and get you out of that bird's nest to let you fall off the mountain. Those people who didn't come back to you must have made it to the other side. They're with their families now."

"I'm scared," Olivia admitted.

"I know, sweetheart, but you're not alone anymore. We're going to stick together and we'll be okay."

The girls took Lacy's hands, and they began walking down the path toward the mountain. But no matter how much they walked, the mountain didn't seem to get any closer.

"We have to keep going," Lacy encouraged, more for her own sake than the girls'. "We have to end up there."

They walked for what seemed like hours without getting any closer to their destination. Then without any warning, a trail head appeared before them, disappearing into the woods. The trees along the path seemed taller and denser than those they'd grown used to. They stepped under the thick canopy of branches and leaves. Was this the burnt woods? Had they made it across the mountain?

The path must have turned, Lacy thought. They only thought there was a mountain. They needed to keep walking until these colorless woods turned into burnt trees and black dirt. Then they would find the bridge.

"I'm hungry," Alice complained.

"I know," Lacy said. "It won't be long now."

"I'm hungry, too," Olivia said. "Can we stop and eat."

"Not yet," Lacy said. "We have to get back to the bridge first."

"We can't go this way," Olivia said. "We can't cross the mountain."

"Keep walking," Lacy assured her. "There is no mountain. We are in the woods now,"

Something rustled in the trees behind them, and Olivia jumped behind her mother. Safe in her mother's care, the older sister could finally let down her guard. Alice and Olivia shuddered. Lacy's heart sank when she saw the terror on their faces. She couldn't bear to think about all the awful and scary things the girls must have seen here, alone on the dark side of Avenrand.

Lacy forced her legs to keep moving. "Tell me about these friends you've met, Trolley, and Digit, and Dumbo?"

"Not Dumbo." Alice giggled. "It's Mumba."

"They aren't elephants." Olivia shook her head. "They are kids like us."

"There are other kids out here? What in the world are other kids doing out here?"

"It's the carnival, right Olivia?" Alice said.

"It's part of Silver Dollar City, stupid. Don't you remember anything I tell you?"

"Girls, be nice."

"People live here," Olivia said. "Isn't that why you showed us how to get here?"

"Of course," Lacy said, "but I thought everyone would stay on the other side of the bridge."

"Oh, that was before the silver gem was stolen," Olivia said.

There was the rustle again. This time it sounded even closer than before. Lacy sped up, moving toward a clearing where she could see light peering through from the trees.

"Galahad, is that you?"

The path widened as they approached, and the tree line came to an abrupt end.

It must be the edge of the burnt forest.

The three of them stood at the end of the path and stared at the opening. The sun shone golden beams along the edge of the canopy and lit up the emptiness between them and the edge of the mountain.

The trail was wider now but less prominent than it had been when it was lined with trees. Now it was edged with a row of white stones on either side. This path seemed unfamiliar. Where were they? Where was the path where Galahad would be waiting for them?

Lacy's gaze followed the clearly marked path as it began a gradual zigzag up the side of the mountain. How she had no idea, but this mountain appeared and blocked the path back to the bridge. Of that, she was certain.

Olivia dug her feet in at the edge of the woods shaking her head.

"No, no, no." Olivia murmured. "Don't go, Mommy. We can't go that way."

"What are you afraid of Olivia? I can see the path where others have traveled before."

"I don't want to disappear in the mountain." Olivia took three steps backwards.

The rustling sound had followed them to the edge of the woods. In the light of the clearing, a shadow of a person appeared but Lacy couldn't see its source.

"Who are you?' Lacy called. "What do you want?"

"I don't want to hurt you," the shadow said.

"Where are you? Show yourself," Lacy demanded.

"I'm a traveler here to warn you." The shadow grew larger, twice the size of a large man.

"It's okay, Mommy," Olivia said. "The shadow helps us. It tells us where to go to be safe."

Lacy noticed that Olivia was calm and no longer shaking.

"What do you want to warn us about?" Lacy asked.

"Turn around before it's too late," the shadow said. "The white stone path leads to death."

"It looks well-traveled. Isn't it true that others have taken this path back to the bridge? We have to get back to the other side of Avenrand,"

"No one can cross Look Back Mountain," the traveler explained. "Halfway across, when you are still looking forward, it will disappear. This path leads to death."

"That doesn't make any sense. We can see the mountain right there. It seems very stable."

"Did you see the mountain on your way in? Have you already forgotten?"

"I don't remember it, but I came in with the black stallion. We were—"

"You are going to have to turn around. If you follow this trail, you will all perish."

"But it will lead us back to the bridge. We must get back there."

"Turn around!" The traveler disappeared.

Olivia pulled Lacy's arm and started walking back into the woods.

Lacy stopped. "Olivia, I know you are scared but we have to turn around. We have to find our way back to the bridge."

"Look! A popcorn patch." Alice pointed to a field of cat tails on the other side of the white stones. But instead of normal brown spindles, the flower tops were white husks of maize.

Olivia took Alice's hand and walked her over to the patch. The girls started pulling the corn cobs off their stalks. When they opened them, the corn began popping in light fluffy puffs in their hands.

"Are you sure these are safe?" Lacy asked. "You can't go eating anything you see."

"The traveler showed us how. Look, Mommy, it pops in my hands." Olivia stuffed a handful of it into her mouth.

Reluctantly, Lacy pulled a cob off the stalk and smiled as buttery corn puffs popped into her palm. The girls ran through the patch chasing the flakes as they blew up and into the air. Lacy joined them, unable to contain the savory treats appearing before her eyes.

"Girls, wait," she whispered. Something moved among the tall stalks. Lacy saw the brown fur and made out the top of its back. "Girls, I said stop," she said a little louder frustrated with how disobedient they had become. "I think it's a bear."

Running between Alice and the creature, she pulled her over next to Olivia and motioned both children to get behind her.

"What's wrong, Mommy?" Olivia asked.

"A bear," Lacy whispered. "Back away slowly."

"It won't hurt us," Olivia said and scooted around Lacy, walking up to the bear and petting it like a dog. It stood up and crammed a handful of puff corn into its mouth. Munching on the popcorn, it leaned into Olivia while she scratched its back.

Lacy was still trying to make sense of it all. Bears that act like dogs.

"Okay…," Lacy hesitated. "I apologize. I didn't realize you were a friendly bear. Sorry to disturb you."

The bear said nothing.

"Again, I'm so sorry."

"Bears can't talk," Olivia laughed. "But he does like back scratches."

Lacy let the girls snack for a while, and the bear wandered off. Then she sat them down on a log and explained her plan to get them to the other side of Look Out Mountain and back to the bridge.

CHAPTER 42

Avenrand

Lacy, Olivia, and Alice set off across the clearing and started down the white, rock path.

Certainly, by the time we get to the mountain, the girls will be convinced that the mountain won't disappear, Lacy hoped. Alice seemed to be willing to trust their mother. Olivia on the other hand, still seemed angry at her for Willy dying and she had been keeping her distance. Lacy tried to give her enough space to pout but stay close enough to ensure she was still heading in the right direction.

The path turned, and they found themselves in a place the girls thought was called the Misty Woods. Lacy took a step under the canopy of bare trees and thick vines to wait for Olivia to catch up. Maybe this was a short cut to the mountain. When they were all back on the path, she and Alice took off in the lead again.

"What was that?" Olivia crouched against a large oak tree that must have been hundreds of years old, she attempted to hide herself in the crook of its large roots.

Lacy turned around, quickening her pace as the roots of the tree seemed to grow larger. The trunk was nearly six feet across and the root system extended out from its base at least three times its width. Squinting as she tried to keep focused on her, Olivia disappeared inside the large trunk.

"Olivia," Lacy screamed, rushing toward the tree. "Where are you?"

A thick mist began circling over the base of the tree spreading out until it engulfed the root system. Like a storm rolling over a field, the tree disappeared in the fog.

"Olivia," Lacy yelled. "Where are you? Olivia? Olivia!"

Lacy grabbed Alice's wrist and ran toward the tree. Alice stumbled behind her, trying her best to keep up.

"Mommy," Alice cried. "You're hurting me."

Lacy's tunnel vision was focused on where she last saw the tree. Before it had vanished, she had snapped a mental picture of Olivia's scared face as the tree engulfed Olivia's tiny body.

"Olivia," Lacy tried to yell, but she was out of breath.

Where was the tree? We should have reached it by now. Large branches spiraled above her while the mist floated up around her.

"Mommy, stop," Alice cried. "I'm getting dizzy."

Lacy's head was spinning. She had been so focused on Olivia that she didn't notice Alice had slipped from her hand.

Lacy grabbed her chest. Her heart was pounding, and she could feel the veins popping out of her neck with each rapid heartbeat. She lost her balance, trying to stop her fall with each step. Butterflies in her stomach felt like lottery balls spinning in a cage, bouncing around until one would try to come up her throat. Her feet no longer supported her and without even trying to brace herself, she hit her head on the ground hard and rolled down a steep embankment landing on the rocky shore of a shallow stream.

Holding her hand to her face, Lacy could feel the warm blood pooling around her right eye. Throbbing pain radiated from her temple, as she struggled to sit up.

"Alice? Olivia?" Lacy yelled in every direction. "Alice? Olivia?"

A twig snapped above her. Lacy saw the steep embankment she had fallen from. Large tree roots protruded from washed-out mud and dirt that once held them. It looked as if the tree roots grew to the stream for a drink. The treetops were covered in large clouds of mist, but the air around the stream was so clear she could see down the stream until the running water disappeared into the side of the mountain miles away.

The wind screaming through the trees startled her.

"Whose there?" Lacy cried.

She tried to pull herself up the embankment by holding onto the large roots. Once she got her feet planted, she slid along the edge toward the trunk of a large tree that appeared to be half in dirt and half over the edge of the cliff. With all her strength, she leaped for the upper plateau and back into the misty woods.

A rustling in the brush was moving closer. "Whose there?" she cried out.

"I told you not to come this way," the familiar voice said.

"You're the traveler, aren't you? You're the one who tricked my girls into coming over to the dark side."

"Nonsense," it rebuked. "I kept those girls safe. Where were you?"

"You don't want to help us find our way back over the bridge. You're trying to keep us here, lost and confused."

"I'm trying to keep you safe. You came in here, and now you've lost your girls again. Why are you afraid of me?"

Lacy stood up and shook the dust off her arms and face. "I'm not afraid of you. I'll find my girls and I am going to get them out of Avenrand."

"If you're not afraid, then why don't you go the way I told you to go? Everything you need is there. Isn't being with your girls enough? Instead, you've lost them again."

"Mommy," Alice's quivering voice startled the traveler and the shadow disappeared.

Lacy ran through the mist toward the voice until she saw her daughter's small frame standing in front of her. "Alice?"

"Mommy, help me," her daughter cried. "I'm scared."

"It's okay, Alice." Lacy took her into her arms and comforted her. "It's going to be okay. Let's go find Olivia and get out of here."

They walked down the path toward where the big tree that swallowed her oldest daughter had been. Another creak in the brush and they both jumped.

"Go away," Lacy yelled into the woods. "Why can't you just leave us alone?"

The creature lurking in the woods continued to follow them. Lacy whipped around and screamed, "Leave us alone."

"I'm sorry," a gentle female voice said. "I didn't mean to frighten you."

As a shadow appeared on the path behind them, Lacy realized it wasn't the traveler. This figure was a light, bright shadow. The translucent figure of a small girl appeared like an angel.

"Who's there?" Lacy asked.

"I couldn't help but overhear you talking to the traveler. He doesn't want any of us to leave, a lonely old soul. I am also trying to find the bridge. May I come with you?"

"You want me to show you how to find the bridge?" Lacy laughed. "I don't know where it is."

"I know how to get there, but I can't go alone. Let me show you—it's this way."

"I can't leave yet," Lacy said. "I have to find my daughter. I can't go without her."

"If you let me go with you, I will show you the girl."

"Why would you want to go with me?"

"I only exist with you."

"Please help me find my daughter and I don't care if you go with us to the bridge."

"Here she is," the light shadow said, encapsulating Alice with her pure light so she radiated like a neon sign."

"I know where Alice is," Lacy grumbled. "It's Olivia I need to find."

She took Alice's hand and huffed away from the light shadow. The fog was lifting, and she could make out the large tree but there was no sign of Olivia. She climbed on the large, protruding roots and stared down into the hold that Olivia had hidden in.

It was empty.

"She's gone," Lacy cried.

"I know where she is," the light said. It floated through the air and into the mist reshaping itself until it took the shape of a child high up in the tree.

The mist lifted and revealed Olivia holding on tight to the large branch.

"Olivia?" Lacy called.

Olivia screeched.

"Hold on!" Lacy screamed. "Don't let go. I don't want you to fall. I'll come up and get you."

"Let go," the light instructed. "If you do, I can help you down."

"No," Olivia cried out loud enough that Lacy could hear. "The traveler told us to not go near the light. Leave me alone!"

As soon as Lacy heard the traveler didn't like the light, her gut told her to take a chance on it. The traveler didn't want them to get out, but the light did.

"Olivia," Lacy said. "The light is our friend. We have to trust it. Please. Let go of the branch."

Letting her fingers drag across the bark, Olivia did as she was told and as if she was an angel herself, the light engulfed her, and they floated down from the tree together. Olivia made a soft landing on the path in front of Lacy and Alice. The light disappeared as quick as it came, and the traveler appeared behind them.

"Why are you still here?" the traveler demanded. "I told you to turn around and get out of the Misty Woods. Why won't you listen to me?"

Lacy saw a distant flashing light behind the trees—a guiding star down the path that led to the edge of the embankment.

Ignoring the traveler, she took the girls' hands and walked away.

"No," Olivia cried. "I'm scared."

"Turn around," the traveler demanded. "That's the way to be safe."

"Olivia," Lacy said. "Don't listen to the shadow. It's going to be okay. You'll see soon, I promise."

"But I can't trust you." Olivia screamed. "You want us to disappear too."

Lacy knew she had grown distant with the girls, especially Olivia, since Willy died. She was so caught up in her own grief and denial. *What was I thinking? Going back and saving someone from the dead. It was no wonder Olivia is pulling away from me.*

"I am not going to make you disappear." Lacy knelt down and set her hand on Olivia's shoulder. "We're going to stay together. No one is going to disappear."

"We're never supposed to go toward the light," Olivia mumbled. "The traveler told us to stay away from it."

It was going to take more than promises to gain Olivia's trust but despite her protests, Lacy had to keep going. She led the girls towards the flashing light as it moved out of reach in front of them. They ducked under low-lying branches and followed the descending path into the mist. A small trickle of water flowed down the center of the creek bed. The river rock clattered as it rolled out from under their feet.

Alice tripped. Letting go of her sister's hand and putting her arms out straight, she caught herself on the loose rocks.

"Are you okay?" Olivia asked.

"She's fine." Lacy reached out her hand to help Alice up and brushed the gravel bits off that had indented into her palms. "Shake it off, babe, we have a long way to go."

Alice stood up and began sobbing. Both her knees and palms were skinned, and droplets of blood began to bead up along the edges of her wounds. Lacy took the edges of her shirt and wiped the blood off Alice's knees.

"Ouch," Alice cried. "You're hurting me."

"Okay, then. It looks clean enough. You'll be fine. We need to keep moving before we lose the light."

"What about the traveler?" Olivia asked. "He told us not to go that way."

"Olivia," Lacy snapped. "Don't you get it. He is trying to keep us here. The traveler doesn't want us to ever get out of here. We have to follow the light."

"There is no way out." The dark shadow appeared on the edge of the forest. "You are being led into a trap."

"And why should I trust you?" Lacy asked. "There's a way out of here or no one would ever have been able to return to Avenrand."

"No one returns to the other side of Avenrand," the traveler said. "There's no way back."

"Follow me, we must hurry," the light reappeared.

Lacy corralled the girls between her arms and ushered them away from the traveler and down the creek bed toward the light.

After what seemed like hours, Lacy began to doubt her decision to follow the light. "Are we getting closer to the mountain? It doesn't seem to be getting any bigger."

"This way," the light commanded. "Hurry, now."

The trail zigzagged back in and out of the dry creek bed. It had so many bends that it appeared to turn back on itself.

Lacy stopped and put her arms out to stop the girls. "Are we going in circles?"

"This way," the light called out. "We must hurry."

Alice sat down on a log. "I'm tired. My knees hurt."

"I'm hungry. Are we ever going to eat?" Olivia sat down next to her sister.

The traveler's dark shadow floated out from a small clearing in the woods. "Come here, I will feed you."

Olivia jumped up and ran toward the traveler in the clearing.

"No," Lacy protested. "Do not follow the shadow."

Olivia motioned Alice to come over and they climbed up out of the creek bed and found a seat on one of the logs in the clearing. There were berries and fruit and nuts lined up on a clean stone in front of them.

"Eat," the traveler said.

Lacy climbed up out of the creek bed as fast as she could but the girls were already enjoying their snack.

"Look, Mommy," Olivia called out. "It's good to eat."

The traveler floated down next to the girls. His shadow took on the shape of a tall man. At the center of his chest, a light flashed.

"You tricked us." Lacy raised her voice with furrowed eyebrows. "Why are you doing this? What do you want from us?"

"Mommy," Olivia cried. "Don't yell. You're scaring me."

"Wait, girls," Lacy said. "Don't eat anything."

"But I'm hungry." Alice tried to sneak a piece of fruit in her mouth, but Lacy blocked her hand.

"Stop." Lacy knelt by the food and inspected it. "At least, let me check it first. I know you're hungry, baby."

"There is nothing wrong with the food. I had the scramblers prepare it for them. They have been feeding the girls for years and they seem fine, don't they?"

Lacy took a small bite of the fruit. Years? The thought of them being out here alone for years made her woozy.

Trying to snap herself out of the dizzy haze, she asked, "How long have they been here?"

"That depends," said the traveler, "on when you've come from?"

Lacy was irritated with the indirect answers and the traveler's deception.

"There is no light is there? No darkness, no light. Only you. You've trapped us here. Making us run around in circles and keeping us turning back from the mountain and I want to know why."

"I am not doing it," said the traveler. "You are. I told you I don't exist without you."

"Quit lying to me," Lacy yelled.

Olivia cowered down behind the log as Lacy's rage went on. She lashed out at the traveler and again called him out on his deception.

"Leave us alone. I don't want you lying to the girls ever again."

Into thin air, the traveler faded.

"It's okay," Lacy told the girls. "We are going to find our way out of here."

"Are you mad?" Alice asked.

"Not at you, precious," Lacy said.

"I don't feel comfortable with you yelling like that," Olivia said.

"I'm sorry, but I don't like being deceived. The traveler pretended to be the light and led us away from the mountain. The path home is that direction."

"I don't want to go there." Olivia said.

"I think he was nice. I'm hungry and he tried to give us food. Now the food's all gone. It disappeared," Alice said. "If Daddy were here, he'd know what to do."

"If daddy didn't disappear, we wouldn't be here." Olivia glared at Lacy.

In a hushed voice so the girls couldn't hear her, she cried out to God or whoever was willing to listen. "First, you take my husband, and then you lead me here? What do you want? I can't do this alone. I can't find my way out of here alone. It's not fair. Why me? All I ever wanted was to be a great wife and a great mom. It shouldn't be this hard." She leaned up against a tree and looked out toward the mountain.

"Sometimes the hardest part is figuring out what you want," a small figure peeked around the tree and looked up at her.

Lacy wasn't startled. She had been talking to birds and shadows and even thought she heard the trees shushing her. Squinting to make out the small creature, it was a walking stick of sorts but larger than a praying mantis she'd seen on their camping trips. It was more of a small branch with legs, bigger than kindling but smaller than a log. It stopped near her face, clinging to the bark on the side of the tree.

"I do know what I want," Lacy said.

"Oh, I don't think you do," the walking wood said.

"I do," she insisted. "I want to take my girls and go home, and everyone else to leave us alone."

"But didn't you come here to save your husband?"

In all of this jumping around to different times and places, Willy was still dead. And Avenrand, the dark side of Avenrand, this wasn't real. Was it?

"I can't save anything," Lacy said. "Not Willy, not my girls, not even Avenrand from this darkness."

"You've already saved your girls," the walking wood said. "You're who got them from the nest and saved them from the winged witch. Everyone is talking about it."

"Everyone?"

"Yes, everyone."

"I haven't saved them yet," Lacy said. "We're still stuck on the wrong side of this mountain, and I have no idea how to find my way back to the bridge, back to Hope and the herd."

"You know Hope, do you? I have heard of this Hope on the other side." The walking wood paused and his feet clicked on the bark and he moved a few steps closer. "You will find what you're looking for when you save the one you are supposed to save. The one you already saved on the island."

Olivia ran up to Lacy with something yellow dripping down her chin. "Mommy, this food is delicious. It tastes like macaroni and cheese."

"Mine tastes like chocolate chip cookies," Alice smiled.

"What did I tell you about eating food from strangers?" Lacy snapped. "The traveler is trying to trick us."

"Never trust that which lurks in the shadows," the walking wood said.

"It wasn't from the traveler," Olivia said. "That tree over there gave it to us. She said that you'd love it and promised it's safe."

Olivia handed a piece to Lacy, and she turned it over in her hands examining it. "You must be careful what you eat, girls. It can be very dangerous to accept food from strange creatures."

She smelled it. It had a spicy scent.

Lacy looked at the walking wood. "I don't guess you eat this food, do you?" Lacy asked, hoping to find a taste tester.

"It tastes like flies to me," the wood laughed. "It's harmless. Try it. Anyone can eat the mystic fruit when it is shiny. Once the sparkle is gone, you better keep your distance."

Lacy held it up to her nose. It did smell familiar.

"Eat up," the stick said. "It only lasts a few hours."
Lacy took a small bite. Her stomach rumbled, and she smiled.

"What is it?" Olivia asked. "What does yours taste like?"

Lacy laughed. "It's crazy, but I think it tastes like my Grandma Lina's spicy chicken."

Lacy and the girls thanked the tree and then accepted as much as they could eat from the tree.

There was nothing like Grandma's kitchen. Lacy remembered. So many unique spices and healing remedies I never got a chance to learn before they sent her away.

"Taste my fruit," Lacy said. "It tastes like my grandmother's spicy chicken."

"I don't like spicy," Olivia said.

Alice took a piece and tasted it. "Yummy. I've had this chicken here before. I like it."

"You've had my grandma's chicken here in Avenrand?"

"Prince Caden's grandma gave me some."

Lacy wondered who that woman was. "Where are all these people you talked to while I was gone? Where do they live?"

"They show up when you need them," Olivia said. "That's why the traveler is trying to help us."

"But he's not trying to help us out of here. He wants us to stay here."

"He said you are the one making us stay here."

Me? It's true. Lacy thought. I am the one who had succumbed to the power of the locket. I am the one who brought the girls to Lina's farm and took them through the portal to Avenrand. I gave them their own portal stones. It was her fault that the girls got put into foster care. She was the one who insisted that Willy take her out that night as well.

Date night. If only, she hadn't insisted on a date night.

Lacy slid down the side of the tree. Her shoulders scraped against the bark, but she didn't feel it. She put another piece of the mystic fruit in her mouth. It felt warm and gooey and tasted like chocolate covered caramel. Despite its sweetness, it brought her no joy.

The girls enjoyed their fruit like nothing was wrong. As long as they didn't have to travel across that mountain, they were happy to hang out in the Misty Woods eating their fruit and playing with their imaginary friends. They had nowhere to be, no obligations, no cares in the world.

Lacy was so deep into her thoughts of regret that she didn't notice the girls stand to offer their fruit to the black stallion. The horse lowered his head so Alice and Olivia could pet his jaw.

"Galahad, you're back!" Olivia shouted with glee. "I thought you were lost forever."

Alice giggled and wrapped her arms around Galahad's head. She squeezed so hard that Galahad lifted her feet off the ground when he looked up. Lacy still hadn't noticed him.

The girls' giggles made Galahad whinny, startling Lacy.

Lacy jumped and Alice lost her grip and fell to the ground. Galahad put his nose down and sniffed Alice.

"Leave her alone," Lacy yelled.

"I apologize," Galahad said. "Are you okay, Alice?"

"Galahad," Lacy said, surprised to see him. "Galahad, it's you! You're alright."

"I'm fine. I am happy to see you found your girls."

"I thought you were hurt."

"It just so happens you left me in a bush surrounded by healing stones. Very fortunate indeed."

"We're trying to get back to the bridge, but this mountain appeared."

"Look Back Mountain. It appears to block your path when you turn to go back. Quite astonishing, really. It is said that if you walk to the top, then on your way back down the other side it will disappear right out from under your hooves."

"I have heard."

"Quite a quandary because some have tried to walk down the other side backward to fool it. But it knows. You can't trick a mountain."

"What do we do? I need to get the girls back to the bridge, so we can find the portal."

"I have also heard there is a tunnel."

"A tunnel?"

"Yes, through the mountain."

"If the tunnel is low enough, when the mountain disappears you wouldn't fall."

"Not very far anyway."

"Okay, great." Lacy looked down the trail out of the Misty Woods. The mountain blocked the horizon. "But it's a very large mountain. How do we find the opening?"

"Follow the creek bed," Galahad said. "The creek flows out of the mountain and is said to have created the tunnel."

Lacy slumped back down against the log. "We tried to follow the creek but it led us in circles."

"I can take you there."

"We get to ride a horse," Alice shouted.

Before Lacy agreed, Galahad knelt and both girls jumped onto his back. He waited for a few minutes but when Lacy didn't climb up, he stood up. He moved over to her and lowered back down.

"Get on," Galahad instructed. "I will take you to the tunnel."

Lacy noticed a slight gimp in Galahad's right shoulder. She knew he was not going to be able to take all three of them at once.

"Take the girls and I will meet you there." Lacy looked down the empty creek bed.

"We'll take our time."

At first, Lacy kept up as best she could. A rustle in the woods made Galahad jump. Another loud noise and he spooked, bolting off down the creek bed.

CHAPTER 44

2036

Chris, Lacina, and David browsed the shelves of Claire's shop. Lacina kept a close eye on David. *What is he looking for? Did he have the silver gem?*

"You know it's scientifically impossible for any of these homeopathic tinctures to work," Chris whispered to Lacina. "There isn't enough potency for your body to even register it's there."

"It's based on the theory that like cures like," Claire explained, having overheard Chris speaking to his wife. The wrinkles that spread out like a cat's whiskers from the corners of her eyes made her look very wise. "The assumption is that if something causes a symptom then a small amount of it will cure it. Sort of like a vaccine."

Chris and Claire exchanged polite smiles.

"Never mind that," Lacina said, motioning Claire over to the gemstones. "Can you tell me where these gemstones come from?"

"I get stones from all over the world. Are you looking for anything in particular?"

"Regional stones," David said. "Anything from Stone County?"

"I do have a collection brought in from the Ozarks. I think many of them come from that county."

Claire led them around the corner and to a narrow aisle lined with wood bins that had been divided into small compartments. They were organized by stone color.

"Where on Earth do you get these? Is it even legal to mine these in the Ozarks?"

Lacina could tell David was ramping up for one of his lectures about conservation and illegal land and mineral poaching.

"Hold on, David," Lacina said, patting his arm. "I am sure Claire runs a legit shop. Let's see if we can find what we're looking for."

"I've been in business for over forty years," Claire defended. "I get my stones from reputable dealers."

"I'm sure that's true," Lacina said. "Can you point out your collection from Stone County."

When Lacina walked by the bin of stones from the Ozark caverns, an electrical spark seemed to pass through them. It even appeared to David and Claire that the stones grew much more brilliant than they had been a moment ago.

David and Lacina looked away, but Claire walked up to the bin. "Hmm?" She sounded concerned. "I thought I saw a flash."

Lacina searched through the bin but didn't find anything. "Thank you, Claire," she said with a sigh.

"I have a new shipment arriving on Tuesday. Maybe you'll find what you are looking for then. The delivery man gets here around noon, but he is never later than two, so come in around four or so."

They spent the weekend in Branson, being sure to attend a couple of shows with Chris so he wouldn't get suspicious, but also exploring as many caves as they could. They decided to extend their stay until Tuesday to look at the latest shipment.

Tuesday afternoon Lacina felt as if she was on a reconnaissance mission.

"I don't know what it is," David said, "but I feel like if there was a place like Avenrand—as Professor Garamondy claimed—there should be an opening that would have been exploited by now. Tours of Avenrand."

"It's sealed by magic," Lacina said. "The gems that call to you can let you in."

David snorted with disgust and brushed by Lacina.

"You guys ready?" Chris asked, stepping back to let David pass. He turned to Lacina, "Is he okay?"

Lacina grabbed a few stones. "He'll be fine. I guess he didn't find what he was looking for." She set her stones on the counter near the register.

Chris read the poster on the counter out loud, "Chakra Reading Sessions every Friday night?"

"It's quite amazing." Claire stepped behind the counter. "The crystals move in different ways depending on what's going on with that specific energy center of your body."

"Interesting," Chris lied.

"I believe it," David said. "My stone is always doing weird things."

"You and rocks have always had a weird relationship, David," Chris laughed.

Claire thanked Lacina and handed her a small felt bag filled with her purchases. She smiled then turned to David, "May I see it?" Claire asked. Reaching out and taking David's hand, she positioned the milky, blue stone in the center of his palm. "Have you found what you're searching for?"

David closed his fingers into a fist and jerked his hand back.

"I'm sorry," Claire explained. "The moonstone. It calls to people on a quest of some kind. I recognize the stone. It belongs to a traveler."

"The traveler?" Lacina asked. That sounded very familiar to her.

"They come from a different realm when you call to them. Often, they have moonstones tied around their neck."

"I've never heard of them," David admitted, "but this does flicker now and again."

"The merchant from Stone County can tell you more about them. He sometimes brings a traveler with him. They come in with special gems that seem to hold very strong magic."

"Where can I find this traveler?" Lacina asked.

"Travelers are very elusive. Rumor has it that they live in a cave hidden deep in the Ozarks. The merchant is eccentric. He's obsessed with finding some specific silver gem. He searches through every bin, all my stones, looking for it when he comes through."

"Silver gem?" Lacina swallowed a lump stuck in her throat, garbling. "Why is he looking for that?"

"Sounds like a crazy old man," Chris said. "Some cave dwelling lunatic."

David and Lacina looked at each other. If everyone is looking for the silver gem, who took it out of Avenrand in the first place?

"That was a good trip." Lacina set her suitcase on the bed and began to unpack.

"It was. We should do that more often." Chris looked up at the pictures on the wall, sighed and took the one with him as a baby down. "My mother was so young. I would have loved to have gotten to know her." Chris motioned for her to look.

Lacina took the picture from Chris and smiled. That place seemed so familiar, that girl holding the baby. Even the flood. Déjà vu. It felt like she'd been there before. She handed Chris their wedding photo and he hung it on the empty hook.

"I'm glad we're giving us another chance," Chris said.

She slid the trunk out from under the bed. "Are you sure you don't want to hang this photo somewhere else in the house?"

"No," he said. "The trunk is full of precious memories. It'll be fine there."

"Okay, great. That's where I'll put it then."

"Thanks. I'll start dinner while you finish unpacking," Chris said.

Lacina couldn't wait to see what else was in the trunk. It had been years since she'd taken a peek. She took her time opening it, waiting for Chris to leave the room. If the locket was there, she was going to take a chance. Her hands were shaking when she tried to dial in the code, O-L-I—She twirled the spindle and tried again, "O-L-I-C-".

Lacina took a deep breath and spun the spindle once more.

"Damn it."

Another deep breath, she tried to stop her hands from shaking, "O-L-I-C-E." She lifted the lid of the trunk, but the locket was gone. As she rummaged through the items within to no avail, tears welled up, breaching the fortress she had built up over the years. Years of denying her past experiences, years of convincing herself she had been delusional, ill, and the tragedy of losing her girls.

There was no locket. No way back.

Streaming down her cheeks, the salt water leaked into the corners of her mouth. She licked them off her lips.

Breathe, she reminded herself. But breathing exercises just brought up years of resentment, years of Dr. Garamondy telling her she needed to stop obsessing over her daughters and move on. Years of collusion between he and Chris convincing her she was delusional.

Anger created pressure in her chest as she gasped under the weight. She put her head in her hands, letting the tears drip off her chin and into the trunk.

"I'm so sorry, girls. I am so sorry I let you go."

A light flashed. She wiped off her cheeks and picked up the small crocheted, pink blanket. It still smelled of babies and felt soft against her cheeks. Another spark caught her eye as she took the blanket out of the trunk, setting it to the side.

The silver stone pulsed as if it was calling to her.

"It's been here all along," Lacina cried. "This is what she— I was after." It's up to me to get it back to Avenrand.

Chris stood in the doorway. "Are you okay?"

Lacina stuffed the baby blanket back in the trunk and placed the picture of Chris and the young woman on top. She closed the trunk and spun the spindle again.

"Spend as much time as you need," Chris said. "I should have known it would be hard for you to look in there again after all these years."

"I'm fine." Lacina smiled. "Everything is going to be fine."

CHAPTER 45

2036

After opening the trunk to her past, Lacina promised Chris that she would check in with Dr. Garamondy. By the time she'd arrived at his office, she still hadn't decided how much she would share with him. She stood in the doorway waiting for him to recognize she was there.

Her breath was intentional and slow. He looked so old hunched over and sifting through the files in his desk drawer. Almost laughing when he jumped, she said, "I'm so sorry. I didn't mean to startle you." I guess I've gotten older, too.

"Lacina? A visit from you was not what I was expecting."

"Who were you expecting?"

"No one. But… we haven't spoken since…" his voice trailed off.

"Since you left so sudden from dinner and accused me of having the locket again? I promised Chris I would check in with you."

"Come and have a seat." Dr. Garamondy stood up and motioned her to the loveseat in his counseling cove. "I would be delighted to chat with you."

Lacina got comfortable as Dr. Garamondy took his seat in his La-Z-Boy recliner.

"I am sure you were right about the locket. But what I am about to share with you is going to sound a little crazy, well a lot."

"It seems to be the week for it. David came by with some crazy talk about a silver gem and a cave and some guy called the traveler. I have no idea what all that was about, but I think he expected my dad to have what he needed."

Lacina's chest tightened up like a vise.

"Breathe," Dr. Garamondy said. "What are you two up to?"

She let out all the air she was holding in and took several slow, intentional breaths. "Okay… I'm not sure I can trust David. Honestly, I don't know who to trust. What I have to tell you…well, please don't lock me away again. Please hear me out."

"Tell me. I promise I won't lock you away. I am a lot more openminded than I was thirty years ago. I'm an old man. What do I have to lose?"

"I think I know why you saw the locket." Lacina squirmed. "This is going to sound very strange—stranger than anything I've ever told you about blinking."

"Okay, go for it. You have my undivided attention."

Lacina shifted in her chair and tried to conceal the smirk on her face. "I am certain that my past self has traveled to this time with the locket. I believe that is why you saw me with the locket on. It's weird, but that's why I have black outs. She comes in my place, maybe even my body. But something weird happened. A glitch or something."

"Because the rest wasn't weird?"

"You promised you would listen. Let me finish."

Dr. Garamondy nodded. "Proceed."

"I saw her."

"Your past self? But—"

"I know. It was weird. But she was in my room getting into the trunk. She saw me too."

"Did you talk to her? What was she doing here?"

"I think she was looking for something. Maybe the silver stone."

"Is this the same stone that Smelsner is looking for?"

"Yes. But I don't know why." Lacina shook her head and stared off toward the windows.

"David said it holds some kind of power that some character—the traveler, I think he called him—is trying to possess. I did read something about the power of gems in my father's work. Allegedly, if you possess the wrong ones, it can cause you to go insane."

"Did you tell David?"

"He did mention it had magical powers. He wanted to know what my father knew about it and something about the caves."

"What did you tell him?"

"Nothing. I promise you. This is not a rabbit hole I want to jump through."

"I have to get the silver stone back to Avenrand. I think it's where my daughters are trapped."

"Ok. Did you not hear me when I said I don't want to go down that rabbit hole with you?"

"But you were curious about the locket. You reached out for it. What is it about the locket?"

It was now Dr. Garamondy's turn to squirm and take long cleansing breaths.

"Okay. Yes, I am growing old and senile and a little more curious about my father's work. I tried to keep my head out of it for all these years but when I saw that locket again... I did open up his trunk and look into his work. But the only thing I saw about a silver gem was on a list he was compiling. He'd started recording gems and their magical properties: the silver gem was about balance and harmony, nothing more. Nothing that should lure David to it. However, it could make you go insane. There was also a rock crystal, which he said was used for time travel, and moonstone which helps you find what you are looking for, maybe true love, as well as protection for travelers."

"Moonstone? David had a moonstone. But why is he looking for the silver gem?"

"If you ask me, he wants to find the cavern that this traveler guy is from. He thinks it will lead him to a lake of some kind, maybe like a goldmine."

"We need to find that cave before he does."

"Whoa! You just heard me say the silver gem can cause insanity. What does finding this cave have to do with finding your girls and how could they have survived for thirty years in this cave?"

"Dr. Garamondy, can I trust you?"

"Of course."

"I mean really trust you? You can't lock me up for being crazy. And you can't tell David or Chris any of this."

The doctor tilted his head. As an old friend of the family and as much as they had been through together, he sighed.

"Of course. I promise I will see this through until we are both deemed insane and locked up in the looney bin together."

"I found the silver gem. I need to get it back to Avenrand. The insanity is happening in Avenrand, not here. But I don't have the locket and the portal from my grandmother's farm has been blocked for years. I have reason to believe there is another portal in the cavern. I think that is what Dr. Smelsner is looking for."

"Is this the same cavern where the traveler is getting gems? Do we think the traveler knows the location of this portal and is taking gems from Avenrand?"

"Yes. And I think your father knew where it was as well. I think David thinks the silver gem will lead him to it."

Dr. Garamondy was onboard and together with Lacy, they searched his father's trunk for evidence of the cave. The only cave mentioned in all his records was a crumpled brochure for Marvel Cave.

"That's in Silver Dollar City," Lacina said. "We saw the entrance when the girls and I were there."

"It's a tourist trap. Do you think it could be the cave?" Dr. Garamondy asked.

"Now it's been commercialized but look here. 'In fifteen forty-one, Spanish explorers entered the cave hoping to uncover riches and hoped to find the fountain of youth. Then, in eighteen sixty-nine explorers descended into the cave looking for priceless mineral deposits.' It looks like they even led parties to the cave by horseback and then descended two hundred feet down from there to search for these gems."

"Is Avenrand the rabbit hole?"

Lacy quickened her pace trying to catch up to Galahad and her daughters, but they had run out of sight. She ran and called after them, but the creek bed seemed to go on forever. Exhausted and despondent, Lacy sat down on a large, flat rock.

How did I let my girls go again, she thought. Is it crazy that I sent them off alone with a talking horse? What is wrong with me? What kind of a mother am I? No wonder they are missing from my future.

Lacy's mind felt like a pin ball machine. Fleeting images bounced off one another.

Willy died. The girls are lost. Horses talk. Am I dreaming all of this? A little boy in a cape. A shadow that is trying to deceive me. Mystical fruit. Time travel. Magic gems. Willy died. Chris. Future husband. Future self. Now I'm supposed to save a future husband I've spent more time with as a baby on a flooding island than as a grown man.

"What is going on?" Lacy screamed.

Her voice reverberated down the creek bed and echoed off the large boulders and cliff walls. The forest walls seemed to whisper back to her but all she could make out was, "…Going, … going."

Then the voice became clear, "Get going, get going."

But Lacy slid off the rock and leaned forward until she was face down in the gravel. "I can't take another step," she cried. "I can't do this anymore."

She heard something flutter in the wind. As she peered up, she saw the cape waving over her.

"Caden?" she asked. Lacy jumped to her feet. "Caden, how did you get here?"

"You called me," Caden said. "Your voice led me here. I don't know how it works, but… here I am."

"Do you know where Olivia and Alice are?"

"I can lead you to the cave. There is a tunnel."

"So, it's real. Will it take us to the other side of Look Back Mountain?"

"I can lead you to the cave," Caden repeated.

Lacy followed Caden as he maneuvered the creek bed, sometimes going right, sometimes left at each fork in the stream. They came to an opening in the side of the mountain. It was a lot faster than walking in circles on her own. Whether there was some kind of magic in that cape or not, they were here.

"Where are the girls?" Lacy asked. "They were supposed to meet me here."

"Galahad will keep them safe," Caden said. "Sir Galahad of Midnight never fails."

Lacy remembered the great stallion when he had been at his worst. Lying in the bushes, telling her to climb that mountain to the bird's nest without him. She'd had to save her daughters on her own.

How did he survive?

"How do I find them?"

"You are their mother," Caden said. "You have a great gift—a mother's instinct. It's that sense of gravitational pull you feel deep inside of you that always drives you to your child. That is why you are here. Even from another time and space, you could feel it pulling you to them. No matter how long you are apart, no matter how much time goes by, you will never let that feeling go."

"I…" Lacy hesitated, pondering Caden's words. She desperately wanted even a small dose of what he was talking about. A mother's instinct, a mother's intuition, a knowing.

"Bring them through the tunnel and I will see you on the other side," Caden instructed.

When Lacy turned around, he was gone.

Staring into the dark cave, Lacy stood still.

It sounds so easy, she thought. Just go in there, find the girls, take them through the tunnel, and then find our way over the bridge and back to the portal. If I can do that, I can certainly be a single parent.

Lacy stepped through the cave opening and began walking down a narrowing tunnel. She went as far as she could with the light from outside. It grew so dark, she had to strain to make out the walls along the way. The footing was bumpy and slimy.

For a second, she froze in place, afraid to continue.

I can't stop. Lacy thought. I have to find my children. I have to get them out of this cave.

"Olivia?" Lacy yelled into the darkness. She shuffled her feet a few more steps over the slick floor.

"Olivia," her voice echoed back.

"Alice?" Lacy yelled.

"Alice."

Lacy kept moving. One step at a time. She tapped her foot on the ground to make sure she had something solid to step on. One hand on the wall, one tiny step forward until she was in complete darkness.

"Olivia," a voice called. "Alice."

Was that Lacy's echo still?

"Who's there?" Lacy called out. "Who are you?"

"Olivia," her echo returned. "Alice."

It sounded like her, but how could that keep happening?

She couldn't move. Her hand against the rock was wet from the moisture dripping down the cave wall. She couldn't reach the other side of the pathway anymore. She couldn't see it either. She thought she felt a slight breeze on the open edge. Was there a drop off?

"Girls, are you in here?" Lacy asked. "Galahad?"

Where was Galahad? Where had he taken the girls? They were supposed to meet in there, but how could Galahad fit through the narrow entrance? Lacy didn't know whether to turn around and go back or keep on going.

Caden had told her she would know what to do, that her mother's instinct would draw her to her daughters, but she felt nothing. But nothing. Maybe she wasn't supposed to go into the cave.

She wanted to go back to her living room, back to when the girls played at her feet while she read a book. If she could get back to that time, she would happily say goodbye to Willy and simply be their mom.

CHAPTER 47

Avenrand

Lacy knew she needed to continue down this dark path. Had the girls made it to the other side? But there were those stories of the ones who had vanished. Those were the stories she had to quiet from her mind. She felt the wall and the floor with her hands and scooted on her seat a little farther into the dark. With each push, she stopped and entertained the idea that all of this was hopeless.

I will never find my girls.

I will never locate the end of the tunnel.

I will never make it to the other side.

Somehow, she managed to convince herself to slide another foot.

And then another. By the time she registered that she was freezing, her whole body was wet. As her pauses got longer and her scoots shorter, her thoughts grew even less hopeful.

What would I do if I give up completely? Would I sit in this cold, wet, dark cave? Scoot.

Lacy shivered with cold.

She was all alone. What was I thinking? How could I parent two little girls alone? I can't even take care of myself. Curling up in a ball, she lowered her head to her chest. Moisture formed droplets that rolled down her nose and onto her folded hands.

Drip.

Drip.

Drip.

The frigid water trickling off her wet hair mixed with warm tears and flowed down her cheeks. It was hopeless. Why had I even brought Olivia and Alice to Avenrand in the first place?

If Willy were here… Lacy thought.

And then she recalled all the times Willy had hurt her or had scared the girls. When she had left him because of his abuse, he had used the girls to get her back. What had she been thinking? Why had I tried so hard to use the magic in the gems to get him back?

It wasn't that she wanted him to die. She simply wanted to be strong enough.

Strong enough to stand up for herself.

To take the girls and leave him.

To not allow herself or her girls to be hurt by him anymore.

She should have let him know enough was enough. Maybe if she had left him… Maybe he would have been able to do some soul searching and get better. Maybe for someone else.

"Olivia," her words repeated again. "Alice."

But this time it didn't sound like her voice. Instead, it was more like a parrot.

"Who is there?" Lacy shouted. "I know you're there."

Whoosh! Something fluttered across the dark room. She listened. Then something approached her, but it was too dark to tell what it was.

"Follow the light," the voice said. Lacy looked around into the darkness.

"I don't see any light," Lacy said.

"Follow me," it squawked.

Lacy followed the sound of the bird until she thought she saw a glimmer of light, maybe a reflection of a wing. She scooted a little quicker, still sliding on her rear. Perhaps it wasn't a good idea to follow a winged creature that she couldn't see, but it felt better than being alone.

"Hurry," the voice said. "Find the light."

Lacy ran her hands along the wall behind her as it began to curve. The ledge was widening, and she shifted back toward solid rock. She slid around the corner and saw it opening up to a large cavern full of cracks letting in streams of light. She stood up on wobbly legs, taking a few seconds to catch her balance, and then she followed the ledge as it descended down to the cavern floor.

As her eyes adjusted, she could make out a large dome over her head. She shuffled across a packed sandy floor and stepped across the bedrock base that led to light radiating around a bend.

A bird of prey the size of a small man flew around the corner and seemed to disappear through a crevice. Lacy ran toward the spot she'd last seen it but was unable to catch up.

"Wait," Lacy yelled. "Do you know where my girls are?"

As she reached the split in the wall, she noticed it was larger than it appeared. If she turned sideways, she could fit through it.

Lacy twisted her body and began to squeeze through the crevice.

"Please, wait."

Lacy stopped. She knew that voice. She slipped out and turned toward the large shadow sitting across against the cavern wall.

"Galahad?" Lacy asked. "Is that you?"

Galahad lifted his head about four inches off the ground. He looked too exhausted to get to his feet. His back was up against the wall, he laid on his side with all four legs sticking straight out.

"Where are the girls?" Lacy asked and then wished she hadn't. "Are you hurt?"

"I'm afraid I am cast," Galahad answered. "The girls are fine. I sent them through the fissure without me. I thought you would have been through already."

"What is cast?" Lacy asked.

"I am stuck," Galahad explained. "I can't reposition myself so I can get out away from the cavern wall to get myself up."

"How can I help you?"

"You need to go get your children. They are looking for you."

"I will not leave you stuck here."

Lacy looked around for something to put under Galahad for leverage and force him to get up. But there was nothing unattached in the cave, rocks upon rocks and then even more rocks. She took off her jacket and wrapped it around Galahad's neck and tried to pull but she could not muster the strength to move him.

"Wrap it around his foreleg and shoulder," the large bird said. "I will pull him free."

"I couldn't budge him and you're just a bird."

"I am a harpy eagle," he said, puffing up his chest and shaking his wings. "I am the largest eagle on the planet—and the strongest I might add. I can crush bone with these talons; I think I can slide a horse a few inches across a wet floor."

And he did.

Galahad stumbled to his feet. "Thank you. Thank you both."

"We need to go," said the eagle.

"But you won't fit through the crevice, Galahad. How will you get back to the bridge?"

"You must go on without me," Galahad said, "and find your children. I have done all I can. It's up to you now to get your daughters home."

CHAPTER 48

2036

Chris had expressed his relief when Lacina said she was meeting with her former doctor again even though he wasn't practicing psychiatry anymore. She let him believe it was for encouragement, but they were actually planning a trip to Marvel Cave.

"In case this plan doesn't work," Mark said, "I am going to write myself a letter. I will tell myself to lock up my father's work and never look at it again."

Lacina chuckled. "Maybe we'd be better off telling our past selves what to do if it's real."

The letters were written, tucked into a journal with his father's work, where Mark would uncover them if past Lacy ever met up with his past self again.

Dear Lacy,

If you've found this letter, I know you are asking yourself a lot of questions right now. I tell you this at great personal cost, even perhaps my own existence. Put the locket away.

If I could go back to you, I would give you a big hug and I would tell you, "You are brave. You are courageous. You can do this."

No one cares more for you than I. Put the locket in this trunk and lock it away forever.

All my love and hope for our future,
Lacina

Dr Garamondy told Chris he wanted to try a therapeutic intervention called immersion therapy. Chris agreed and had helped him plan an impromptu road trip to Silver Dollar City for the next morning. With an early start, they could be there by the afternoon. It wouldn't be official therapy, but it would be helpful. Mark would help Lacina retrace her steps through Silver Dollar City while Chris dropped off demo CDs at recording studios in Branson.

Lacina and Mark went to the entrance of Marvel Cave. They got in line between the velvet ropes that helped visitors form a single queue. As the line moved forward, they weaved around the posts until they reached an opening into a small room where their young guides welcomed them.

After a little speech on the history of the cave, their tour guide took them to the stairway that led down under the entrance to Silver Dollar City.

As planned, it was the last tour of the day. They waited for their tour guide's commentary to end at each stop along their way down into the large cathedral. "Look up, this is the hole where the eighteen sixty-nine explorers had lowered themselves in search of marble. When they'd discovered that there was no marble in the Marble Cave—only bat guano—the name was changed to Marvel Cave."

"Interesting," Mark said. "Were our parents explorers from a long line of explorers that never found what they were looking for in this cave?"

"My grandmother found something. It's not going to be obvious."

As the group finished coming down the stairs, Lacina noticed a curtain just behind the stairwell. She tilted her head, making Mark aware of her plan. They meandered over there as soon as everyone was distracted. As the others lined up for a picture with the ancient cavern column, Lacina and Mark slid behind the thick black curtain.

Behind the curtain there was a podium and some folding chairs, set aside for a large event held here in the main room. They glanced at each other without a word, confirming that the area was the perfect place to hide.

Mark peeked out. He relayed to Lacina that the group was moving on for the rest of the tour and they would soon be left behind. Alone in the large cavern room, they begin looking around for the portal.

"You know, we didn't talk about this, but if we are wrong and there is no portal to Avenrand… We're going to be trapped with no way out until the first tour group comes through in the morning," Mark reminded her.

"You still doubt me, yet you came all this way," Lacina retorted.

As the groups moved to the next section, the lights were turned off in the main cavern. The only light in the room peeked in through the hole in the ceiling. Like the explorers before them with small lanterns, they switched their flashlights on and began searching along the cave walls.

The tour continued across the bridge over a little creek that ran through the cave. Mark pointed his flashlight down where the creek led. "I think we should follow the water."

"Any particular reason?" Lacina asked.

"The gems come from a lake, right? If this cave is a portal to Avenrand, then the stream may be a tributary."

The creek flowed through the main cathedral, under the bridge, and through a small opening in the cave wall. They ducked down to peer under the arched opening that led to another room. Wading through the gentle flowing water a few feet, they found themselves under a dome that felt like a walk-in closet.

"Now what?" Lacina asked.

"This is your rabbit hole, Lacina. Where should we go?"

"I guess we continue to follow the water."

And they waded through two more rooms, each a little smaller than the last until the water seemed to stop.

"How does a stream quit flowing and turn into this puddle?" Lacina asked.

"That's how cave systems work. Water seeps down through the rocks. It looks like it ends up in an underground spring of some sort."

"It's a dead end." Lacina sounded discouraged.

Mark swept his flashlight around the room. As far as Lacina could tell, there were no clues to be found there. As the doctor continued to move around the room, the light reflected off a set of eyes staring at them from where they'd entered. A small rodent-like figure scurried off before they could react.

A few moments later, Lacina heard movement there again and pointed her own flashlight at the archway. There she saw a small, brown creature in the opening. Bending her knees and leaning forward with one hand reaching to the animal with her palm up, she gave a weak smile.

"It's okay," she tried to soothe him. "We won't hurt you."

"Are you Lina?" the otter asked.

"No, Lina is my grandmother. I'm Lacina. Who are you?"

Mark shook his head in disbelief. "Did that marmot just speak to you?"

"I believe it's an otter. Did you hear it?"

"Lacy?" the otter questioned. "I think you need to follow me."

Then, it ran by them, jumped into the small pond, and disappeared.

They waited for it to come back up, but after ten minutes it still had not.

"I think we've found the portal. It called me, Lacy." Lacina said.

"You can't jump in the water," Mark cautioned. "We don't know how deep it is. You could drown."

Lacina peered into the puddle. Brilliant blue water reflected her face. She watched as her gray hair turned blond and her wrinkles disappeared.

"Blue makes me look decades younger don't you think, Dr. G?"

Lacina held the silver stone close to her, contemplating jumping in. Her hands shook. Her choices weren't great. Either she sits in a cave all night or she jumps into the bright, blue water.

"I don't have any choice." Lacina continued staring as the image in the puddle widened, and she saw a younger version of herself standing on the end of the bridge as two small figures appeared beside her.

"It's Alice and Olivia!" she yelled. Then without any more hesitation, she squeezed the stone and jumped in.

Dr. Garamondy watched in disbelief as Lacina disappeared into the puddle.

This is the stuff psycho thrillers are made of. A man takes a woman into a cave, and she disappears, he thought.

He knew if he didn't join her, he would be the number one suspect. He jumped but only made a splash in the shallow puddle.

It's not my rabbit hole, he realized. I am going to have to append my letter.

Avenrand

Following the harpy eagle, Lacy slid back through the tunnel along the cavern wall. He led her through the darkness with the sound of his wings echoing off the limestone. Her back was cold and wet. She pressed so hard up against the solid rock, bruises formed along her spine. Side stepping out of the dark, she inched toward what she hoped was the other side of the mountain and into the light from the next room.

The cavern opened into another large cathedral area. Although there were towering stalagmites along with stalactites that almost reached the floor, what she desperately wished to see was missing.

Her daughters weren't there.

Was this bird misleading her? Surrounded by tall, solid rock walls, there didn't seem to be a way out at all. The room was filled with columns. Behind them, where the stalagmites and stalactites joined, she could see a creek that ran through the formations and trickled into a narrow tunnel. Other than the one she'd entered through, that appeared to be the only opening.

"Hello?" her voice echoed. "Is anyone here?"

"I told you not to come here," replied the familiar voice of the traveler. "And now your girls are gone."

"Where are they?"

"Gone," the traveler said. "That horse you were with sent them through the Looking Pond. No one comes back from the Looking Pond. They are gone forever."

"You just don't want people to leave. You are afraid of being left alone out here. He didn't lead them, Galahad was trapped. He couldn't fit through. How could he have sent them through anywhere."

"You are a foolish girl. What happens when you turn around? Then you are looking forward, the horse is ahead of you."

Lacy pondered his words until she felt dizzy. "I can't focus on Galahad right now. I need to find Alice and Olivia. Can you show me where they went through?"

"It leads to nowhere. Many have disappeared from it. You go in, but you can never come out."

"Galahad must have sent the girls through to get to the other side of the mountain."

"You should have never trusted him. I tried to warn you."

"Please," Lacy begged, "show me where the Looking Pond is. It doesn't matter where it leads. If my daughters are there, then I need to be with them."

"I truly want to help you, Lacy. You have a beautiful life ahead of you."

The traveler led her near the creek. Together, they crawled through the small opening where the water flowed into the tunnel.

"But know this," he continued, "you could be making a grave mistake."

The tunnel grew larger as they crawled through, and soon Lacy could stand up and walk. Where it looked like the creek disappeared into the rock. a large puddle formed. It was the brightest, most brilliant turquoise blue she had ever seen.

"It's beautiful," Lacy said.

"That is how it deceives you. It lures you in. Best not to look into it."

But by then Lacy was already mesmerized. At first, she saw her reflection, a young woman with flawless skin and bright blue eyes. Small ripples moved across the puddle, shifting the image until the woman aged. Her hair turned silver and wrinkles formed around her mouth as she smiled. Her bright eyes dimmed.

"Look away," the traveler advised.

Lacy couldn't stop. The woman seemed to call out to her, pleading with her eyes. The reflection began to fade as the view widened. She could see the woman was standing near a bridge. Lacy leaned forward as two small figures beside the woman formed in the ripples.

"It's Olivia and Alice!" Lacy said.

"Don't!" The traveler warned. "This is how it lures you in! You will never return."

"It's the girls; they've made it to the bridge." Lacy said. "I think she wants me to join them."

"No, don't ju—" the traveler cried out, but he was too late.

Lacy closed her eyes and jumped feet first into the puddle.

It wasn't like jumping into a pool where she needed to hold her nose and push off the bottom, gasping for air as she broke through the surface. It was more like closing her eyes and appearing in a different place, much like when she blinked with her locket. The shift was instantaneous.

Lacy stood looking over the bridge. The older Lacy—the woman from the reflection—stood on the opposite side, returning her gaze. They both stared at each other with the same heartbreak and confusion.

Olivia and Alice were nowhere to be seen.

Lacina felt dizzy as she landed on the bridge. Her legs wobbled like limp noodles with the force of the impact. Looking across the bridge, she caught a glimpse of her reflection. Trying to catch her balance, she grabbed the rail and stared at the figure staring back at her.

It was definitely her, although a much younger version.

"Hello," Lacy's voice was shaking.

"Where are we?" Lacina asked.

Lacy looked around. "Is this the bridge that connected North and South Avenrand?"

"It's been too long. Have the girls been lost in here all these years?"

"I thought the girls were with you. I saw them…" Lacy began to cry.

Lacina grabbed the rail and took a step toward her, her legs still shaking from the landing. "I saw them with you before I jumped."

"They are lost in the crack in the mountain. I must have left them. But the traveler told me that they had jumped through the Looking Pond." Lacy gasped in between sobs. "But I thought I saw them with you. They were behind you in the reflection."

"I came to Avenrand through a back portal." Lacina took a step toward her younger self, and then another. "But Dr. Garamondy was with me. I guess he didn't jump in."

"Dr. Garamondy? He turned us in! He tricked me."

"No, he helped me," Lacina explained. "We found a back portal in Marvel Cave. David is the one after the locket."

"David Smelsner wants the locket? Do you know where the locket is now?"

"I thought you had it. You took it out of the trunk."

"I lost it in the burnt forest. How did you get here without it?"

"I jumped through a pond in the cave. You didn't happen to see a river otter come by before I got here, did you?"

"I think we ended up here at the same time. I saw your reflection. That's why I jumped. I was in Look Back Mountain."

"I remember..." Lacina began to weep. "I wasn't dreaming all of this after all. For decades, I've tried to convince myself it was a dream made up by a poor grieving widow who wanted her kids back. But here we are. It's real and the girls... They were here. I saw them."

At first, Lacina wanted to run to her past self. She imagined them hugging and crying over their missing daughters. But that's not what she did. Her anger got the best of her.

"How in the hell did you ever leave them here?" Lacina yelled instead. She knotted up her fists. "This is all your fault."

Lacy braced herself gripping the railing. Tears puddled in her eyes. She stumbled backwards as Lacina stomped across the bridge toward her.

"I thought they were with you," Lacy said. "I saw them with you in the reflection."

"You should have never left them here." Lacina brushed her grey hair off her face and pushed by her younger self. "I have spent my entire adult life in grief because of you."

A red streak flashed by and both of them turned toward the center of the bridge. Prince Caden slid across and landed in a playful gesture of triumph, "You made it."

"Prince Caden?" Lacina asked.

"You do remember," Lacy said.

Caden stood tall on the highest point of the bridge. "Lacys, you made it. Did you bring the silver stone?"

"Where are the girls?" Lacy asked. "We have come to find the girls."

"I have the stone," Lacina said. "But no one is getting it until Alice and Olivia have been returned to…well, to that Lacy." She pointed to her past self.

"You stole the silver stone?" Lacy turned to her future self. She furrowed her eyebrows. "We've been accusing Dr. Garamondy of that all this time."

"Technically, you did," Lacina replied. "Dr. Garamondy is on our side. It's Smelsner you shouldn't trust. He wants the silver gem for himself. I found it in the trunk. You put it there. You stole the silver gem from Avenrand."

"Lacys, please." A familiar voice tried to quell their bickering as Hope clomped across the bridge. He passed them and stood in the dark, dry dust of South Avenrand. Hope looked up, gasping at the air with his gapping nostrils. "Please. We don't have a lot of time. You must take the silver stone to the south Gem Lake. And Lacy, you must take the locket as well."

"I no longer have the locket," Lacy confessed.

Caden walked up to her, holding the chain in his hand. "I promised that I would find it," he said.

Lacy knelt, and Caden slipped it over her head.

She stood up, careful not to touch it.

"But," Lacy shook her head, "without the locket I won't be able to go home. I will be trapped in Avenrand."

"You're always worried about yourself," Lacina scolded. "What about Alice and Olivia? If you'd have been worried about them in the first place, we wouldn't be here at all, would we? We are not taking the stone anywhere until those girls are back with us."

Hope turned toward the Lacys and lowered his head. Lacy reached out and scratched his long muzzle.

"It's good to see you, Hope," Lacy said. "But I'm afraid that she is right. We can't give up the silver stone until we find our girls. I have been here for…I don't even know how long—searching for them. I've found them and I lost them again and again. They're stuck somewhere in a crack of the mountain."

"Good grief, Lacy!" Lacina yelled. "How could you let them fall off Look Back Mountain. That is Olivia's greatest fear."

"No one fell off Look Back Mountain," Hope assured her.

"And how do you know this?" Lacina asked. "You've never left North Avenrand."

"She's right," Lacy said. "You were too afraid to even come near the bridge."

"Well," Hope lifted his head and pranced around in a small circle. "I am over here now, and I will return… find your daughters. You must take the stones—both the silver one and the one in the locket and throw them into the Gem Lake. Then I will meet you here at the bridge with the girls."

"I've seen the future," Lacina said. "How am I to believe anything you say?"

"You both saw the girls standing here on this bridge and you will see them again," Hope assured them.

The walk to south Gem Lake was difficult for both Lacys. It was hot and muggy. The land was dry and hard. They had to jump across large cracks in the earth where lack of rain had deprived the land of moisture for years. Lacy kept her fears to herself and kept putting one foot in front of the other.

"I need to rest," Lacina constantly complained.

"We'll find some shade," Lacy encouraged. "Just keep moving. One step at a time."

Looking around for anything to block the blistering sun—even a dead tree—Lacy realized it was unlikely they would find any in the barren wasteland that continued to stretch for miles ahead. There was nothing to indicate life had ever sprouted there.

"I can't," Lacina said. "You go ahead."

"We have to go together," Lacy said.

Lacina collapsed. "I'm too out of shape for this. I know my fate. To have lived in a lie my whole life, and now I will die in the desert of the land I denied for over four decades."

"You're not going to die out here." Lacy reached out her hand and helped her future self up out of the dirt.

Lacina stumbled as she tried to stand. The ground rumbled beneath her. "It feels like an earthquake. If we aren't quick, we will be sucked into the cracks in the earth, into the eternal abyss where no one lives or dies."

"You don't believe those old stories Grandma Lina told you, do you?"

"You are so young. By now, you'd think I would know the difference between myth and truth but look at us. I don't know what to believe anymore."

"Look! It's a dust devil." Lacy pointed across the barren ground to a swirling cloud speeding across the flat land.

"It's coming right for us!"

And it did. The whirlwind sped to them, stopping a few feet in front of them. As the dust settled, a black stallion with a white blaze down his nose emerged.

"Galahad!" Lacy shouted. "You're alive!"

"Of course, I am alive. You saved me."

"I thought you were trapped in the mountain."

"When you jumped through the looking pond, a tunnel opened up through the mountain and I was able to walk out. I will take you to south Gem Lake."

Lacy stood beside Lacina atop the highest point they were able to find. It was at least 350 feet above the last bridge they'd found. That one had crossed over a dry creek bed. Everything was dry in South Avenrand.

They looked out over the South Gem Lake. The ground was cracked and barren.

The bottom of the lake was black like charcoal, and the gems that Galahad said once glistened through clear water were dull and lifeless.

"So, we throw the stones into this dark pit, and magic happens?" Lacina sounded skeptical.

"Yes, Prince Caden said returning the silver gem to South Gem Lake would restore Avenrand…I think we should throw them at the same time." Lacy unlatched the locket from her neck and grasped the stone, letting the chain dangle from her hand.

Lacina pulled the silver stone from her pocket and held it in her left hand. She kissed it as if for good luck. "Whenever you're ready."

Lacy counted to three and both Lacys stretched their arms back in a similar stance. Three. Lacina let the silver stone fly high in the air as far toward the middle of the lake as she could throw. It sparkled as the sun reflected off its brilliant surface.

Lacina's arm came back as Lacy released the locket. its chain stretched out behind the stone like the tail of a comet. Lacina reached over and grabbed it. She reeled the locket in and pulled it toward her chest. Her eyes ghost like and sorrowful were the last thing Lacy saw. Lacina vanished into thin air.

"What have you done?" Lacy shouted.

Beams of light radiated from the silver stone as it fell down into the lakebed.

A bolt of lightning shot out, hitting a boulder high on a ledge to the east. It rolled down the hill to the lake and behind it, a rush of water. The waterfall roared and began to fill the lake with clear spring water.

The silver stone sent a bolt of light to the west and one to the south. Another hit the ledge and jarred Lacy onto her knees. The gems in the lake sparkled and the full color spectrum glistened along the shores until they radiated across the surrounding land.

Lacy stood frozen in time, taking it all in. South gem lake was restored, but the locket and her future self were gone. A whinny from below broke the trance. She slid down the ledge.

"I guess that's it," Lacy said.

"Just one rides home," Galahad said. "It was meant to be."

Lacy didn't reply. She climbed up onto his back in silence.

The trip back to the bridge was much more colorful. Lacy watched as the burnt forest came back to life as Galahad walked past. He took her back along the same bridges, now arching over the rushing springs, bursting with bright colors.

"Thirsty?" Galahad asked as he knelt to let her off for a drink.

Lacy sipped the cool water, and Galahad nibbled some green grass nearby until she was ready to get back on. "Do you think we'll find them?"

"Hope promised, they will be there."

"It will be up to me to get them home. To take care of them. I'm scared."

"Be brave," Lacina's voice whispered, and Lacy looked up and saw Olivia and Alice standing on the north side of the bridge. She hopped off Galahad and ran across the bridge to greet them.

The herd was also there to meet her. Crowding and neighing. Pushing and shoving. They all wanted to see South Avenrand restored to its former glory.

"I thought I would never find you," Lacy cried. She held them both so tight that Olivia squealed.

The girls interrupted each other talking about their adventure through Look Back Mountain, and the harpy eagle that lifted them off a cliff. They talked about how excited they had been when they were reunited with Hope.

"We even saw Prince Caden," Alice said.

Lacy stood up and turned toward the bridge. She stood in the very spot where Lacina had seen her in the Looking Pond. The girls stood behind her. Lacy took a moment to look across the bridge where she had once stood and smiled.

She had taken her place once again. A tear rolled down her cheek.

"What's wrong mommy?" Olivia asked. "Why are you crying?"

"I'm fine, girls." Lacy smiled. "I am just so happy to see you both."

CHAPTER 52

2001

After searching for over an hour, Raelynn still couldn't find Lacy. She couldn't help wondering if something bad had happened to her friend. What would she do if Lacy was hurt?

Praying that this wouldn't be the last straw that destroyed the tenuous bond they still had, Raelynn pulled out her phone to call for emergency services. Before she could start dialing, a black car approached, spitting out rocks as it lost traction on the hill.

Raelynn didn't recognize the car as it crested the hill and paused in front of the house. It proceeded to the corral and pulled up alongside Lacy's car. A gentlemen got out and approached her.

"You must be Raelynn, Lacy's friend. I'm Dr. Garamondy. Lacy's parents said I might find Lacy here."

"She was here, but she went down this path into the woods and I haven't been able to find her."

"Were her children with her?"

"No, it was just the two of us. Are the girls alright?"

"The children are missing from foster care, and there is a warrant out for her arrest."

"She doesn't have them." Raelynn insisted. "She wanted to show me her grandmother's farm."

"I'm sure they ran away but there are rumors that she—" Dr. Garamondy shook his head. "I don't believe any of those stories. She would never harm her daughters, but the sooner we find her the better. There are a whole lot of people wanting to know where she is."

The walk to the portal path was quiet with the exception of two giggling girls. The herd escorted them. Hope stopped long enough to show her the entrance. The second path would come out along the west side of the old farmhouse not up into the corral.

"Thank you." Hope moved away from the path. He turned toward Lacy and paused. "You have saved Avenrand from the darkness and restored the land to all of its beauty."

"I didn't do anything. The other—"

Hope stopped Lacy. "It doesn't have to make sense. It is as it is supposed to be. Just enjoy the time you have."

After a few long goodbyes, Lacy took her daughters by the hand and stepped onto the path into the woods. When they emerged, there were two cars parked in front of the barn. Strange, *I don't know anyone around here.*

She saw Raelynn standing with a man. Was it social services? Why was Raelynn still there? How long had they been there?

The last time she'd seen Raelynn had been when she'd tried to take her friend into Avenrand. The girls hadn't been with her then because they'd been in foster care.

What would she think now that she is returning with them?

Be brave, Lacina's voice echoed in her head.

Lacy clasped the girls' hands even tighter and went to greet Raelynn in the corral.

"Raelynn! You're still here?"

"Of course, I am. But I was getting worried."

Dr. Garamondy turned around and nodded at Lacy. "I am glad you found where they wandered off to."

"Yes, everyone loves Grandma Lina's farm," Lacy said. "But we are all tired and ready to go home."

"Isn't anyone concerned about how the girls got up here?" Raelynn's inquiry was cut short by Olivia and Alice's hugs and giggles.

"You should have seen it, Aunt Rae. Hope saved us." Olivia grabbed Raelynn's hand and squeezed.

Alice twirled in front of them as they walked back up to their cars.

"Did they come up here with you?" Raelynn pointed toward Dr Garamondy's car. "I didn't see them get out."

"How about we get a couple rooms in Branson, check out early, and head back to Florida in the morning?" Dr. Garamondy redirected their attention to Lacy. "I have some exciting things to show you. I found some letters you will definitely want to read that might help us."

"From whom?" Lacy asked.

Dr. Garamondy winked. "I am officially releasing you from counseling. However, I am afraid we're going to have some explaining to do to social services."

"You came all the way up here to tell me that?"

"I think it's best if I show you when we get back."

When they got back to Florida, Lacy convinced Raelynn, with the urging of Dr. Garamondy, to tell social services that the girls had run away and found him. Raelynn would tell them she had met up with Lacy and Dr Garamondy for some immersion therapy at her grandmother's farm.

Lacy was relieved to read the letter from Lacina. She remembered Avenrand and that her girls were missing in Lacina's future. She would heed her warnings and not return to her grandmother's farm. Dr. Garamondy read his letter to her. It explained how he knew he had to find her. It took the help of a local man named, David Smelsner, who knew a lot about the area's cave systems. However, he felt David had seemed pretty obsessed about a silver gem he thought Lacy had "borrowed" from him. As intriguing as his father's work would be now, they both agreed locking the trunk and throwing away the key was the best thing to do.

"Messing with time is a dangerous endeavor." Dr Garamondy stated the obvious.

Lacy heeded his advice and was determined to do everything possible to make life as a single mom work. She shared the safe parts of her story at her grief support group. The part about being afraid of being alone with two young girls. She was encouraged to journal her progress and it was there she put her thoughts about time travel and Avenrand to rest. She wrote her last story, the trip with Lacina to the South Gem Lake, her disappearance, and bringing her girls home. Then she closed the book and wrapped a string around it. She tied it in several knots and tucked the book into one of her grandmother's old trunks.

Dr. Garamondy had insisted the support group would help, and Lacy agreed to go for one year.

Lacy released a deep sigh. Staring into the mirror at her reflection, almost hoping the locket was hanging from her neck. She rubbed her hands together under the warm water until the flushing sound from the farthest stall near the wall jolted her back to reality. Would this be the same meeting I had attended in the past? Will I meet Chris again? Her heart raced as she anticipated seeing him again, knowing their future, and feeling anxious about what she would do if he wasn't in attendance this time.

Chairs were set in a full circle and Lacy tried not to draw attention to herself as she took her seat. She didn't seem to recognize anyone and the more she looked for Chris, the more she doubted herself. Were her time traveling adventures conjured up in the imagination of a grieving widow? Was he ever here? There was something very familiar, however, about a woman as she spoke about crying every day and longing for her late husband. When she confessed that he had died over five years ago, Lacy knew she had heard her story before.

After the break Lacy took a glass of lemonade off the refreshment table and found a quiet corner in the room to wait. Contemplating whether to stay or sneak out the door before she had to share, a voice startled her.

"I don't want to be in this dark valley in five years," he said.

Lacy jumped, "Chris!" she slipped out.

"Yes, Chris Manning"—he held out his right hand—"and you are?"

"Lacy Donathon." She stopped herself right before she almost told him she had been looking for him. Trying to cover up her familiarity with him, she lowered her eyes. "It's difficult but I don't want to be crying every day in five years." She peeked up at him, "I think that is motivation to figure a way out."

"I couldn't agree more," Chris said as the leader called everyone back to their seats. "It was nice to meet you, Lacy Donathon."

"You too, Chris." Lacy said as they found their seats. He didn't call me Lacina.

Assuming he'd say yes, Lacy invited Chris to have coffee with her the next morning. That began the courtship that Lacy had missed with her time jumps. She was eager to fill in the missing parts of this love story now that the locket was safely out of reach. From now on, she would discover where life would lead her one day at a time.

CHAPTER 54

Chris pulled out her chair and smiled as she took her seat. The candle in the center of the table flickered, as he laid a red rose across her place mat. He leaned over and kissed her cheek.

"Happy anniversary, sweetheart."

Still madly in love with this man, Lacy grinned. "Happy anniversary, my love. You are the absolute love of my entire life."

"Are you trying to show me up?" Chris smiled as he poured the wine.

Lacy picked up her glass and held it under her nose. The smell of tart black cherries stung in the back of her nostrils.

Chris held up his glass and she reciprocated with the clink of their glasses together.

"Wait," she said, "Shouldn't we cross arms or something?" Laughing as they struggled to wrap their arms together across the table they met in the middle. The sip of the wine was full bodied, and she loved how it burnt a little on the way down.

The restaurant where Chris had brought her on their first date was quiet tonight. They had the full attention of the staff who wasted no time taking their orders.

"Would you like another bottle of wine, sir?"

"One more?" Chris looked for Lacy's approving nod.

When the waiter had left, he slid his chair around the table to be next to her. Another toast, and then a kiss. Lacy kept her eyes closed a little too long as she tasted the red wine from his lips even after he had pulled away.

When I open my eyes, she thought, I'm afraid he won't be here. As much as she had tucked Avenrand and time travel away in a journal, that feeling of blinking and being in another time and place had never left her.

Her heart was racing, and she mustered up the courage to open her eyes. He's gone. No longer sitting across from her, it startled her for a second.

"I have something for you," Chris whispered in her ear, and she remembered he had moved next to her.

"We said we weren't going to exchange gifts." Lacy frowned. "Now I feel bad."

"Please don't." Chris put his right hand on her leg and slid the black velvet jewelry box in front of her. "With you by my side, I have everything I could ever want. And besides, I got this for you before we decided on the rule. I was just waiting on the perfect time to give it to you."

Lacy smiled.

"Thank you, dear, I'll owe you one." She opened the box so slowly the hinges creaked. Peering inside she saw something familiar about the necklace inside.

"This is…"

Lacy stared at the locket. The gem sparkled as if it was calling out to her. It was Lina's Locket. How could Chris have gotten the locket? How was it possible that she was sitting here staring at it again after all the trouble she went through to return it to Avenrand?

She whispered, "Is this my grandmother's locket?"

"I wish it was your grandmother's locket. You were so upset that you lost it. When I saw this at the antique mall, it called out to me, and I knew you had to have it. Let me help you put it on."

THE END

ABOUT THE AUTHOR

K.S. Brixey is a novelist based in the "Show Me" state. She was born in Missouri during a tornado which explains a lot about her life.

A lifelong lover of walking in the woods, Kim feels more at home in the outdoors than stuck inside. It took way too many decades for her to discover that the cause of her debilitating social anxiety was trying to fit in in all the wrong places. When she found her people at an outdoor wilderness retreat, she knew where she belonged.

Kim's favorite place to write is the screen room of her lakeside home. She loves watching the birds come to her feeders and listening to the chipmunks chirp at her cat in the window.

When she isn't writing a crossover of women's fiction and portal fantasy, she may be sharing about personal transformation on her blog. She is a certified life coach and has a Master of Science degree in counseling psychology. If she isn't in front of her computer writing, she may be out on an adventure with her grandchildren.

If you want to know what she is up to next, escape to her website at ksbrixey.com

TALES FROM AVENRAND

BY K.S.BRIXEY

BOOK ONE: THE LOCKET (2023)

BOOK TWO: THE KEY (2024)

BOOK THREE: THE ROSE